Also by Dennis Fisher

Motherless Children

BE GONE

Dennis Fisher

Copyright © 2022 by Dennis Fisher
All rights reserved.

"Be good and you will be lonesome."

— Mark Twain

One

As I recall, the story goes something like this.

I was lying on an inflatable alligator in the small pool behind a large rented house on Key West. A pair of high-fidelity, high-priced speakers mounted on the outside wall of the pool house was playing a mix of Tom Petty, Will Kimbrough, and Zac Brown, while four stray roosters scratched and pecked at a patch of dirt behind the pool pump. I flail-paddled my way to the wall to take a pull from a can of beer that was warming quickly on the cement deck.

Before I could get to the edge, a shadow moved across the deck and I heard squishy footsteps approaching. I looked up in time to see JD swoop down, grab the can, and launch himself over my head into the pool. I cranked my neck around, watching him spread-eagle in the air, aiming for a giant swan float on the far side of the pool. He realized a half-second too late that he had overestimated the distance, tossed the beer in the air, threw his head back and executed the saddest back-flop in human history, missing the pool coping with his head by a fraction of an inch. The beer landed right-side up on the swan and bounced, hanging in the air for hours until JD burst out of the water and grabbed the side of the pool with one hand and snagged the can with the other just before it hit the surface. He tipped the beer all the way back, finishing it.

From behind me, a slow, rhythmic clap and low whistle. Caroline, lying on a lounge chair. JD hoisted himself onto the swan, bowed from the waist, and held up a hand. From the second-floor balcony a new can arced across the sky, down toward the pool, through JD's hand and hit him square in the forehead. He blinked twice, reached down and scooped the beer out of the water and laid back on the float with his legs wrapped around the swan's neck.

The sun was low and our spirits were high.

We had been on the island for the better part of two months, the last stop of a slow, aimless cruise down the east coast and along the eastern edge of Florida on JD's boat, the *Buffer Overflow*. The three of us--myself, my girlfriend Caroline, and my old friend JD--had left Massachusetts with no particular destination or itinerary in mind, wanting only to clear our heads and put some distance between us and the wreckage of the previous few months. We had largely succeeded, although I wasn't sure how clear JD's mind was at the moment.

We'd made a good run at it and a few weeks into the trip we'd stopped in Hilton Head to restock our food and beer supplies. It was meant to be a one or two hour stop, but we had ended up in the Salty Dog for lunch and then lunch had led to afternoon cocktails and then the happy hour crowd rolled in. Somewhere around sunset, we lost track of JD for a minute so Caroline and I had moved down the dock a bit to talk. We stood and watched a couple of guys on stand-up paddleboards mosey around the inlet until one of them badly misjudged the height of the Dog's outdoor deck and smacked his head on it with a solid thunk.

We followed the crowd to the end of the dock where a group of guys had helped the unfortunate paddleboarder out and had him sitting upright on the deck. A young woman who said she was a nurse made her way through the onlookers and squatted down next to the dazed man, whom we now realized was JD. He'd somehow commandeered the paddleboard and decided he should race another paddler, despite the fact that he'd never been on one of the boards before. After four beers.

Perhaps it was sympathy or the heat or the drinks, or a combination of all three, but JD's somewhat eclectic charms had worked on the nurse, whose name was Savannah, and she'd decided to join our traveling party. That was three months ago. Caroline, my girlfriend of nearly a year, and Savannah had become fast friends, bonding over a shared love of art and terrible pop music.

We had fallen into an easy rhythm during our time on Key West, sleeping late into the mornings, walking into town for lunch, and then hanging by the pool at the house in the afternoons. JD and I would go fishing once or twice a week and usually catch enough for a few dinners and some seafood omelets on the days we woke up early enough to eat breakfast. Key West had turned out to be the perfect antidote to the poison we had left behind up north.

Now, laying on the alligator float with nothing to do but watch the clouds go by, I could feel myself getting antsy. I loved doing nothing as much, if not more, than the next guy, but it was getting to be that time. I floated over and kicked JD's swan in the throat.

"So. Is there a plan?" I asked.

"Man plans, the gods laugh," he said.

"Psych 101 in the form of a mediocre white guy," Savannah said.

"I'm hardly mediocre," JD said.

"What I meant is, it might be about time to think about heading home. I'm in no hurry, but some of us do have some adulting to do at some point," I said.

"Why start now?" JD asked.

I didn't have a great answer. Or any answer.

"That's what I thought."

Caroline: "I do have a commission for that painting I'm supposed to deliver by the fall…"

"And since it's about to be full on swamp-ass season down here, it wouldn't be a terrible time to make our way home," I said.

"OK, so then maybe we head out in the next few days, hit Hilton Head, deliver Miss Savannah, and then point this thing north and spend a few days getting back to Massachusetts," JD said.

"Was anyone planning to ask me about this?" Savannah said. "Maybe *I'd* rather not go back to reality yet. Maybe *I'd* like to go to Boston for a spell and see my brother. Maybe *I'd* like to extend this little junket a while longer."

The three of us looked at her, then at each other and we all smiled. Caroline went into the house and came back with three shot glasses and a bottle of Don Julio 1942, which had about three inches left in the bottom. She set the shot glasses on the table, filled each to the brim and then kept the bottle. We lifted our shots, Caroline grabbed the bottle and hoisted it.

JD cleared his throat and said, "Here's to friends, old and new, good times in the sun and leaving the world behind. It's been a great trip." He lifted his shot glass and we all clinked: "If they're not here…"

"Fuck 'em!" we all said in unison.

Two

So: Rather than moving due east for South Carolina, JD took a big, slow turn to port over the course of the next two days and we headed back up the east coast with no particular haste. After short stops in Tybee Island, Annapolis and a town in north Jersey that I'd rather forget, we made it to the Cape by the first of July. It was late in the afternoon when we reached Chatham and JD decided to stop there for the night rather than go out and around P-town and up to Boston. I called an old friend and we were able to wrangle a spot at a marina in town, something that's more valuable in Chatham in July than a tee time at Cape Cod National.

"It only cost you a dinner at Eastern Standard," I told JD as he eased the *Buffer Overflow* into the borrowed slip.

"You mean cost *you*."

"Ain't my boat."

After we tied up, we walked a few blocks into town and found a small restaurant with a deck looking out at the water. It was full of summer revelers, about half tourists from the look of them. The rest were various characters from the boaty crowd: owners, charter captains, a few crew guys mixed in. A deeply bored, deeply tanned twenty-ish girl led us to a table near the rail that only had three chairs. When Caroline asked her to bring over another chair, the girl sighed deeply and slouched away, finally returning with the chair.

"So nice to be back in New England," Caroline said once we were seated.

"Land of the free, home of the dumb," JD said.

We ordered a round of drinks and the girls shared a dozen oysters as an app. I leaned back against the deck rail and scanned the crowd. I felt relaxed and at ease. The trip down south had been a great distraction for me and Caroline, and being away from Massachusetts for so long had felt good. I'd never totally felt at home here. I'd lived most of my life in Virginia and still thought of myself as a southerner, despite having settled in Plymouth several years ago. I loved the town and enjoyed my life there, but the events of the last year had tainted all of it for me.

My own actions, and those of Paolo DeSilva and Joao Alves, had hurt a lot of people and had changed the direction of my life, at least for the time being. I wasn't sure yet whether that was a good thing, but I'd chewed over every bit of that episode dozens of times in the last few weeks and I always came to the same conclusion: I couldn't be sure I'd done the right thing. At the time, it had felt right, and more than that, it had seemed like I had no real choice.

I had been a state trooper, and my partner Tex and I had built a case against DeSilva and Alves for the murder of ten young women. They had killed them and then dumped their bodies in a swamp along the side of a highway, in the same way that a passing driver might toss an empty Coke can out the window. It was an inconvenience to DeSilva and Alves for these women to remain alive, and so they'd killed them. We knew this, and we knew that DeSilva had been trafficking in women—girls, actually--for years with impunity.

But we couldn't prove it. DeSilva and Alves had been careful enough that they were probably going to walk on the murder charges and DeSilva might get only a minor sentence for the trafficking ring. The prosecutors had no confidence that they could get them for the killings, and I had decided that wasn't an acceptable outcome.

So I forced their hands. I had painted them into a corner, playing one against the other and watching to see what would happen. Alves and DeSilva had both died and that was fine with me. At the end, Caroline had asked me whether I could have stopped the killings, and I said I probably could have.

But I didn't stop them and I was glad I didn't.

In the months that had passed, I had realized that if things had gone differently that night, if I had found DeSilva and Alves a few minutes earlier, I likely would have killed them both and left them in that same swamp. I didn't know where that put me on the moral continuum, but a small bit of evil had been removed from the world that night.

After dinner, we lingered on the deck, enjoying the warm night air. A competent bar band was playing inside, moving easily through the standards: Allman Brothers, Van Morrison, James Taylor, like that. It was after eleven by the time we decided to call it a night, but we had a problem. At the beginning of the meal, we'd all placed our phones on the table in a pile with the stipulation that whoever gave in to the temptation to check their phone first had to pay the tab. Somehow we'd gotten through the meal with no one giving in. While the waitress was back inside getting the tab, one of the phones rang and we all leaned forward to see whose it was. Savannah hung her head and grabbed her phone showing us all the screen, which read: Mom.

Caroline clapped her hands and we all laughed as Savannah dropped her credit card on the table and then stood up and moved down the deck to take the call. We gave the card to the waitress and when she came back, Caroline signed Savannah's name. As we got up to leave, I saw JD's face change and his eyes darken. He pushed past me, walking toward Savannah. I turned to see what was going on and saw Savannah slumped in a chair, her head in her hands, shoulders shaking. JD bent toward her, his arm around her shoulders. Whispering, head shaking, snuffling into tissues.

Caroline and I watched silently until JD stood up and walked back to us, his eyes not meeting ours. He sighed and sagged into a chair.

"Her brother was found dead today. Sounds like he was killed. They found him a couple of hours ago in his house. She didn't have all the details, said her mom was incoherent and she couldn't get much out of her, but it sounded gnarly," he said.

JD stood up, looked around for a second, then sat back down and ran his hands through his hair. I touched Caroline's arm and nodded toward Savannah. She walked over, pulled a chair next to Savannah's and sat down, not saying anything, just waiting.

"What did she say exactly? Remember everything you can," I said.

"She said the police were still there and trying to figure out the exact situation. Her mom wasn't sure how he'd been killed, because the police were kind of holding back on the specifics."

"What else?"

"His roommate found him when he came home from work around six. He was in the bedroom. The roommate called the cops and then went back outside to his car. Cops found him there shaking and sort of babbling. They couldn't get him to say much, but her brother didn't go to work that morning because he wasn't feeling well, so the roommate didn't see him or talk to him since about seven-thirty this morning when he left."

I glanced over and saw Caroline and Savannah huddled together, 's shoulders still shaking. Caroline is smart and has the kind of instinctive feel for people that is such a rare thing. So she would sit and listen and nod and wait. Lost skills, those.

"Where was this?" I asked JD.

"South End somewhere."

"You know anything else about him?"

Shake of the head. We looked out across Nantucket Sound, south toward the islands. The night was clear and star-filled, with nothing more than a few ripples on the water. The loud boozy voices of people in the bars and on their boats carried and collided and as I looked around, the scene that had just minutes before been benign and celebratory now looked sour and petty. People laughed and drank and told stories and made plans. And would have to deal with the fact that while she'd been out cruising with us, her brother had died. While we were doing shots and deciding whether to have the lobster tail or the filet, he was already gone.

Caroline came back over and gave the full report. His name was Wyatt Austin and he was an artist. He'd gone to art school and had had some minor successes with shows of his sculptures and paintings in Miami and Atlanta and he'd thought it was only a matter of time before the world discovered his talent and rewarded him for it. But as many generations of artists have learned over the years, it turned out that the world was a little slow about doling out its rewards. So he had taken a job at an ad agency in Boston on the word of a friend. It was meant to be a temporary thing, as most such jobs are, but the money was good and the hours were flexible…and so he'd stayed. He did commercial art, the kind of stuff you see on the sides of buses and buildings. Huge fabric things promoting celebrity fragrances and rum and organic dog foods. But he still thought of himself as an *artist* and had been thinking about taking some time off from the ad agency to concentrate on a series of aquatic sculptures he wanted to finish.

    Wyatt and Savannah had been close throughout childhood and their teenage years, Wyatt being two years older. Their parents had divorced when Savannah was six and it hadn't been pretty, so she and Wyatt had clung to each other, shutting out the chaos and tension. They had remained close after Wyatt went to Georgia from their home in South Carolina and he had even helped pay Savannah's way through nursing school when their mom couldn't. And when Wyatt had been stricken with meningitis several years ago, it was Savannah who had spent three weeks nursing him back to health, his low-budget health insurance provider having thrown him out of the hospital after a few days.

They didn't see each other as much these days, with their work schedules and distance getting in the way, but they talked often and Savannah still thought of Wyatt as her closest friend. She had been scheduled to come up to Boston and see him earlier in the year, but had canceled in favor of a last-minute trip to Playa Del Carmen with some girlfriends for the weekend. And now…

"She's lost," Caroline said. "Just…lost. When she told me her brother's name, I knew who he was. He's sort of locally famous I guess you'd say. At least in the art community. People know him."

"I think you need to talk to her, Danny," she said. "I don't really know what to say and I feel like anything I do say could just make things worse."

"Consolation isn't really my specialty," I said.

"Maybe not, but empathy is," she said. "You know what she's going through and you know what's coming next and maybe you can help her prepare."

I shook my head. "There is no way to prepare. It's different for everyone and what I went through won't necessarily match up with what she's got coming. She doesn't need me trying to compare grief with her. She just needs people to listen and to know that we're here."

Caroline looked at me, her eyebrows raised, hand on one hip. So I went.

Savannah retold the story, recounting what her mother had told her and what the police had told her mother, adding a few details that JD and Caroline hadn't mentioned. She had calmed down some, but her hands shook as she spoke and when she reached for her water glass, she spilled it on the table and the water dripped down through the metal grate of the table top. I watched the water pool on the deck as she continued to talk. A slivered golden moon hung over the water. As I listened, I noticed a small oddity in the way that she was describing her feelings about the death and what it meant to her. Most people in these situations talk about them in terms of their own feelings, how sad they are, how they don't know what to do now and how it's going to affect them. Savannah was talking about how it was unfair to Wyatt, that he had so much more to do.

"This isn't right, Danny. It's not right," she said quietly. "He was supposed to matter."

"He did matter. He mattered to you and to your parents and to a lot of other people," I said. "This doesn't change that."

"You're not going to give me a lot of shit about how every life has meaning and I need to remember the good times, are you? Because you can sell that somewhere else. Right now, I can't remember a single good thing and I can't believe there's one single good person in the world. I'm looking around this place

"And I'd guess that you were not necessarily interested in justice."

"That's something that the lawyers and courts deal with. I'm interested in what's actually right and wrong, not what the courts might say."

"And you're the one who decides what's right or wrong."

"For me, yeah."

She nodded again. "Well, I guess I'm glad I'm not a cop right now. That way I don't have an option of doing what you did."

"No." *You* don't...

Back on the boat, JD got Savannah in bed in the master suite and came back out after a long while. We all went topside and sat on the deck, our legs dangling off the side as we looked out across the sound. The lights of Chatham winked in the dark, and we sat quietly for some time. The boat rose and fell on the gentle swells, the insects made their nosedives, swooping in from high above looking for exposed flesh. Merrymaking sounds drifted in on the breeze from the shore and the other boats. Caroline leaned against me, her head a warm comfort on my shoulder. JD picked up a stray bottle cap and threw it out into the night. He looked over at me, his face half-shaded in the lights from the boat.

"Danny, we…"

"Nope."

"Tobin. This is…"

"No thank you."

"Danny! Shut the fuck up for a minute, would you?" he said. "This is something we need to help her with."

"No, it's not. This is what the cops do, not what we do. They're good at solving murders. Sometimes. We're good at… other things."

"The cops are not good at solving murders. You were good at it. Tex was good at it. But most of them aren't. They spend a couple of days knocking on doors and writing reports, and if they haven't made an arrest by then, they move on to the next thing."

"Some of them do."

"Most of them do," JD said. "It's a business like everything else, and they need to make their quotas. If it looks like a dry well, they start losing interest. We need to…"

"No, JD, we don't. We need to let the cops do their jobs. If we go in there and start messing around with stuff, talking to people, stirring shit up, it's just going to distract them and slow the process down. Trust me. I saw it from the other side for a long time. Anytime the family brings in an outside investigator, it ends up causing trouble, one way or another. It also pisses off the cops, and that's not what we want. We want them focused on finding the killer, not dealing with us."

"So what do we do?"

"We see what happens. Let things play out for a while. It was in his house, so this doesn't sound like a random murder to me. Odds are it's someone he knew, and so the pool of suspects is already narrowed for them. There's a decent chance they'll have someone hooked up for it within a couple of days, a week at the outside."

"And if they don't?" he asked.

"Then maybe we consider it. Maybe. But I don't even see what the angle is for us right now. There's no paying client, there's no technical piece to it and no one's asked us to play."

We sat quietly again for a while more. Finally, sometime after midnight, JD stood up and said he was going to bed. Caroline and I stayed outside for a bit longer.

"I hope the cops find the guy in a couple days like you said," she said. "But if they don't, and if it starts to get stale, I think you guys need to help."

"I didn't think you'd want me in on this kind of thing anymore."

"It's the last thing I want," she said as she stood up. "But it's what you do."

So we made the short trip out around the tip of the Cape, past Provincetown and up to Boston. Savannah had arranged for her mother to fly up from South Carolina and she met us at the marina. A sturdy woman in her early 50s, she had the same fine black hair as Savannah and I could see that she once would have given her daughter a run for her money all the way around.

JD and I carried Savannah's gear to the waiting cab, gave Mrs. Austin our condolences and then I went back to the boat while JD said goodbye. There was a long hug, some nodding and then Savannah climbed in and the cab pulled away, headed for South Boston and an afternoon of painful questions and few answers.

Caroline and I had our gear piled on the dock and stood nearby and watched as JD walked back, head down. He came over and sat on a wooden piling and was quiet for a minute.

"I am not good at this goodbye business. It could be for one day or for five years, it doesn't matter. I suck at it," he said.

"Yeah, I think Amy would probably agree with that," I said. Several years earlier, JD had been engaged to Tex's sister, Amy, but had seized up when he thought about the loss of freedom and so he had bolted in the middle of the wedding preparations and just never went back. That had gone over…poorly with Tex and with their parents. But Amy actually understood it and had moved on without much trouble. It had taken Tex a bit longer. Like years.

"Thanks buddy. You know how to twist the knife," he said, pushing himself up off the piling.

"Danny, you hush," Caroline said, wrapping JD in a tight hug. She held him close for a few seconds and then pushed him away, holding him at arm's length. "She'll be fine. She will. Savannah's a tough girl."

JD nodded, looking off to the south, toward the apartment in the South End where Savannah and her mom would have to clean out Wyatt's possessions and try to ignore the smell of death and disinfectant and pretend not to see the dark stains on the wood floors.

"Listen, thanks for a great trip. It was just what we all needed," she said. "Stay with her, JD. Don't let her fade away. She's one of the good ones." Caroline raised up on her tiptoes and kissed him sweetly on the cheek. She then made herself busy double-checking our bags while JD and I talked.

"Let it play out for a while and I think you'll see that things will work out, one way or the other," I said. "But if they don't, then we see what we can do."

"Yeah?" he said, sounding weak and tired.

"Yeah. It's been a while since I got to fuck with the police. I'm overdue," I said.

We said our goodbyes and JD went back aboard the *Buffer Overflow*. He planned to stay in Boston for a few days until Savannah and her mom were finished with their business and had figured out the funeral arrangements. Then he was going to take the boat back around to Nantucket, wanting to stay close by in case something happened or Savannah needed some help.

I had left my Jeep in a long-term garage a few blocks away from the marina, so we had a cab drop us there and then piled all of our stuff into the CJ-7 and pointed it south. It was a fine, warm July day, a few high clouds hanging around, but no threat of rain. So I put the top down and we took our time heading back to Plymouth. The traffic was heavy on Route 3 as we passed through Hingham and then Marshfield, the highway full of cars and SUVs headed to the Cape for the weekend. We were plodding along at about twenty-five miles an hour as we rounded a bend in Duxbury and came up on a swamp.

Caroline was dozing in the passenger seat beside me, and as I downshifted she woke with a start, looking around to get her bearings. When she saw where we were, she turned her head away from the swamp and pulled her faded Boston University cap down over her eyes. She made a hurry-up motion with her right hand.

"Get going. Hate this place," she said.

I accelerated and caught up to the traffic ahead of us, and as the swamp receded in the mirror, a cloud passed in front of the sun casting a greasy shadow on the water.

It was nearly five by the time I turned off of Warren Avenue and into the sand and dirt road that lead to Plymouth Long Beach and my house. The public parking lot was filled to overflowing and I could see hundreds of people lining the beach, getting a head start on the weekend. We bounced along the rutted track and finally turned in to my crushed-shell driveway. It had been months since we left and the house looked like it had come through the early summer in fine shape. After dragging our bags inside, Caroline headed upstairs to shower while I unpacked and separated the dirty clothes from the filthy ones. By the time everything was in its place, I realized I was starving and began foraging. When we left, I hadn't known how long we'd be gone, so I'd emptied the fridge and left just the dry goods in the pantry and some steaks and burgers in the freezer. I pulled two big steaks from the deep freeze, filled a large bowl with hot water and put the meat in the bowl to defrost.

    Caroline was out and dressed by then, sitting on the small deck off our bedroom upstairs, her hair wrapped in a coral-colored towel. I showered and dressed and then went out and sat with her, looking north across the marshland and dunes that lined the inland side of the Long Beach peninsula. We talked for a while about the trip, avoiding any discussion of Wyatt Austin's murder. Then we went down and made dinner, me cooking the steaks on the Weber while Caroline put some sweet potato fries in the oven. When it was ready, we ate outside on the deck. We stayed there for a long time, listening to the surf crash on the rocks on the far side of the house and watching as the sun slowly eased its way down below the tree line to the west. When it got dark, I lit the tiki torches to ward off the insects and we sat and talked some more, enjoying the relative quiet after weeks aboard the humming, noisy boat.

After a time, we took the dishes inside, cleaned up and went upstairs, both of us falling asleep within minutes, exhausted from the journey and, perhaps resting for what was to come.

Three

I spoke with JD the next day, checking in on the progress of things with Savannah. He had given me some of the details of the crime scene.

The apartment had been torn apart, papers, books and clothing strewn everywhere. Wyatt had been found in his room, tied to his bed, a pair of underwear shoved in his mouth as a makeshift gag. He had been shot once, in the forehead.

The Boston cops told Savannah that they were confident they'd make an arrest within a few days, that they had a couple of solid leads they were pursuing. But that's just what cops tell families to give them something to hang onto. The killing was clearly personal and if the cops didn't find a likely suspect in the next day or so, it would be a long road to nowhere.

That morning, while Caroline worked on a painting that had been commissioned by one of her mother's friends, an intricate landscape, I walked over to the beach with a book, hoping to put some of the ugliness out of my mind for a while.

I was lying on the beach a couple of hours later, about halfway through *Right as Rain*, when Caroline appeared next to me holding my iPhone. She had a smudge of light green paint on her cheek and her honey brown hair was pulled back in a loose, low ponytail. She wore tattered cutoff jean shorts and an old Foo Fighters shirt of mine. It was covered in paint.

She held out the phone and said, "It's JD."

I thanked her and said to JD, "You coming by for dinner?"

"Matter of fact…"

I sat up and laid the book down on the cooler beside my chair. "What's going on?"

"Savannah called this morning and laid something on me that I want to run by you," he said. "I'm just over in Dennis now. Can you fix it with your friend at the yacht club to let me tie up there tonight?"

"Sure. It's two now. Say five o'clock at the club?"

"I'll be the one with the big boat."

I called my neighbor down the beach who was on the board of the Plymouth Yacht Club and he said it would be no problem. I gathered my things and walked back across the road to the house and found Caroline in the living room glowering at the canvas on the big wooden easel. It looked like a meadow with a smattering of what might be llamas, or perhaps horses, standing around in the far background.

"Coming along," I said.

"It sucks," she said.

"The true work of art is but a shadow of the divine perfection."

"It sucks."

"Rome wasn't built in a day."

She turned the dead-eyed stare on me. "Any other clichés you'd like to try out?"

"Umm, just because an artist made it doesn't mean it's art," I said, and sprinted for the stairs. A paperback book whizzed by my ear as I hit the first stair and took them two at a time on the way up. I called down when I reached the top, "We're three for dinner. JD is coming."

"Oh goody, a playdate."

I cruised into town and pulled into the yacht club parking lot just before five, tires crunching on the gravel and seashells. I put the Jeep in a spot beneath a massive live oak whose branches reached well across Union Street and then walked into the club and found JD sitting at the bar. He'd already made friends with a group of old timers and was buying a round of shots.

"Danny!" He slapped me on the back and hooked his arm around my neck. "I was just telling these gentlemen about the time in college when you were coming home from the bar at two in the AM on your bike and decided to stop for nachos."

"Grab a stool," one of the men said. And another one slid a shot of Jameson's in front of me on the scarred oak bar. I took it, raised it in salute, clinked glasses with the others, and threw it back.

"So," JD continued, "here's our hero on his Trek, drunk as a Kennedy on election day, and he's got this big mess of nachos balanced on his handlebars…"

"Wait wait wait," I said. "If you're going to embarrass me, at least let me tell my part."

JD made a dramatic bow and flourish with his hand. "By all means, my good man."

"So I'm pedaling along, doing pretty good, when I come to the train tracks about a block from our apartment. Remember, I'd had a beer or two at this point. Maybe eleven. So I start to get all wobbly and next thing you know, the front tire hits the tracks sideways, wedges into the gap by the rail and here I go right over the handlebars. I hit the ground, and look up and I see the nachos coming at me in slow motion. I can see the chips spinning in the air and the chili and cheese sauce separating into these big globs, and it's like I'm in a bad kung fu movie. I couldn't move. So the whole mess lands right on my chest. Cheese, jalapenos, chili, all that shit."

The old timers are cackling now, tears running down their cheeks. "Oh Christ, you're lucky no cars were comin'. You'da been dead for sure," one of them said.

"Oh yeah. I laid there like a moron for a good two minutes. So I finally get up, get my act together, and very calmly walk the bike down the street to our apartment complex. We were on the third floor, so I hump this thing all the way up the stairs, banging it around. I get to the top floor and there's JD on the landing and he looks at me, looks at the bike, sees my shirt and just steps aside and holds the door open. There's a few people in there hanging out, but I just walk through the living room to the back deck, open the sliding glass door and walk over to the railing and heave the bike off the deck. There's a big-ass maple about ten feet outside our deck, so the bike goes crashing down through the branches, sounding like Vince Wilfork falling down a flight of stairs carrying a bunch of pots and pans. It finally hits the ground and I walk back into the apartment and there's this guy"—I pointed at JD—"and the rest of them giving me a standing ovation."

Laughter echoed through the old wood-paneled room and the men gathered around the bar were red-faced. One of them signaled the bartender for another round of shots and I watched as he poured them and handed one to each of us. We touched glasses and put the shots down, slamming the glasses on the bar.

"Best night of my life," JD said, nearly hyperventilating from the laughter, hiccupping every few seconds. "That was the night I got to know Krissy whatshername."

"In the biblical sense," I said.

"Hey now. She just wanted to cuddle," JD said.

"Sounds like my wife," one of the men said.

"That's your Viking out there on the end of the docks?" another one asked JD.

"It is. Had it for about three years now. Made a nice deal with a charter service owner in Tybee who was retiring."

"Lemme guess. She was named *Southern Charm* or *Sweet Georgia Brown*."

JD laughed. "Even worse. *Hope Floats*."

"Fine boat. She's a seventy-four? That's a lot of boat for one man."

"I'm a lot of man," JD said.

As I swung the CJ-7 onto Main Street and headed for home, I said to JD, "So tell me."

"You see the papers today?"

"Nope. Been on the beach all day."

"Tough life."

"Says the guy who lives on a boat and hasn't owned a winter coat in ten years."

"Don't hate the player. So, the *Sunrise* had a cover story this morning saying that Wyatt was part of a child exploitation ring and that the cops are working under the theory that his murder was related to that."

"Whoa, where did that come from?" I said. The *Sunrise* was an alternative paper in Boston that published twice a week. It was known more for its lists of the top body piercing shops and reviews of food trucks than crime reporting.

"From the ever-helpful 'sources close to the investigation'. The money quote was from an anonymous source who said that the cops had data linking Wyatt directly to this ring and that they were almost positive the killing was somehow linked to that."

"The guy said 'data'? Not information or evidence?"

"Yup. That tripped me up too. What's the translation in cop-speak?"

"It says to me that they found something on his computer or something like that," I said. "They would have taken any computers in as evidence and searched them pretty quickly, within a day or two, along with his phone if they found one. That's what I did for a couple of years. The homicide guys usually push for those reports double quick because even if there's nothing weird on there, it might give them a list of people to talk to or angles to go after."

"So...pictures?"

"Could be. Or maybe browser history files. Or both. There's a lot of stuff that could point to something like that. But the word 'data' tells me they have something concrete and not just supposition."

He thought about that for a minute. "Savannah saw the story and she tried to keep her mom from seeing it, but she's been obsessive about following the news on the case. She has a Google Alert set up with Wyatt's name, so the story was in her inbox this morning. She was pretty upset, and loud about the fact that the story was horseshit."

I slowed as we neared the turn in for the beach and waited as a column of bikers passed by on their way into town. I made the left after they rumbled past and then picked my way through the haphazardly parked cars in the beach parking lot. "So it looks like there are about two or three possibilities here. Either Wyatt had a secret life, which would put him with about half of the American population."

"Or whatever the cops found on his laptop wasn't his," JD said, finishing my thought.

"Right. We used to call it the entourage defense."

"Why?"

"Because, you know how whenever a musician gets pulled over and the cop finds a dime bag of weed in the glove compartment the guy says it isn't his?"

"Sure."

"And then the next day one of his boys or his guitar technician steps up to say, 'It was my weed, sir. I was driving that car earlier in the day and just forgot I put it in the glove box. I'll take the charge.' The entourage defense."

"I know what you're saying about that, but this feels a little different, you know?"

"How so? If I was the cop looking at that evidence, assuming they have pictures or something equally incriminating, I'd reach the same conclusion they did."

"Think about it this way, though: We both know how easy it is to hide things on someone else's computer. If Wyatt's laptop was compromised, it's possible that someone was using it as a file dump. Happens all the time with cybercrime gangs using laptops or servers inside some random network as a staging or storage area. Could be the case here. Just thinking out loud."

"That's a possibility. Not a good one, but it's there," I said. "So what does Savannah want from us?"

"She wants us to take a look," JD said.

"At the laptop?" I asked, hoping that's all it was.

"At all of it. She feels like the cops are completely on the wrong track and that they just found an easy way out. The stuff about the laptop is freaking her out, not to mention her mom."

"So they want us to prove a negative?" I asked.

"That's about right. But they also want to know why this happened. None of it makes any sense to them. The guy was about as harmless as I am."

"The last thing you are is harmless." I sighed. "Let's go eat. I can't think about this on an empty stomach."

We talked it through some more over fish tacos with homemade mango salsa. Caroline asked a few questions as we talked and then as we were clearing the dishes, she said, "Is there some way to prove that a computer belongs to someone? Or that they created the files on it?"

I looked at JD and he shrugged. "Not really," he said. "I mean, the best you can do is nail down which user account created the files. But that doesn't tell you who actually did it. Most people just have one user account on their computers and do everything under that. So no matter who's using the machine, they're using that account."

"The same goes for the ownership part," I said. "You might be able to track down a receipt and prove who bought it, but again, it could have been a gift or a shared machine that a bunch of people in a family or office use. What are you thinking?"

"Well, you guys were talking during dinner about the ways that hackers or whoever sometimes hide files on other people's computers. That makes sense for them since they're trying to avoid getting caught with bad stuff. And people do that in the real world too, right? They hide their weed in their brother's room or something."

"Ok…" I said.

"So, is there some way that the stuff on Wyatt's computer could belong to one of his friends or someone like that? I mean, people let their friends use their laptops all the time. Danny, you use my MacBook every day and it's not like I'm sitting there looking over your shoulder the whole time. I don't know what you're doing."

"Well, I'm not doing *that*."

"She makes a good point, though," JD said. "Say he's at the coffee shop with some friends, he gets up to make a phone call or take a whizz, leaves his laptop on the table…that's plenty of time."

"I guess so, but it would have to be done over and over."

"And how often would one person have that kind of access?" JD said.

We were back out on the deck, sitting in the fading light. A big brown hawk glided silently overhead, twisting and wheeling on the warm summer currents. Caroline and I sat in a pair of Adirondack chairs, our feet up on the deck railing and JD was pacing around the deck, chewing on the problem. He stopped in the middle of a lap and looked at us.

"What?" I said.

"He had a roommate, right?"

"Yeah…"

"That's someone who would have pretty easy access to Wyatt's laptop on a regular basis."

I pointed at him. "Shoulda thought of that. The cops would've talked to him right away though. He'd be the first interview, since he found the body."

"But they didn't have this information when they talked to him," JD said.

"I'm sure they went back to him, then. It's the logical move."

"But," Caroline said, "they might not have reached the same conclusion you guys did. They found the files, assuming that's what it was, on Wyatt's laptop, so they're not going to go out of their way to prove they weren't his files. It's easier for them if the stuff is his."

"I want to see that *Sunrise* story," I said. I went inside and got my iPad and came back out on the deck and found the paper's site. The home page was only rendered halfway, with a lot of missing images and videos.

"Flash. Are you fucking kidding me?" JD said, reading over my shoulder. "What year is this?" He pointed to the second lead story on the page. "There's the story right there."

I brought up the piece on Wyatt's murder, which ran under the headline, "Cops: Slain South End Artist Tied to Child Porn". The piece was relatively short, but brutally effective. The anonymous quotes and another from some retired prosecutor painted a pretty damning picture of Wyatt. The "source close to the investigation" didn't come right out and say that the cops had found pictures, but the use of the word "data" in his quote, along with the tone of certainty in the piece left little doubt. Caroline was reading over my other shoulder and made a couple of small sounds of disgust as she read.

"Why did it take them so long to come up with this theory if they've had the laptop all this time?" she asked.

I looked at JD and said, "I can think of one possible reason. If whatever they found on the computer was encrypted, that would explain the delay. It could have taken them some time to get at that."

"For sure," JD said. "I was them, as soon as I saw an encrypted drive or files, that's what I would've spent my time on."

Caroline looked confused. "But I thought the whole point of encrypting something was so that no one else could read it. Don't you have to have a key or passcode or something?"

"Sure, but people do all sorts of stupid things with those keys," I said. "They keep them in a Word file on the computer. They write them on a sticky on their desk. I once found a key written on a piece of paper taped to the bottom of the laptop. It's just like any other key. If you're not careful with it, anyone can find it and use it."

"Also, depending on the strength of the encryption he used, there are tools out there that will brute force the key for you in a few hours," JD said. "Meaning, they will run through all of the possible combinations and find the key."

"I got that. Thanks," Caroline said.

"But we don't know for sure that's what they found," I said.

"That's what Savannah wants us to find out," JD said, hopping up to sit on the deck railing in front of us.

I looked at Caroline. "I think we need to talk to your dad."

The next morning, the three of us were sitting at a corner table in Water Street Café sipping orange juice when Scott Nelson, Caroline's father, came in. A trim, fit man in his early fifties, he wore jeans and a blue polo shirt with the Boston police seal on the left chest. He kept his steel gray hair cropped close and he had the calm, confident manner of a man who was used to being heeded. He had been on the force for more than twenty-five years and was now on the city gang unit. If you had brought a first grader into the restaurant and asked him to pick out the cop, knowing nothing about anyone in the room, the kid would point straight at Scott Nelson. He came over to the table, kissed Caroline on the cheek, shook my hand and did the same with JD when I introduced them.

I had only met Scott on a few occasions since Caroline and I had gotten together last year and I would be hard-pressed to describe any of them as enjoyable or even cordial. He was a hard man and a hard man to know.

After the waitress came and took our orders, I gave Scott a little more of the detail about Wyatt Austin's murder and why Savannah and her mother were concerned with the investigation so far. And I explained the problems they had with the *Sunrise* account of Wyatt's supposed private life and proclivities. He snorted at the mention of the newspaper story. Few cops have any use for the media, until it comes time to use it for their own purposes, as the investigators on Wyatt's case apparently had done.

"Never was one for putting people's shit in the papers," he said. "You can't do your job without using the papers, you need a new job."

"You know anything about the reporter?" I asked.

He glanced down at the article. "Louis Andino? Doesn't ring a bell."

The waitress came back with our food and once she'd gone, Scott pointed his fork at me and said, "Tell me again exactly what it is you two do."

"We help people who might not have other avenues open to them. We work the edges," I said. "A lot of the work we've done so far—and it's only been a few months now—has involved online investigations. Helping people figure out what their wife or husband is doing online, tracing online affairs, things like that. Not things that the police are going to do. It's mostly word of mouth right now."

"But that's not everything you do, is it? I heard you guys were involved in that thing back in the spring with the FBI and Interpol and the cybercrime ring in the UK. That right?"

"It is. We helped them with some of the attribution, putting real names to the aliases the group was using. And JD worked with the FBI team on tracking exactly where their malware was going and what countries were involved."

Scott looked at JD with a bit of surprise on his face. JD was wearing board shorts, flip flops and a t-shirt from Jimmy Buffett's Chameleon Caravan tour. It was easy to take him lightly, and people often did. But he'd built and sold a Web security company for eight figures before he was twenty-seven and had been doing high-end computer forensics and security consulting for the last few years. And he never needed to look for work.

"Ok, so what can I help with?"

"Just a little perspective," I said. "What do you know about the guys running this investigation?"

He pushed his plate away. "I know one of them pretty well. Chris King. He was on the gang squad for about six months, two, maybe three years ago. He's police all the way. Dad was a New Hampshire state trooper, brother is a highway patrolman out in Texas somewhere. Single, no kids, no real hobbies I ever heard of. Worked his nuts off, from what I saw. He wasn't on my team, but we worked on a couple things together here and there and you couldn't ask for a better worker."

"Six months is a short rotation."

"He wanted homicide and he had some pull in the department. Guess his old man worked with one of the deputy commissioners a ways back," Scott said. "A spot came up and he threw his name in the hat and somehow it magically got pulled out."

"What about the other guy?" I said.

Scott shifted in his seat and leaned forward across the table. "Dave Henderson. Him I don't know very well, just met him once or twice. But he's got a tail on him."

"Tail?" JD said.

"A bunch of shit that follows him," I said.

"Shit is right. He's had four or five partners in as many years from what I've heard. Lots of talk about him not necessarily caring if he gets the right guy, as long as the skin color is right."

"I thought they'd washed most of those guys out," I said.

"Most being the key word there. Henderson is pushing sixty, already has his thirty in, but they keep him around because he clears cases and makes the bosses look good. You keep them happy and you can live a long and fruitful life in the Boston police."

"Would he cut a corner to make things fit?" I asked.

"That's the picture I get of him. I don't think he's been taken to a review board or even reprimanded more than a couple of times, so whatever he's doing isn't getting under the wrong people's skin."

"That's a skill you could've probably used, Danny," Caroline said.

"Little late for that," I said. "So, what's the best way to approach these guys? I doubt they're going to be very happy with us coming onto the scene."

"They'll probably be outright hostile. At least Henderson will. King, as long as you guys don't get in his shit and aren't holding anything up, I don't think he'll care. May even help you out, if it advances the case. I'd say just come at them straight, let them know who hired you, what you're trying to accomplish."

I cleared my throat and looked over at JD. He was busy counting sugar packets. "Well, mostly what we're trying to do is prove that their case is bullshit," I said.

"How's that?" Scott said.

So I explained. He frowned when I got to the part about the child abuse imagery allegations and pulled an empty, tarnished .45 shell out of his shirt pocket and began spinning it on the table as I spoke. When I was finished, he kept spinning the shell before finally putting it back in his pocket.

"That sounds like a Dave Henderson production all the way," he said. "King would push the reporter in front of a bus before he'd talk to him. Your problem is that if they found what you think, then their theory may be the best explanation. And they have the evidence."

"And we don't," JD said.

Scott Nelson took a ten out of his wallet and placed it on the table and then stood up. "Come up to the city tomorrow and I'll introduce you two to King and Henderson." He looked at JD: "And put some damn pants on."

When we got home, Caroline and I made some sandwiches and a salad, packed it all in a cooler with a six of beer and headed across the dirt road and down to the beach. JD had decided to go back to his boat and sleep for a bit. It was late in the morning and the sun was almost directly overhead and the beach was beginning to fill with families and groups of young couples setting up grills and settling in for the day. We found a good flat spot for our chairs and sat quietly for a while, watching the tide recede as roving bands of kids dashed in and out of the small waves, squealing each time the frigid water hit them. Caroline had brought along some supermarket detective novel, the cover of which was graced by a fountain pen writing in blood. She had been reading it for about six months now and was only about fifty pages into it. Just looking at the cover made me sad.

"You know, reading that stuff will make you dumber by the minute," I said. "There have been studies."

"You're saying I'm dumb?" she said, without looking up.

"No. I'm saying *that* book will make you dumb. There are no words with more than two syllables in that whole thing. I'd bet a hundred bucks."

"But in order to get *dumber*, I'd already have to be dumb. You see the problem?"

"That's not what I meant," I said, scrambling a bit to recover. "I'm saying…"

She looked back down at the page. "Keep explaining. You're doing great. Really."

I sipped my beer instead. At least I knew how to do that without getting in trouble.

After a while we ate the sandwiches and I had some salad while Caroline looked on in disgust. Despite her trim, athletic figure, she lived on a diet that would give an NFL lineman the meat sweats. She hated vegetables with a passion and, if left to her own devices, often ate dessert before dinner. She was eating a salami, pepperoni and ham sub covered in hot peppers and Italian dressing. I had turkey and lettuce on whole wheat and was munching on a large dill pickle.

"Have I mentioned my theory on pickles?" she said between bites of the hoagie.

"Not today."

"They're just cucumbers dipped in evil."

"But you don't like cucumbers either."

"So maybe they're more like evil dipped in evil. I'll have to work on it some more."

We had finished eating and were on our second beers when my phone rang. I checked the screen, not real interested in talking to anyone at the moment, and saw the photo of my brother standing in St. Peter's square in Rome. I hadn't spoken with him since we'd gotten back from Key West.

I answered. "Brendan, what's going on?"

"Nothing. Just checking in on you. Making sure that you weren't swallowed up by the Bahamas triangle down there."

"It's the Bermuda triangle, B. And I'm fine."

My brother was a priest assigned to a parish in Palo Alto, California, and did not know much about the real world. I had once had to fly out there to help him set up a bank account. When I got to the bank, the woman helping us explained that Brendan had been bringing in his small paychecks for several months and just asking the bank to hold them.

"Good. You working? I don't want to bother you."

"Dude, you're never bothering me. I'm just sitting on the beach with Caroline, not doing much of anything." I could tell something was on his mind, but I knew he would get to it at his own pace.

"Ok...so I wanted to ask a favor. It's entirely acceptable if you say no. I would understand, of course."

"B, stop dancing around. Whatever you need."

"Well, I was thinking of maybe coming back east for a little while. I, ah, need a break and I haven't been back to grandpa's house in a few years, and so I was just thinking maybe I'd come. But I don't want to inconvenience you two."

The house that Caroline and I lived in had been built by my grandfather, passed on to my dad when I was a child and then I'd bought it from him a few years back, after my mother had died. Brendan still thought of it as grandpa's house for whatever reason and would probably call it that even if he owned it. I covered the phone and said to Caroline, "He's coming out for a couple weeks. Ok?"

"Of course! I can't wait!" She had never met Brendan and had been bugging me to rectify that situation.

To Brendan: "That sounds great, man. We'd love it. When are you thinking of coming?"

"I have a flight booked for tomorrow. I hope that's not too soon." His voice sounded a bit shaky and watery.

"That's totally fine. Give me the flight info and we'll meet you at Logan."

"Thanks Danny. That's…thanks."

I ended the call and leaned back in my chair, looking out at a pair of teenage boys making expert use of a skimboard along the waterline. They darted in and out of the shallows, looking for just the right moment, then slapping the flat wooden football-shaped boards onto the thin film of water and riding as far as they could, arms pinwheeling as they worked to stay upright.

Although we had been close when we were young, Brendan and I had taken different paths as young men and adults and I had to admit to myself that I didn't really know him very well right now. Brendan had always been introspective and quiet, and often would spend hours in his room thinking about one sentence in a school essay or how to approach a problem in his personal life. He had been one of those kids in high school who got along well with just about every clique without belonging to any of them. Smart without being arrogant or showy about it, Brendan had had his pick of colleges and when it came time to make the decision, he surprised just about all of us by choosing Notre Dame and then going on to the seminary from there. Our family was Catholic, but none of us, aside from our mom, was especially serious about it. She was devout but never pushed it too hard on the three of us kids. My sister Erin hadn't seen the inside of a church for more than ten years by the time she died and I had moved on from religion long ago. What I had seen in my years as a cop had pushed me even further down that path, removing any small notion I might have had that there was some amorphous being with a grand plan for all of us. There was just too much hate and chaos in the world for that to be possible.

Our divergent views of the world and life had put Brendan and I at odds at various points in recent years, but we were still brothers first. Everything else came in a distant second. We talked fairly often, but usually not about anything deeper than our work, how our father was doing and whether the Orioles had any chance of finishing above last place this season. During the most difficult days of the investigation last year into DeSilva and Alves, I had talked with Brendan several times about my struggles with the ideas of justice and right and wrong. He had said he knew I'd make the right choice and that the concept of earthly justice should not be of any concern to me. God would take care of that, he said.

I took care of it myself instead.

I chewed my lower lip and found that I was more than a little disquieted by the call with Brendan. Whatever was bothering him was bound to be something relatively thorny. He didn't often ask for help with his problems, preferring to trust in God to show him the right path. It had been his way for most of his life, and it had given him a contented life so far. The idea that he was having enough trouble that he needed to fly three thousand miles to see me did not sit well.

"Did he sound ok?" Caroline asked.

"Not really. He seemed…off somehow. Like something had spooked him."

"Well, hopefully a couple of weeks out here in the sun will fix him up. Oh! I just thought of something…" She was up, moving toward the house.

"What?"

"Does he know I live here? I mean, do I need to go stay at the motel or something?"

I laughed. "No, babe. He's aware that I don't share his views on cohabitation."

Brendan was coming in the next afternoon on the United direct flight from San Francisco, which gave Caroline less than twenty-four hours to freak out about what a mess the house was, clean it, clean it again and then tell me she was embarrassed at the way we lived.

"Honey, he's a priest, not a monk," I said, after we'd collapsed onto the couch in the living room at the end of the cleaning marathon, well after ten that night.

"If I had just one more day, I could make this place look like humans lived here," she said. "The floors need waxing, the counters need to be done and our room is just a wreck."

I didn't mention that our room looked far better than at any time since I'd owned the house, nor that I had never mopped the wood floors, let alone waxed them. I wasn't interested in setting her off again.

"But you're the first human to live here for a long time," I said.

Four

I slept badly that night. I dreamt of dogs, black and grey, their muzzles slick with foaming saliva. They moved in groups of two and three toward my house, picking their way soundlessly across the marshy land to the west. A yellow moon lighted their path and they moved with purpose and direction, not pausing to look for markers or listen for sounds. Though the moon was high and full, it gave no reflection off the dogs' eyes. Instead, the sockets were blank and colorless. Not black or even dark, but simply devoid of coloring and substance. It was as if they all had been born without the need for sight.

As the animals moved closer to the house, they picked up speed and one of them toward the front of the pack, not the largest by the look of him, but clearly the leader, moved naturally to the center as the others fell in behind him on either side. In the dream I stood on the back deck of the house, watching as the dogs moved across the marshland. Though the tide was in and the inlet at the rear of the house was filled, the dogs trotted across it, seeming to float above the water as they ran. As they neared, I felt no fear or anxiety, only a sense of inevitability, as though these animals had been on their way for a very long time and now they sensed that their journey was almost at an end.

The lead dog crossed onto the land at the back of the house and he accelerated again, this time moving into a full run. As he covered the sandy ground between the house and the inlet the moonlight caught him full in the face and I saw that what covered his muzzle was not water or saliva but frothy blood, bubbling up out of his mouth. His tongue lashed out and licked his chops clean, but still the blood came up, covering his muzzle again as soon as he cleaned it. The other dogs were fading into the background now, dropping back as the leader closed in on the house. They blurred and began to disappear from view even as the lead dog came into sharper focus and seemed to grow in size as he neared the house. I saw a shadow pass over the lone dog's face and looked up to see a long-winged egret moving in wide, lazy circles overhead. The dog, sightless though he was, sensed it too and raised his face to the sky. He faltered for a second, his hind legs catching in the deep sand. He quickly caught his balance and pushed forward with renewed purpose. I saw the shadow once again, larger now, and then a third time as the bird circled lower. The dog was twenty yards away now and I could feel him, smell his scent. I made no effort to move, though I was sure this animal meant me harm. I could see the dog gathering himself for the leap up to the deck, his muscles flexing and tensing. But just as he reached the edge of the yard, he stopped short, his paws just on the other side of the grass.

The animal, which I now clearly saw was a wolf, lowered his head and licked his chops once again, wiping away the bloody foam, and let out a low, primal growl. It was not a threatening sound or the sound of fear. Instead, it sounded almost like disappointment. He crouched there for a long minute, teeth bared and cast his empty eye sockets directly at me. I shivered, though the night was warm and humid, and watched the foam drip from his jaws onto the sand as he began to back slowly away. He retreated into the marshland and gradually faded into the darkness.

In the morning, I stood on the small deck off the bedroom that Caroline and I shared as the sun rose over the water and looked down at the marsh and the inlet, studying it for signs of movement. While Caroline slept, I dressed quietly and went downstairs and out into the back yard and walked to the spot where I'd seen the wolf stop in my dream. A small pile of rocks fashioned into a crude pyramid stood on the grass there, marking the place where I'd buried Reggie, my black lab, last year. I squatted down to put some of the stones back in place and saw that a dark stain was spread over the grass in a short line leading to the sand. I stood, feeling dizzy and weak, and moved around Reggie's grave to find a dark stain on the sand as well. I reached out a shaky hand and touched the sand and brought it up to my nose. Blood.

"Wolves?" Caroline asked. "I don't think we have wolves around here."

"Did I mention it was a dream?" I said. "They're usually not that accurate on regional animal populations."

We were a couple of miles into a seven-mile loop that we ran a few times a week, keeping close to the edge of the road to take advantage of what little shade there was. I had recounted to Caroline the dream and my discovery earlier in the morning of the blood in the backyard and she had listened quietly. I wasn't much for reading deep meanings into my dreams, mostly because it seemed to me that they were usually just my subconscious taking bits and pieces of things going on in my brain and throwing them into a blender and showing me the resulting movie. I treated them as a way for my brain to keep itself occupied while my body rested, not as some window into my psyche or predictor of events to come. Caroline tended to share that view, but this one seemed to have her a little more concerned.

"What do you think it was about?" she asked.

"The same thing all dreams are about. Nothing. It's just my brain fucking with me."

She was quiet for a minute or two, then: "I don't like the blood thing. That's creepy. You're sure it was blood? Maybe it was just some oil from the lawn mower or something."

"It was blood. But who knows where it came from? There are hawks and egrets back there all the time. One of them could have caught a rabbit or a squirrel and killed it there and then taken it away to eat it. Or it could have been some other injured animal. It's just a coincidence."

"You don't believe in coincidences," she said.

She had me. I believed in coincidences about as much as I believed that O.J. spent all those years looking for the real killer. Coincidences were for intellectually lazy people too simple to figure out what actually happened.

"Um, I do when they support my theory," I said.

"Ok. So let's say that part is a coincidence. Why did the wolf stop at the edge of the yard in the dream? What was it scared of?"

"I don't know that it was scared of anything," I said.

But I did know. The animal had stopped at Reggie's grave, sensing his presence. I had rescued Reggie a couple of years earlier from a shelter, and he had been the perfect dog for me: low maintenance, easy going and amiable. He had been killed by Joao Alves during the height of our investigation into the human trafficking operation Alves and DeSilva were running. Reggie had taken to Caroline immediately and his death had hit her hard, as it had me. When I'd found Reggie's body one night when Caroline and I came home late, it had broken my heart as well as hers. I had considered getting a new dog recently, but it still felt too soon. Maybe next year.

Caroline and I ran along in easy silence for a while, keeping a comfortably hard pace, she letting me keep up without hurting my ego too badly. We passed through the Eel River marshlands on Jordan Road, pushing hard on the rolling hills and on through to Long Pond Road where we turned north toward town. Caroline led the way as we ran single file along the sandy shoulder past the light early morning traffic. I thought some more about the dream and Reggie and wolves, and felt a little tickle at the back of my brain, a fraction of a memory. It slid away before I could bring it forward, though, so I let it go and switched my mind off, letting it float along as we ran.

Some people do their best thinking in the shower or on the crapper or while they're driving. For me, I've always been able to work things out best when I'm running. Whenever I come up against something in my work or elsewhere that I can't seem to work through, heading out for a run usually helps me figure it out. I'm not sure why that is, but I'm happy that it still seems to work. The mechanics of it don't interest me; only the results.

"Are you guys going to get into this thing?" Caroline said as we ran down South Street past a small group of houses on our left and the town library on our right.

"Not sure. Right now, we're just trying to figure out who knows what and see if maybe we can't help out Savannah. I don't think there's much more to it than that for us."

"Yet," she said.

"Who's to say there will be?" I said. "The Boston cops know how to work a murder. They don't need me and JD in there confusing things. We just want to see if we can make some sense of the, uh, stuff on Wyatt's computer. If we can figure that out and make Savannah and her mom happy, then we're done."

"Or not," she said as we made the right back onto 3A and headed south toward the beach. We ran in silence the rest of the way home.

An hour later, I rolled the Jeep into the lot at the yacht club. JD was waiting outside, dressed, as Caroline's dad had suggested, in pants. They probably weren't the ones Scott Nelson had in mind, however. I stared at him as he climbed into the Jeep and tossed his laptop bag in the back.

"What?" he said. "I was told to wear pants. So I'm wearing pants."

"You sure?"

What JD had on his legs could only be called pants under the loosest, most generous definition of the word. They appeared to be made of one of those fabrics that's advertised in the back of Sunday newspaper magazines as "space age" and "flame-retardant", though I had serious doubts about that last adjective. The pants bore a checkerboard pattern of alternating squares of dark blood red and a shade of yellow that I'd only seen in a toilet in a bar. They had no belt loops but sported a clever system on one side that allowed the wearer to adjust the waist size as his fortunes waxed and waned. The pants ended about six inches above JD's ankles and had some sort of logo with a medieval shield and a lion holding a trident. JD had chosen to finish the ensemble with a pair of Sanuk sandals and a red t-shirt with a picture of a sandwich that said "The McRib is Back".

"You're gonna get us shot," I said.

"I don't have any pants, so I met a very nice English gentleman at the bar last night and I explained my dilemma and he was nice enough to lend me these," JD said.

"Why didn't you bring any pants? You're in Massachusetts. It'll be winter by sundown."

"No, I don't *have* any pants. Don't own any."

"Of course you don't." I put the Jeep in gear and pulled onto Union Street and made for the highway. "I thought this might be a problem. Reach in the back there and grab my backpack. There's some jeans in there for you. And a polo."

"Aw hell. A polo? I'm gonna look like fuckin' cell phone salesman," JD said as he pulled on the clothes.

"Better than Ronald McDonald," I said.

We met Scott Nelson near the carousel on the Greenway, the long, narrow park that the city of Boston had given to its citizens as a long-overdue apology for the Southeast Expressway's reign of terror. The hideous goose-shit green elevated highway had cast a long shadow over the eastern part of the city for decades, and had separated the North End from the rest of Boston, providing a physical border to go along with the sociological and mental ones that had always existed. Nelson was standing in the shade of the carousel with two other men, whom I took to be Chris King and Dave Henderson. Nelson introduced us and we shook hands all around. Henderson had the kind of handshake common in steroid cases and overly enthusiastic car salesmen. He held the grip a second or two longer than was necessary and seemed to be studying me as he released my hand.

We all walked over to a pair of benches under a trellis covered with pink and white blooms and sat. All except Scott.

"Tobin, I explained to the guys your connection to their case and what you two are trying to do here. At least as best I could," Nelson said. "The floor is yours."

"Thanks, Scott," I said. I stood and faced King and Henderson, who sat on one bench, while Nelson took my spot on the other next to JD. "Detectives, thanks for your time here. As Scott mentioned, your victim is the brother of a friend of ours. A good friend. She's a sister to us. She and her family obviously have had a tough time with this, just with the murder by itself. But then they read the news like everyone else and they see this stuff about Wyatt being involved in child exploitation and they start thinking that something has gotten mixed up. Because that's not the Wyatt that they know. Not at all. So they asked me and JD to see what we can find out. We're not here to get in anyone's way or double-check your work. We just want to see if we can help Wyatt's family understand what happened."

Henderson and King looked at each other and King shrugged. Henderson studied his nails.

"Not a whole lot to tell you that you don't already know," King said. "We got the call a few minutes after the roommate called nine-one-one. A pair of uniforms were close by and they went in and saw what was what and then called for homicide. When we got there the roommate was out on the curb with some of his friends who had shown up. He was shaking pretty bad and not making much sense, so we didn't bother with him at that point."

"How long had Wyatt been dead when the roommate found him?" I asked.

"Coroner says about five or six hours, which would put the time of death around midday. Roommate, whose name is Martin Simms, says when he left for work that morning Austin was awake but said he wasn't going to work. Was feeling a little sick, something about a stomach bug. So this was around seven-thirty, seven-forty-five. Simms goes off to work, doesn't hear from him during the day, goes out for a drink with some co-workers and then goes home and finds him. You know the rest."

"Was it unusual for Wyatt to stay home like that?" I asked.

"Yeah, sort of. Simms says he had been living with Austin for more than a year and had only seen him miss work once or twice before," King said.

"And the apartment…what was the scene like?"

King glanced at Henderson, who had been quiet the whole time. Henderson sighed and leaned back against the metal trellis support.

"What do you think?" Henderson said. "Guy was tied to the bed, shot. Not much to it, really. Aside from the dead asshole."

JD came off the bench quickly and was in front of Henderson in two steps. I got my hand on his elbow and Scott Nelson stood next to Henderson and eyed JD carefully, waiting for him to make a move. Chris King stayed on the bench. Henderson never moved and just looked at JD curiously, interested to see what happened next.

"Easy, easy," I said.

"Fuck easy," JD said, his teeth gritted. I could feel his muscles tense under my grip. He pointed at Henderson: "You don't know shit about Wyatt or his life. And from what I can tell, you don't know shit about his death either. You've already made up your mind about him and put your stupid theory in the paper. Some fucking cop you are, using the media to do your dirty work for you."

Henderson stood up slowly, fully engaged now. He wasn't a tall guy, a little under six feet, which put him on about equal footing with JD. But Henderson was solid and had the cop attitude, not to mention two other cops standing next to him.

"Look here, son. I haven't talked to any damn reporter, not now and not in years. Got no use for them," Henderson said, a small smile on his face. "Media can suck it. So that information didn't come from me. You're talking about the *Sunrise* story, right? Yeah. He got one thing right: your boy was into that shit up to his ears. That much is for sure."

"He wasn't my boy," JD said. "He was my girlfriend's brother and he was a good man, regardless of what you think. But then again, I wouldn't expect you to go much farther than the obvious. You put two and two together and got nine."

"This wasn't even two plus two, son. It was already four," Henderson said.

"Bullshit. You're just looking for an easy way out of a case that makes you nervous," JD said.

I looked at King, who was standing by quietly, his face unreadable. Scott was watching Henderson intently, a look of disdain on his face.

"We got plenty on Austin to make the connections we've made. And that puts him in the middle of a bunch of shit you don't want to hear about. Believe me."

"Yeah, you mean aside from having no evidence and no suspect? Sounds solid as a rock to me," JD said. "Fucking stellar police work."

Henderson moved in closer to JD, their faces inches apart. I tightened my grip on JD's arm, ready for the worst.

"Listen, boy. Until you know what we seen on that computer, don't you say another fucking word to me about evidence. Not one. Hear? Because what we seen will curl your fucking toes. So unless you're interested in taking this up a notch, you shut your fucking mouth. Clear?"

"We'll see," JD said. "We'll see."

King's shoulders slumped at the mention of the computer and I felt JD's muscles relax as he backed away from Henderson and wandered over to the carousel where he stood and watched the children whirl around in circles on top of plastic lobsters and seahorses. Henderson stayed where he was and turned his gaze on me.

"And what's with you?" he said. "You think we're just taking the easy way out over here?"

"No idea," I said. "I don't know you or anything about how you work. Like I said before, I just want to help our friend get some answers. I'm not here to judge your investigative skills. I'm sure you're good at your job."

He just sneered and turned away and walked down the Greenway toward Rowe's Wharf. I looked at King and Scott Nelson, both of whom had remained calm and quiet during the confrontation between Henderson and JD.

"Didn't see that coming. Sorry guys," I said.

King shrugged. "Dave's a tough guy to deal with sometimes. But I wouldn't recommend your friend try that trick again," he said. "If we had been in a parking ramp instead of a public place, it would've gone differently, I think."

"On both ends," I said.

"He'd hit a cop?" Nelson asked.

"Nope," I said. "Not him."

Five

"That was fun," I said.

We were back in the Jeep, heading south on Atlantic Avenue on our way out of the city. JD had calmed down some but was still tenser than I was used to seeing him. He looked out at the passing traffic and the streams of people pouring in and out of the subway stations and high rises in Boston's financial district. I had known JD for the better part of twenty years and I had rarely seen him that upset. He was an even-keeled guy who normally didn't take anything too seriously, especially some bullshit from a clown he didn't know. But something had dug in deep on him back there with Henderson.

We crept through the light midday traffic in the South End, winding through the streets lined with brick row houses that were older than most of the towns in New England. We crossed over Tremont on West Newton Street and found Wyatt Austin's address in a block of neatly kept houses near the O'Day Playground. His apartment was on the ground floor of a building in the middle of the block and I could see from the street that it was unoccupied. The windows showed no blinds or curtains and though the sun shone through the windows, I could see no furniture inside. I found a spot up the block a bit and we walked back to the building where Wyatt had lived and died. It was an unremarkable building in every way, on a block with a dozen more like it and on a street with a hundred others. A visitor without an exact address could spend hours wandering up and down these streets searching for the right house. We stood in front of Wyatt's house, peering inside as people walked by, oblivious.

"What are we doing?" JD said.

"Don't know. I just wanted to take a look."

So we looked. From the sidewalk, all we could see was the front room, which probably looked like the front room of every other apartment like this in every other rowhouse on the street. Wood floors, overhead lights, white walls.

A nice tidy house that just happened to be a murder scene.

"We going in?" JD said.

I looked at the lock on the door—a simple handle and deadbolt—and thought about what might be in there. The crime scene crew would have processed it the day of the killing and pulled out everything of any use, and then the cleaners would have gone in and done their best, trying to restore the place to some semblance of normalcy. I'd been in dozens of houses like that, with the dried blood ground into the hardwood floors and the smell of the cleaning fluids seeping into my nostrils and burning my eyes. I thought about what would be inside the apartment, even this long after the murder, and I had no desire to go in there. It would serve no purpose.

I turned and walked back toward the Jeep. I was two steps from the vehicle when I heard a loud crack, the sound of wood splintering. I crouched and spun around. The door to Wyatt's apartment was hanging off the hinges and JD was standing in the doorway, peering around the corner into the front room.

"I guess we're going in," I said.

I looked up and down the street and saw no one who seemed to have any interest in what we were doing. I scrambled off the sidewalk and followed JD into the apartment. The interior was dark and clammy, despite the midday sun. JD was in the middle of the front room, turning in a slow circle, taking in the surroundings. He did two revolutions and then stood stock still, looking down the short hallway to the back bedroom. I could feel the air in the apartment, full of moisture and dust and the residue of the death. The smell was awful, a mix of coppery dried blood and mustiness. I wanted to be out.

After a few moments, JD began edging down the hallway, walking with the slow, tentative steps of a young boy going down into a dark room. He moved past the smaller guest bedroom on the right that had belonged to Martin Simms without giving it a glance. I could see the sweat stains on the back of his shirt as he approached the open doorway to what had been Wyatt's room. He stopped on the threshold, one foot in the hallway and one in the room. I was twenty feet behind him with no view into the room, but I knew what he was looking at. Wyatt Austin's bed rested against the far wall, facing the open door where JD now stood. The room was remarkably clean, save for a small, dark stain about the size of a quarter on the back wall. JD was staring at the stain, and he remained still there for so long that I began to wonder whether he'd fallen asleep on his feet.

I put my hand on his shoulder. "We've seen it. Let's get—"

I felt him crumble under my hand and he sat down heavily on the floor, his legs straight in front of him. The collapse surprised me and I wasn't quick enough to catch him as he slumped to the left, his head thudding against the doorframe, and then lay crumpled in the hall, curled in a fetal position.

I squatted on my heels next to him, checked for a pulse and breathing. All signs go. His eyes were half open, as though he were just waking up.

"Hey man. You ok? You took a little spill there," I said.

No response. The breathing came steadily and the eyes opened and closed regularly. So I waited. In about ten minutes, JD sat slowly upright and tried to struggle to his feet. I went over and got him under the arms and we walked like that out of the apartment where I sat him on the brick stairs and waited some more. In a while, he began to look around and seemed to be getting his bearings. He looked over at me with a mix of curiosity and embarrassment.

"Why are we sitting out here?" he asked.

"You had a little, ah, thing inside there."

He turned and looked slowly at the apartment's front door. When he turned back to me, he said, "We went in?"

"For a minute or two. Then you decided to lie down for a while on the hall floor and now we're back out here," I said. "How do you feel?"

JD scratched his head and looked out at the passing foot traffic. He was quiet for a time, watching the students and workmen going here and there. The sun was glinting off the windows of the brownstones across the street and JD shaded his eyes.

"Fuzzy," he said. "I remember us driving here and then standing down there in front of the door…and then we were sitting here. How does that happen?"

I shrugged. "Not sure. You never said a word in there. You walked into the living room and then down the hall to Wyatt's bedroom, and then you sort of slumped down to the floor slowly and ended up lying in the hall. I got you up after a few minutes and walked you out here and now we're watching Berklee kids walk back and forth. You ever fainted before?"

"Not that I remember."

"Well, you don't remember this one either, so I guess that doesn't mean much," I said.

JD rubbed the back of his neck and stood up. "Let's go," he said. "I don't like it here."

We had a couple of hours to kill before Brendan's flight landed at Logan, so we drove over to the Yard House, a nice dark bar in the shadow of Fenway Park. The Sox were out of town, so we had no trouble finding spots at the rectangular bar. The bartender dropped a magazine-sized draft list in front of us and walked down the bar to help some other customers.

"Stone IPA for me," I said, when he came back.

The bartender looked at JD. "Lemme get a yard of Dale's and a shot of Jameson," JD said.

"Good enough," the bartender said, and went away to get our drinks.

"Irish breakfast," I said.

"Feeling a little shaky over here," he said.

When the drinks came, JD drank the shot straight down and chased with a small sip of his beer. We watched an inning of the Sox and Yankees on the TVs above the bar and sipped our beers in silence. I finished my beer and ordered another. JD was still working his way through the yard.

"You've seen a lot of that, I guess," he said.

"Stanton striking out on four pitches? Yeah."

"The blood, the smell, all that."

"Yeah."

"It was the smell that got to me," he said. "The blood was just…blood. But the smell was so bad. It's like the cleaning stuff is worse than what they're trying to clean up."

"It's not," I said.

"I don't know if I'm fit for this kind of thing. Not like you."

Brendan was standing on the concrete island outside the arrivals area at terminal C at Logan. He wore dark jeans and a light wool sweater despite the summer heat and had a small leather satchel clutched in his right hand. He gave me a long, tight hug and shook hands with JD and we loaded his small rolling suitcase into the Jeep. I had the top off the Jeep and Brendan sat in the back, his face tilted up toward the sun, the wind playing havoc with his hair. I noticed that his hair was longer than when I'd seen him last and it had gained quite a bit more grey. He looked calm but somehow disquieted. When we pulled onto the beach road, Brendan opened his eyes, looking out at the ocean. Caroline was waiting on the porch when we turned into the driveway. We piled out of the Jeep and up the stairs and introduced Brendan to Caroline. She looked nervous and tense, but when Brendan wrapped her in a warm hug, the tension drained from her face.

"Well, Miss Caroline, it is lovely to finally meet you," Brendan said.

"Danny never told me that the handsome one of you two went into the seminary."

"It seemed unfair to limit myself to just one woman, so I chose the church instead," Brendan said. "I'm quite sure Danny has made up for my absence."

I cleared my throat. "Okayyy, what do you say we move this party inside and let Brendan get settled?"

Caroline and I offered the upstairs, but Brendan insisted he was fine on the couch. A little discomfort was good for the soul, he said. He went upstairs to get cleaned up after the flight while Caroline and I got dinner going. JD begged off, saying he was tired, so he took the Jeep back to the yacht club.

I had stopped at Wood's and bought four lobsters on the way in from the airport, knowing that Brendan loved the giant bugs and didn't get them much out west. While the water boiled, Caroline set out the big mound of shrimp I'd gotten and covered it with Old Bay. By the time Brendan was ready, Caroline and I had already put a dent in the shrimp and were halfway through our first beers. I handed Brendan a can of Mayflower New World IPA and he tipped his can to us and had a deep swallow. He held the can back, examining the label for a minute.

"Made in Plymouth? Never would've thought there'd be a brewery here," he said.

"Things change," I said.

"That they do," Brendan said. He walked around the kitchen and living room area, picking up framed photos, touching a small throw pillow that our mother had crocheted when we were boys. He spent several minutes standing in front of the landscape that Caroline was working on, moving back and forward to get different angles on it.

"You're quite talented, Caroline," he said. "There's something I really like about the way you're using the blues and greys in the trees over here on the right side. They're cool colors but somehow are conveying a kind of warmth there."

"That's very nice of you." She smacked me on the arm. "Danny said that it looked like a herd of llamas. What was the line you used? Just because an artist made it doesn't mean it's art?"

"It was a joke! I love it. I think she's done a great job with the llamas."

We took the shrimp out on the deck and sat at the table, munching and drinking. The air was cooling and there was a hint of breeze coming off the water. When Brendan and I were young, we'd always come to the beach house with our parents for Labor Day weekend. I'd always secretly dreaded that trip, knowing that it meant the beginning of the end of something that I loved. Now, as an adult, I'd grown to love the onset of fall, even though it signaled the end of the warm weather. Because it also promised months of time to myself on the beach without the roving pods of loud, sunburned tourists. The bars and the beaches of my town were once again mine.

I looked over at Brendan as he and Caroline chatted about the changes in Plymouth since our childhood. He was clearly at ease here. Even though it had been years since his last visit, he had slipped easily back into the relaxed persona he'd always had here when we were boys. His phone call had unsettled me and I wasn't sure what to expect when he got here, but if anything he seemed to be calmer than I'd thought he'd be.

I went back inside and lowered the squirming lobsters into the roiling water. Brendan came in and stood next to me at the stove, and we listened as the bugs squealed their last and finally quieted down.

"Not a good way to go," Brendan said.

I shrugged. "Eh, good or bad, we're all fertilizer," I said. "Doesn't matter much in the end."

Brendan smiled weakly. "Ah, there's the fatalism I remember. I've missed that."

"I do bar mitzvahs and funerals. Just let me know."

One of the lobsters poked his head above the water and bobbed up and down a couple of times, looking for all the world as though he had designs on climbing out of the pot, scurrying across the road and heading for the safety of the ocean. Instead, I sent him back under the scalding water with the tongs and turned the flame down a bit. Brendan leaned against the counter, looking out the back door to where Caroline stood at the deck railing.

"How long have you guys been together now? A year?"

"About that, yeah."

"She's quite in love with you, you know," he said.

"I told you she was smart."

"Which is why it was so surprising to realize how taken she is with you."

"It really is pretty shocking."

"You're about to hit your expiration date though, aren't you? A year is more like a decade for you."

"Like you said, things change."

He nodded and drank some beer. "For everyone," he said.

The lobsters were done, so I turned off the flame, moved the huge dented black pot to a back burner and let the water sit for a minute while I got the plates, utensils and butter ready.

"Is that mom's old lobster pot?" Brendan asked.

"Yeah. Dad brought it up a couple of summers ago. Said he couldn't find any lobsters worth a damn in Virginia, so I might as well have it here."

"I saw mom's pillow in the other room, too. It's nice that you have some of her stuff here. It makes it still feel like our house."

"It *is* our house," I said. "I'm just the one living here right now, that's all."

"Not the only one…"

I looked at my watch. "Damn, Caroline had over three hours before you mentioned that. I owe her ten bucks."

"I'm not going to get on you about it, Danny. You know my feelings. End of discussion," Brendan said.

"That's it? You sure?"

"Something else you need to discuss? I'm sure it's been a while since your last confession."

"I'm good."

"You look good," he said. "You seem happy, content."

"I *am* happy. I'm not sure whether content is a word that I'd use to describe myself at any point," I said. "But yeah, things are good with Caroline, work's going along pretty well. Not too much to complain about right now."

"That doesn't sound like you."

"Gimme a minute. I'll find something," I said.

He was talking in circles, working his way around to the reason he came out here. Brendan had a deliberate way about him, doing things in his own time. Trying to rush him wouldn't actually speed up the process, it would just fluster him and stretch things out even further. So I waited. We took the lobsters and corn out to the deck and ate and drank and talked and drank some more and talked some more. And Brendan and Caroline got on like they'd spent a summer together fifteen years ago and hadn't seen each other since. I ate the better part of two lobsters and enjoyed watching the two of them discuss books I'd never read and painters I would never care about. By the time they had exhausted themselves, the sun had been down for an hour, the crickets were in full song and I was fading fast.

Caroline stood up from the table, kissed Brendan lightly on the cheek, did the same to me, and went up to the bedroom. Brendan pulled his chair around to face me.

"Good meal, Danny. I didn't know you'd become such a good cook."

"Out of necessity," I said. "If I hadn't learned to do it, I would've starved to death years ago. And Caroline can't make a peanut butter sandwich, so it works out."

"Maybe you can teach me someday. I might need to learn how to take care of myself," he said.

I stared at him. "Why?"

"I'm in a bit of a tough situation right now. As you know, my faith and my work are everything to me. They are the reasons that I get up in the morning and why I can sleep peacefully at night. I know that God has a plan for me and that the work I do every day with my parishioners makes a difference in people's lives. I've never wavered in that belief, and I never will. It's what defines me. I am my faith."

I nodded. "I know."

"Without that faith and that knowledge of what's in store for me, here and in the life to come, I would not be able to endure what I see and hear from my parishioners each day. Danny, I know you have been through a lot and seen your share of bad things, evil even. But the pain and despair that I see in the eyes of my people every day, I can't tell you how much it hurts me. I see their faith being shaken by the things they have to deal with in their lives. The family problems, financial pressure, marital issues. They see all the bad things happening in the world and they pray and they come to Mass and they wonder why there's so much pain and mayhem and hate. They ask me, Why does God let this happen? How could He let my little girl die? Why did my husband cheat on me? And I've always had an answer for them, and it's always been the same answer for all these years: God has a plan. As long as you remember that, the bumps and bruises that come along the way are just that. And that's truly my belief. If I don't know anything else, I know that. I put my faith in that plan," Brendan said.

"B, if you're here to try and bring me back into the fold..."

He waved his hand at me. "No. I'm finished tilting at that windmill. I know where you stand and I know you're a good person, and that's enough for me now."

"So what then? I'm missing it."

"Me too, Danny. Lately, I've found that something is missing for me. I haven't felt right in quite some time, now. I've been a bit at loose ends, trying to figure out what it is. I've talked with my fellow priests and even our bishop, looking for some answer to this quandary. It's been months of prayer and discussions, but I've reached a decision."

I said nothing.

"I believe God's plan for me has changed. I'm planning to leave the priesthood at the end of the year," he said. His voice was quiet but firm. It spoke of resolve.

Brendan was the most thoughtful and careful person I knew, and if he had come to this decision it had been, as he said, a long, contemplative process. He was not one for rash decisions or gut reactions. His worldview was at the opposite end of the spectrum from my own, and where I was impulsive and judgmental, he was calm and understanding. So I knew that something major must have happened for him to have made this choice.

"Nothing to say?" he asked.

"I have a lot to say. I'm just not sure where to start."

"With the obvious question," he said.

"Ok. Want another beer?"

"Oh, thank you for that. Yes, in fact, I'd love another one."

I went into the kitchen and brought back two more Mayflowers. I handed one to Brendan and he took a long drink.

"Ok, now the real question," he said.

"What's changed?" I asked. "If there was anything I knew for sure, it was that you had found your spot in the world."

He nodded. "Indeed I have. I *had*. Gosh, it's hard to say that. It wasn't any one event. I guess it began when Erin died. I have counseled many of my parishioners over the years who had had to deal with the loss of a loved one, sometimes from violence. It's an ugly part of our world and a distasteful part of a priest's life. But it's an important one, as well. I looked at it as a chance to remind people about the joy and love that awaits the faithful after death. But when Erin was killed, I found myself wondering what purpose her death could possibly have served. She was a beautiful, loving girl who had put her trust in the wrong person. And it had gotten her killed. Erin and I weren't as close as the two of you were, but her death sent me into what I later recognized as a deep depression. I began having a hard time taking joy from the daily routine of priestly life that I've always loved so much. I would avoid confessional duty if I could, something that I would never have done previously. I couldn't stand to listen to other peoples' problems. After all, I had my own to deal with. What could any of my parishioners have to tell me that was more important than Erin's death? Nothing. So I stayed in this state of self-pity for months, thinking that I was the only one who had ever had a sibling or loved one die and that how it affected me was the most important thing on earth. And for the first time I began questioning whether a truly just God could allow something like this to occur."

"You never let on," I said.

Erin's murder had been difficult on all three of us—me, Brendan and our father—but Brendan had seemed to handle it the best at the time. He'd spoken at her funeral about Erin's love for us and the beauty of her life and the beautiful legacy she'd left in the form of her friends and family. Privately, later that night, with an empty bottle of Jameson standing on the table in our father's kitchen, Brendan had spoken of the God of the Old Testament, the vengeful God who tolerated no insults and meted out justice in swift and certain terms. That God, he said, would ensure that Erin's death did not go unpunished.

And it hadn't.

"I knew that was not the time to come to you or dad with those concerns," Brendan said. "We were all deeply hurt and it was my place to hold fast. And, truth be told, I was more than a little embarrassed and ashamed by the doubts I was having. I spoke of them to no one, not even my fellow priests. Those topics are not talked about openly, as you might expect."

"But I'd bet my ass—sorry—that there isn't one of them who hasn't had the same thoughts at some point," I said, maybe a little too forcefully.

He smiled, nodded. "Not a single one. Whether they ever admit to even themselves is a separate question, but I assure you that all religious have these doubts. It's called faith for a reason, Danny. There's still a lot of unknowns out there, as you often remind me."

"I never thought I'd see the day when your faith wavered."

"You haven't. And you won't. What's changed is my faith and trust in the church, the institution that is supposed to function as the instrument of that love here on earth. The last few decades have been…difficult for the church, to say the least. Modern society has little time for our message, and I've always seen it as part of my job to help deliver that message in a way that people can understand and appreciate, in any time. But the problem we now face is, how do you continue to ask people to believe in the church, and by extension, God, when that same church has been responsible for sheltering some of the most vile, predatory criminals of the last century? I've watched as this all has unfolded, Danny, and it's sickened me. At first, I was like everyone else, and I couldn't believe that the church had done the things that the newspapers said it had. It just wasn't possible. But it happened. Bishops and others, who knew what these men—and I will not call them priests—had done and they not only didn't punish them, they helped hide them! They moved them from parish to parish, allowing them to continue their crimes and running countless lives in the process. We are taught as priests that no sin is unforgivable in the eyes of God, so long as the sinner is truly sorry and repentant. What I've learned through this process, Danny, is that I have different ideas about that than God might. To me, what these men and the church have done is truly unforgivable."

"This scandal isn't new, B. It's been going on for years now."

"You're right. But it showed up on my doorstep earlier this year. There was a man transferred from a parish in New Hampshire to my parish in Palo Alto. I didn't know anything of his history or his career, only that he was close to retirement. Our bishop had told us that the man was given this assignment in California as a kind of pre-retirement present, a thank you for years of faithful service. And we all took it at face value and went about our business until a few weeks later when a woman in our parish, someone I've known for years now, came and told me she had heard some horrid stories about the new man and was pulling her son from the altar server program. My parishioner has a sister in New Hampshire, you see, and she had filled her in on the real reason for the man's transfer. I won't recount those stories, but you can fill in the blanks, I'm sure. Well, by the time I worked up the courage to speak with the bishop, the new man was already gone and there were three families in my parish with sons whose lives were irreversibly damaged. These were altar boys all, Danny. Boys in my care. And this… this demon had taken them all into his confidence and ruined them. Ruined, Danny. Absolutely *ruined*. That was a week ago."

Brendan sighed, his shoulders slumped, and took a deep swallow of his beer, then stood and went to the railing of the deck and looked out over the inlet. The sky was clear and the stars were bright enough to illuminate the inky surface of the water. I said nothing for several minutes, wondering what exactly I had to offer him. Everything I thought of sounded trite or too clever so I opted for the direct approach.

"How can I help?" I asked.

He shook his head. "I just needed to get away from the situation and sit with my decision for a while and make sure that I wasn't being rash or dramatic."

"I've never known you to be either of those."

He shook his head sadly. "Things change," he said so quietly I wasn't sure it was meant for me to hear.

Six

In the morning, I woke to an empty house and a note on the kitchen counter from Caroline saying that she and Brendan had walked over to the beach and would be back by lunch time. That left me with a few hours to kill, so I called JD and asked him to find out what he could about Wyatt Austin and his roommate. I wanted to be sure that we had the right idea about them.

I ate a quick breakfast and then went for an easy ten mile run through downtown, up into North Plymouth and back around through some back roads. After a shower, I spent the next hour reading what little there was online about Chris King and Dave Henderson. Neither one of them came up too often in news articles, even though they'd both been involved in some fairly high-profile cases over the years, particularly Henderson. His time on the gang unit had been short, but he'd been part of a major undercover operation that had helped take down much of the leadership of one of the larger Irish gangs in the city. The crew had been working the lower end drug trade and serving as freelance head-knockers and killers for some of the other gangs in town, particularly the Italians, who were so low in numbers these days that they couldn't even muster the manpower for their own hits.

That case had been all over the papers and TV, but Henderson's name was only mentioned several weeks after the news broke when he was promoted and moved out of the gang unit. The case later fell apart when the defense attorneys showed that several key witnesses had been coerced into making statements, but by that time Henderson was up and out of there. Aside from that, there was virtually nothing to see on him, despite the problems that Scott Nelson said Henderson had had dealing with his partners and controlling his emotions over the years.

Chris King didn't register much more in the media, although I found a few old Globe and Herald stories where he was quoted as an official spokesman, but that was pretty early on in his career. The quotes were mostly innocuous, the kind of stuff that's vetted nine ways from Sunday before it's given to the press. Even those statements dripped with disdain, though, and the one TV clip I found of King consisted of him staring into a camera silently for forty-five seconds while a reported tried desperately to get any bit of information from him at a murder scene. The clip ended with King giving the camera the bird over his shoulder as he walked back to his car.

So, it looked like Nelson's assessment of King and Henderson's dealings with the media was pretty accurate. King was the picture of the cop who only wanted to do his job and saw the media as an obstacle, not an ally. If information needed to be

released, that was someone else's problem. Henderson, though...
I'd known other cops like him who had no official relationship
with the press, but somehow their cases always seemed to get big
play, even if they weren't the most newsworthy. Funny how
things worked.

Caroline and Brendan wandered in from the beach just past
noon, sun-baked and smiling. Caroline came over and stood on
her toes to kiss me hello. She tasted like a pleasant mix of salt and
lime.

"Someone's had a couple Coronas," I said as she dropped her
beach bag on the living room floor and went straight for the
refrigerator. She came out with the bowl of leftover lobster meat,
a lemon and some Cholula hot sauce.

"Correction: three Coronas," she said. She shoved the food at
me. "Lunch, please. I'm gonna shower."

"Yes'm." I dumped the lobster in a bowl, minced some fresh
garlic and celery and mixed it all together and then hit it with a
liberal dose of the lemon juice and Cholula. I took some fresh
Romaine from the fridge and made salads out of it all for me and
Brendan and then just put Caroline's portion on a plate. Brendan
and I sat down to eat and Caroline arrived from upstairs, freshly
scrubbed and trailing lovely girl scent. She dug into the plate as if
someone was threatening to steal it from her, and was finished

before I was halfway through mine. She sat back in her chair and patted her flat stomach.

"Hit the spot," she said and followed it with a long burp that caused Brendan to drop his fork. "Ha! Listen to me. Sorry, Brendan. A girl can get used to acting like a savage living out here. No one around to hear my gross sounds."

"It's quite alright. Our sister Erin had the same capacity for, um, noisemaking," Brendan said.

"I think I would've liked her," Caroline said quietly.

Brendan looked at me and we both smiled. "You most certainly would have," he said. "You two share a number of traits."

"Like what?"

"Well, your sense of humor and sharp wit, to start with. Erin and Danny would get in the loudest, most profane arguments about the silliest things, like who was going to wash the dishes after supper or who had played Sam the butcher on the Brady Bunch."

"The what?"

I sighed. "It's a TV show that had these two families...oh forget it. The point is, Erin and I were really close, but we argued all the time, too, and Erin was usually the one who came out on top. She was smart as hell and had this way of backing me into a corner with her arguments that frustrated me to no end. I hated it."

"Oh I bet. What else?" Caroline asked. She was leaning forward on the table, her hands propped under her chin.

"She was a helper, one of those people who is always taking on some project, usually a person who needs a lot of help," I said. "But she did it with dogs and rabbits and whatever else she could find that she thought needed her. She had friends who I couldn't see any redeeming value in at all, but she would stick with them no matter what. Almost to a fault."

"That's no fault. It's a virtue," Brendan said. "None of us really knows what we're doing in this life. We're all just wandering about, bouncing off one another, hoping to find some happiness along the way. And it's a lot easier when you have people to help you along the way. That's who Erin was. She would help anyone who needed it and worry about herself later. History is full of those kinds of women and it's something that I loved her for."

Caroline gave a wan smile and reached out and put her hand on Brendan's wrist. He returned the smile with a small laugh. "I think the two of you would have been quite a pair," he said.

"Quite a pair."

Caroline gathered up the dishes and took them into the kitchen and Brendan and I wandered out to the front porch and looked across the road at the sun bright beach. A pack of feral kids came clambering over the dunes squealing with laughter and scattered in all different directions. A moment later three older boys appeared atop the dunes, each holding one of those massive water guns that run on small car batteries and opened fire on the smaller kids, soaking them from thirty or forty feet away. The targeted kids ducked behind cars and used each other as shields as the streams of water continued. I saw one of the smaller boys pop the hatch on the SUV he was hiding behind and climb in. A few seconds later he came back out with a beach bucket in each hand. He crab-walked across the road and filled one with water from the inlet and scurried back, pulled several tennis balls from the other bucket and dunked them all in the water. He then began handing out tennis balls to the other boys and they rolled them in the sand and crushed shells on the beach road. I could see what was coming. They all sat on their heels behind the cars and as soon as they heard the click-click-click of the water guns going dry, they sprinted at the older boys, waiting until they were within easy range at the bottom of the dunes and then began hucking the tennis balls.

    The water gunners didn't register the counterattack quickly enough, standing their ground on the dunes and laughing as the horde of third-graders came at them. But when the first crustacean-crusted ball hit a tall, thin boy in the chest, bright red dots of blood appeared immediately, a perfect red circle marking his pale skin. The boy yelped and soon the others were hollering too as they tried to run down the dunes while protecting their exposed backs. The tennis balls hit with a soggy thump and each one elicited a painful cry from its victim. When the younger kids reached the top of the dunes, they all threw their arms in the air and screamed, a long high-pitched yawp.

"That was a pretty clever strategic move there," I said. "I don't think those guys will be coming back with the water guns anytime soon."

"Squirt gun attacks should be a young boy's biggest worry. Nothing more serious than that," Brendan said.

"Don't let it eat at you, B. How many people are in your parish? Thousands? You can't know what's happening with every one of them."

"But I didn't even know what my own priests were doing, Danny. And it's not so much that as it is the larger problems with the church. I can forgive myself, but forgiving those men is something I just can't do."

"There is no forgiveness for what they did," I said. "Hopefully, only punishment."

He grunted noncommittally and went inside.

That night we drove downtown and met JD for dinner at Dillon's Local. It was a small, homey spot done in rough wood with comfortable booths, a few high-tops, good service and a great rotating tap list. Our waitress, a friendly girl in her mid-20s with lots of red hair pulled back in a long ponytail, was named Ally and had worked with Caroline a couple of years back at the British Beer Company down the street. They chatted for a bit about Caroline's painting and Ally said she was making good tips at Dillon's and almost finished with her degree in restaurant management and was hoping to move to California when she was done next year and see if she could do any good out there. We ordered Philly cheese steak eggrolls to share. The bar was full but not overcrowded and the guy playing good acoustic covers in the corner was quiet enough so we could talk.

"I talked to Savannah today," JD said after Ally had come back with our drinks. "She said a group of Wyatt's friends is planning to have a little memorial for him this weekend. The funeral was basically just for the family so none of them got to say good-bye, I guess. Some of his friends from home are going to come up and they're going to have it in a little gallery in the South End that has shown some of his work. Savannah's going to come up, but I don't think her mom is going to make it. Once was enough for her, I guess."

"Should we go?" Caroline asked.

"I was planning on it, but you guys shouldn't feel obligated. I know that's not your favorite thing, Danny."

"We'll be there," I said. "Couldn't hurt to see what his friends are like, get a better sense of who he was. Did you have any luck with the research on him and his roommate?"

JD nodded and produced a small black Moleskine notebook and flipped through it until he found the right page. "By all appearances, Wyatt Austin was just as Savannah described him. Talented artist, had some good early showings and got some encouraging notices from the local critics down south. His painting got more of the attention, but the sculpture seems to have been what he really loved. I found an old interview with him in a free weekly where he talked about the feeling of creating something with his own hands, making something out of nothing. He'd been working on a new series of sculptures when he was killed. I'm not sure what became of them or where they are. But apparently he was working in a shared studio space a few blocks from his place, so maybe they're in there. He hasn't had any public shows since he moved to Boston, or at least none that I could find. He took the ad agency job for the money, and ended up being pretty good at it, so the more artistic stuff probably fell to the side at that point."

"Sculpting is a tough specialty," Caroline said. "Most of the people who make real money at it do it all on commission. Maybe they do some of their own stuff on the side, but the big pieces they have buyers for before they even start. Otherwise it's a great way to go broke. It's really time consuming and to get any good at it you have to really work, like years and years. Painting, mostly anyone can do if they get some good instruction. But sculpting is brutal."

"What about friends?" I asked.

"His Instagram account is sort of a mess at this point, with all the memorial messages and all that. But he had a ton of friends on there, and I couldn't see much in the way of a common thread. People from all over and all different kinds of professions. Lots of pictures of parties and road trips and Sox games. What you'd expect. His roommate is a bit of a different story, though."

"How so?"

"I found his Instagram page too, and there were cobwebs on that thing. What's his name—Simms? He was posting shit on there night and day, about his boss being an asshole, how much he hated his job, why it's so unfair that other people were getting record deals and he wasn't, blah blah. I guess he thinks he's some kind of musician. Anyway, as much as he posts, there's like no one else on his page. He has about thirty friends on there, but not a soul responds to his posts. And this is the internet. People respond to stupid stuff like that like it's their job. But not for this guy," JD said. "Same story on Twitter. He's posting a dozen things a day and they're just falling into a bottomless pit. No one cares."

"That's how everyone should treat Twitter," I said.

"What's Twitter?" Brendan asked.

"The saddest place on earth," JD said. "So, I checked out Simms a little more, employment history, credit, bank, RMV records, all of that. He's been all over the map in the last five years. San Francisco, New York, Dallas, Vegas. Doesn't seem to stay anywhere more than about a year or so and he mostly works restaurant jobs. Waiting tables, bartending, whatever he finds. He grew up in Washington State, outside Seattle. Both parents are still alive as far as I could tell. No siblings. Went to UW for a couple of years and then dropped out and went to San Francisco and he's been bouncing around ever since. Finances look fairly stable for someone with no real career. Aside from the fact that he doesn't seem to have any friends, he's fairly normal, I'd say."

"How did you find out all of this information?" Brendan asked.

JD smiled. "It's why I get the big bucks. What's our fee for this gig again, Tobin?"

"Somewhere south of nothing. We play for the love of the game."

"The picture you just painted there, JD, is of a lonely, rootless man," Brendan said. "Tell me: Did you find anything in his past about him being associated with any sort of religious group or anything like that?"

JD looked surprised. "In Texas. He was part of some bunch of fundamentalist nutjobs down there. They were building a replica of Noah's ark and were planning to launch it at the end of 2012 to avoid the apocalypse."

"From Dallas?" I said.

"I *said* they were nutjobs. Anyway, Simms left out of there a year before they ever got close to finishing."

"What made you think he'd be part of something like that, Brendan?" Caroline asked.

"I see it quite often. People move from place to place, from thing to thing, searching for some kind of base that they can build from. They often drop in and out of various religious groups, trying to discover something about themselves. Or perhaps trying to forget something. Either way, it's a common behavior and one that psychiatrists will tell you is rooted in childhood issues."

"Abandonment, that sort of thing?" Caroline said.

"Could be. Especially in single-parent families or other difficult situations," Brendan said.

"But that's not his background, at least from what I found," JD said. "He had a pretty normal set of parents, doesn't have any arrest record or anything like that. Just a boring guy drifting around the country. Plenty of people doing the same thing out there."

"Where is he now?" I said.

"Quincy. RMV records have him living in an apartment up there."

Ally came back with our egg rolls and we ordered a couple of the night's special pizzas, flatbreads with buffalo chicken, Monterey jack cheese and ranch dressing.

I thought about the information that JD had found on Wyatt and his roommate and realized there were a lot of blank spots. We didn't know how the two of them had become friends, whether they'd known each other before they moved in together, who Wyatt's real friends were or what he liked to do for fun. We had the outlines, but not the details that made up the people inside the silhouettes. The pizzas came and we devoured them and when we were done, we paid Ally, Caroline insisting we leave her thirty percent on the bill.

We stepped outside onto the sidewalk into the cooling evening air. Caroline gripped my arm and pulled me close and gave a small shiver. I looked down the street to where the white steeple of St. Peter's Church was just visible above the storefronts. Brendan followed my eyes and smiled weakly.

"When was the last time your shadow darkened that doorway?" he asked me.

"Years, brother. Years."

We stopped at the yacht club to drop JD and he jumped over the side of the open backseat and then leaned in to give Caroline a kiss goodbye.

"Tomorrow, let's go find this Simms guy and see what he has to say," I said. "I want to get a better picture of him. And of Wyatt."

"Ok, but not before eleven. It's unhealthy to be up that early."

The next day was a Friday and when I came downstairs in the morning, the house was quiet and still. Brendan had asked to borrow the Jeep to go to morning Mass at St. Peter's. Caroline was still upstairs in bed, trying to hold off the morning as long as possible. I opened a couple of windows to let in the sea air and then walked out on the front deck and watched a trio of fishermen stand on the beach talking as they cast occasional glances at their poles buried in the sand, looking for signs of a hit. The morning was bright and clear and the ocean calm.

Before going to bed last night I had spent an hour or so looking at Wyatt Austin's work online. Caroline had said he was sort of locally famous and that she thought he had a good reputation in the community, and I could see why. I knew next to nothing about art, except what Caroline told me, but I could see why people might be attracted to Wyatt's work. I scrolled through a series of abstracts that did nothing for me but then found a pair of street scenes that were remarkable. One was from the perspective of someone standing on a sidewalk, looking down a long, tree-shaded avenue with a wide median. The sun, unseen, shone through the leaves, casting small shadows along the street and sidewalk and on the faces of the pedestrians strolling toward the viewer. It could have been Comm Ave. or any one of a dozen streets like it in Brooklyn or Philadelphia or Washington. The detail work in the painting was so precise and so realistic that it took me a full minute to be sure it wasn't a photograph. Each car and tree and leaf and brick was perfectly rendered, down to the tiniest pockmark in the sidewalk.

But it was the faces in the painting that held my eye. Or rather, the lack of faces. While the bodies and outfits of the people, as well as the purses and packages they held, were as precise and well-imagined as the rest of the painting, each face was a blur. The kind of fuzzy, unidentifiable features you might see in a photo taken from a moving car. One face was indistinguishable from the next, all lines and dots like a close-up of an old comic strip.

All, that is, save one. On the right side of the scene, a tall, willowy woman stood near a lamppost. She appeared to be pushing a bike down the sidewalk and had stopped to look back over her shoulder, toward the viewer. Her chestnut hair gleamed in the sunlight filtered through the leaves and her face was lit by a broad smile. It was a grin of recognition, the kind you give someone seen unexpectedly, a look of pure delight. The woman's eyes were a deep green, the color of grass after a spring shower, and were crinkled with the joy of seeing…someone. The painter, I presumed. With fair cheeks reddened by the sun, the woman was stunning. Not the kind of manufactured looks you see in movies or magazines, but the kind of natural, effortless beauty that makes your breath catch in your throat and turns heads on the street. I sat on the couch in the dark and stared at her face for a very long time, willing her to tell me something about the man on the other side of the canvas. But she remained silent.

The skill and artistry in the painting, which was titled "Afterglow", were evident even to a casual viewer like me, but beyond that it gave me an important window into the things that Wyatt may have been interested in. My time with Caroline had taught me that artists generally don't waste their time and effort on subjects or projects about which they're not passionate. Art is difficult enough without trying to manufacture interest for something. I supposed that could change if there was a lot of money involved, but this painting wasn't done on commission and had sold for a modest sum.

The screen door creaked and Caroline came out onto the deck, stretching and yawning. She leaned against the rail and looked up and down the beach, taking in the morning view.

"You're missing a nice day," I said.

"Mmm. Not as much as I would've missed the last couple hours of sleep. Are we going to run?"

"I was thinking of a long swim instead."

"We could do that."

"Come inside for a sec first. I want you to look at something," I said.

Inside, I opened my MacBook and brought up the image of Wyatt Austin's painting. I didn't tell her who the artist was. She leaned her elbows on the counter and looked closely at the image, studying it for several minutes and zooming in on a few sections of it to get a better look. She finally straightened up and looked at me.

"Ok. Really nice work. What about it?" she said.

"I want to try something with you. Just from looking at the painting, what would you be able to tell me about the artist?"

"What do you mean? Like age, influences, things like that?"

"Anything at all. Whatever comes to mind."

"Well, the first thing I'd say is that it's almost certainly done by a man. And not just because of the obvious focus on the woman. That's one thing, and the artist is clearly making her the focus of the piece, even though she's off to one side. But there's also a kind of masculine quality to it. The brushstrokes are broad and bold and the colors are almost all primaries, which is something you'd usually associate with a male artist. The style is fairly straightforward, not a lot of flourishes, but it's clear that the artist has had quite a bit of formal training. This is the work of someone who is confident in his craft. He knows the fundamentals of composition and structure and the perspective is excellent. As a viewer, you get a very good sense of being in the scene, but also of having stumbled onto a private moment between this woman and whoever she's looking at."

"Can you tell me anything about the mindset of the artist?" I said.

"Like his mood? That's going to be guesswork, Danny."

"Give it a try."

"Well, a simplistic view would be that it's a bright piece with a lot of light and a beautiful woman as the focus, so the artist is conveying a sense of happiness, an upbeat mood," she said. "He could have had her standing under that streetlight at night, caught in the glow of the light, but he chose the middle of the afternoon on a sunny day. To me, at least, that's an important part of the whole piece, showing a kind of pleasure I think. How's that for AM radio psychiatry?"

I smiled. "Frasier Crane would be proud. And you confirmed several things that I was thinking."

"What's this about?" Caroline asked.

"That painting is by Wyatt Austin," I said. "It's one of the last ones he finished before he died."

She looked at the image on the screen again and nodded. "He was talented. I would've liked to work with him. But why the psych profile?"

"I'm trying to figure out some things about him and I wanted to see if I was crazy."

"I mean…"

"About this, smartass."

"Can I hear the theory?"

"Not yet. It isn't even a theory, just some ideas. I'll tell you more when I have something to tell."

After a light breakfast, Caroline and I changed into our wetsuits and waded out past the surf line and dove in. We swam side by side, falling into an easy rhythm in the cold fall water. She was a stronger swimmer than I was, but I had the advantage of longer reach. Every time she pulled ahead by a bit I'd reel her back in. We went out for about a half mile and then turned around. With the shore in sight, Caroline surged past me, digging hard for the last fifty yards. I tried to cover the move, but she was standing in knee-deep water by the time I paddled in out of breath.

"Sucks getting old huh?" she said.

"I'm not *old*. Just older."

I picked JD up at the yacht club a little past noon and we headed up Route 3 toward Quincy. I exited the highway near the massive Braintree mall and went down onto a surface road that was splattered on both sides with strip centers and car dealerships and squatty brown office buildings. Just past the entrance to the Blue Hills Reservation was the apartment complex where Martin Simms now lived. A sign out front announced its name as Beacon Hill South. It was a newer development with a half dozen three- and four-story buildings, each with a small balcony that overlooked either the parking lot or the VW dealership down the road. The buildings and grounds were clean and neatly landscaped and it was impossible to tell one apartment from the next. I had the sense that even a resident who had lived here for several years could come after dark and find himself walking into the wrong unit and only realize his mistake when he saw the wrong brand of mountain bike rusting on the balcony. I was sure that whatever leasing company had the complex's business advertised the units as having sweeping views of the Blue Hills and an easy commute to Boston. It had neither.

We found a visitor spot in front of the building closest to the road and followed the signs to the building that housed Simms's apartment. It was on the third floor and the door was one of four facing in on an open-air staircase. I knocked and we waited a minute or so. Just as I was raising my hand to knock again, the door opened. The man on the other side of the threshold was no more than five feet tall and rail thin. He probably weighed about ninety-five or a hundred pounds and his eyes were sunk so far back into their sockets they were nearly invisible. Dark circles surrounded the eyes and his ears were far too small for his tall, lean head, atop which sat a sad, greasy slick of dirty blond hair. He was sweating profusely and the thin yellow polo shirt he wore was stuck to his chest. His jeans were filthy and appeared to be several sizes too big, with the legs puddling around his bare feet. The man had a wad of cash balled in his right hand and his left hand went to his nose every few seconds to wipe a persistent stream of snot. I knew from JD's research that, if this was Austin, he was not yet thirty, but the man in front of us could easily pass for forty-five.

"Bout time. Where the fuck have you been?" he said in a shrill voice. He looked us over quickly, going from me to JD and then back to me. "You're not the pizza guy. The fuck is he? I hate that place. I don't even know why I order from there. Bunch of potheads can't get the order right once. How hard is it to remember bacon and jalapenos? Not that goddamn hard. Same order every time, you'd think they'd get it one or two out of ten times. So far, zero out of a hundred. Dicks. I don't know why I expect decent pizza out here in the fuckin sticks anyway. What'd you guys say you want?"

"We didn't," I said. "Is your name Martin Simms?"

"Nah, mine's Clarence."

I considered my options. It was a fair bet that this guy was jacked on something. At least I hoped he was. No one should look that bad straight. A guy like that wouldn't be likely to let us in if he thought we were police. So go the other route.

"Well Clarence, we're investigating the death of Wyatt Austin. We're trying to figure out what exactly happened."

He seemed to collapse in on himself. His face fell and his chin hit his chest. The sweaty clump of money slipped out of his hand and fluttered to the floor. He backed out of the doorway and stumbled to the side and sat wearily on a wooden stool next to a breakfast bar. He covered his face with his hands and mumbled something I didn't catch.

"Come again?"

"I already talked to the cops. Why do I have to go through it again? I can't. I'm not doing it again," he said.

"We're not cops," I said. "We're friends of Wyatt's sister, Savannah. She's asked us to see if maybe we can't find out a little more than the cops did."

He looked up at me. "Bullshit you're not a cop. Look at the size of you. And the little package you're carrying under your shirt on your belt. You're a cop all day long."

He slid off the stool and went around into the small galley kitchen and pulled a can of Bud Light from the fridge. He drank half of it down in one go, wiped his mouth with the back of his hand and then came back into the living area and stood in front of us. He pointed at me, his finger shaking.

"I told that big, dumb cop everything I knew, which isn't shit. I only knew Wyatt a few weeks before we moved into that apartment and we didn't hang out that much anyway. He was a friend, but it's not like we were buddies from college or something. We both needed a roommate and it worked out. That's all there was to it. I'm not going to sit here and go over all this shit for you two. I already did it and I'm not doing it again. Not for you, not for anyone."

"How did you meet Wyatt?" I asked.

Simms waved his hand. "How does anyone meet anyone? We were in some of the same social groups, knew some of the same people and we just ran into each other here and there."

"Where is here and there?"

He finished the last of the beer. "Christ, I don't know. Parties, concerts, galleries, whatever."

"Are you an artist, too?"

"No."

"But you hang around galleries?" I said.

"Some."

I looked at JD. Simms's answers were getting shorter by the second. JD cleared his throat and pulled a straight-back wooden chair over in front of where Austin had settled on the couch.

"Listen, no one is here to accuse you of anything," JD said. "All we care about is finding out what really happened to Wyatt. Like Danny said, we are not cops, and that's the truth. He used to be, but not anymore. I know he looks like he'd just as soon throw you off the balcony as look at you, but he wouldn't be here doing this favor for Savannah if he didn't care. He'd be doing something that paid, which this doesn't. I'll tell you straight: I want to find whoever killed Wyatt and I want to beat him to death with my hands. I'm not a violent person. I can't even remember the last fight I was in. Probably fifth grade or something. But I've been having dreams about taking this guy out on my boat, into the middle of the ocean, and listening to him beg for mercy while I kick the shit out of him for a couple of hours and then dump him overboard. Not real nice, I know, but that's the way it is. And I never even met Wyatt. All I know is that Savannah loved him, and that's enough for me. She asked us to find out what we could, so here we are. It would be a lot easier for us if you'd help us out, but I get it if you don't want to. If it was me I would probably tell two guys like us to go screw. But that's not going to help Wyatt's family. They want to know who killed him and why."

Simms walked back into the kitchen and got another beer. He raised the can to us and we both nodded. He came back and handed us each a beer and we both took a drink and then waited. He took a long swallow of his beer and looked out the windows that overlooked his small porch and gave onto the parking lot. He cracked his neck loudly and then looked at JD, who was still sitting in the chair in front of the couch. I settled on one of the wooden stools near the counter.

"The way it was, Wyatt and me, we were friendly but I wouldn't say we were friends, you know? He had his work and his friends and his girlfriend, and I had my job and my friends. We'd hang out sometimes, but it wasn't like we were together all the time. He spent a lot of time at the work space over the last few months. He was busting his ass to get this set of sculptures done for some reason. I don't know whether he had a buyer or what, but he was there all the time. Sometimes he'd be gone before I got up in the morning and wouldn't come back until after I was asleep at night. I could go four or five days without even seeing him."

"What kind of work do you do?" JD said.

"I teach music. Or taught, I guess. I haven't been working."

"Where do you teach?"

"I give private lessons. And do some fill-in work at a couple of high schools."

"That's enough to pay the bills? I didn't think teachers made much, especially subs," JD said.

Simms snorted. "Pays plenty if you're teaching spoiled little fuckers in Brookline to play Heart and Soul. Their parents just want them occupied for forty-five minutes. They don't care what it costs."

"So what were Wyatt's friends like? Was it all the artsy crowd?"

"Not all. He had friends from all over. Plenty of artists, but some guys who worked in the financial district, a couple of girls who run a gym, a dude who cooks at a place in Fort Point. Different groups. He was one of those people who got along with just about everyone. He was easy to like. He had that thing of where you always felt like he was totally focused on you whenever you were talking to him. I thought it was kinda phony at first, but I realized later on that's just how he was. He was a good guy. He really was."

"Did you know his girlfriend at all?" I asked.

"Leigh. Yeah, a bit. They met at the work space a while back. She's some sort of agent or consultant or something like that. Helps artists find patrons and galleries and buyers and shit like that."

"What's she like?" JD said.

"Cool as shit. Think of someone's cute, funny older sister from high school and that's Leigh. No pretense with her at all. I'll tell you a story. A couple of nights after they met, a bunch of us were out in the Seaport. We went for an early dinner and then hit a couple of bars for drinks. By ten or so we were all ready to bail, except Leigh. She kept badgering us to stay for one more shot until we all caved. So she goes to the bar and orders a round of tequila shots. Not good ones either. The waitress brings them over and everyone sort of muscles up and gets it done. Then another round comes. And another. And another. In like thirty minutes we were all absolutely housed. Just *hammered*. Everyone except her. We got outside and it took us twenty minutes to get a cab because none of us could speak coherently enough to tell the cabbie where to take us. It was a massacre. Next day I'm lying on my bathroom floor moaning and I hear Wyatt yell and then Leigh laughing like a crazy person. Wyatt busts into my room and starts yelling and waving his arms and I can't understand anything he's saying. When he finally calms down, he tells me that while we were drinking tequila shots Leigh was drinking water. She had told the waitress when she ordered the first round just to give her water every time. Leigh was standing behind him in the doorway while he was talking, and she had this look on her face that was like, total glee. I wasn't sure whether to strangle her or hug her."

JD looked at me and I tried to suppress a smile.

"I think I'm in love with her," JD said.

Simms nodded and finished his beer. "She's the goods. I didn't see her all that much, but whenever she was around it made me happy."

"He was with her for a while?"

"Most of a year I guess."

"What happened?"

"I'm not sure. Like I said, I didn't see them that much, but I got the feeling that they just sort of hit that point where it's either take it up a notch or let it go. Wyatt was still young and was really grinding on his work and that was taking a lot of time so I guess he just let her go."

I cleared my throat. "The police think he was involved in something with kids. Like child exploitation."

Simms stood up and walked back into the kitchen and came back with three more beers. He opened his and took three quick swallows. "Kids. Wyatt wouldn't…he wasn't…no. I mean, who told them that? Why would the cops think that? I didn't say anything to them. Who would say that?"

He was talking rapidly and his voice had gone up an octave. He picked up his phone, which had been lying on the coffee table, and began spinning it in his hands.

"I don't know. Maybe no one. The cops made it sound like they had some evidence. Do you have any idea what that could be?" I asked.

Austin was shaking his head, looking down at the floor. He didn't say anything for a long while, and then looked up at JD and then me. "They have it wrong," he said. "They're wrong. Wyatt wasn't that guy."

"That's what we're—" I began, but he cut me off.

"I don't want to talk about this anymore. I don't have to, and I don't want to," he said, and moved to the front door and opened it. "Please leave now."

We walked out and left him standing there in the doorway, his scarecrow frame lost inside the outsized clothes, greasy hair sliding down his forehead. I heard the door close as we walked down the stairs and in the parking lot we passed a fat young man in a red windbreaker carrying a pizza box. He stumbled on the curb and dropped the box flat on the ground before picking it up and heading up the stairs toward Simms's apartment.

Seven

We rode out of Quincy and back south toward Plymouth. I was thinking about what we'd learned from Martin Simms and decided that it didn't amount to much. Mostly just confirmed things we knew already. Wyatt was a good guy, lots of friends, passionate about his art.

And clean.

The cops had taken one piece of information—whether it was pictures on his laptop or something even weaker—and jumped straight to the end of the story without bothering to see where else it might lead. I knew how that went and I even understood their thinking and the need to clear cases, especially ones like this that could take an ugly turn. But it was that kind of reasoning that landed innocent people in jail for years and continued to undermine whatever trust the public might still have left in cops.

Simms said he had told everything to the cops, which I figured meant Chris King and Dave Henderson. So they had the same information that JD and I had. And they had still decided that Wyatt was involved in something unspeakable that had gotten him killed. I needed to find out what they had seen on that laptop. As much as I doubted it, I still had to consider the possibility that King and Henderson were right and that Wyatt had somehow hidden this portion of his life from everyone who knew him.

It was unlikely, but certainly not impossible.

We pulled into the beach road and wound down among the dunes to the house. The sun was still high in the sky but it was close to high tide, so there weren't many people on the beach, just a few fishermen and a couple of families waiting out the tide sitting on top of the massive boulders that defended the beach against erosion. I made some chorizo and mushroom pizzas for a quick lunch and afterward we sat on the front deck and listened to the steady rhythm of the tide banging against the rocks.

A small black lab puppy was wandering among the rocks, splashing in the tidal pools caught behind them and poking his head up between the boulders every so often. I watched as he tried to scramble up the side of a rock, his paws finding no purchase on the wet surface, and he tumbled backward and dropped into a sizable pool. A second later, I saw his head pop up and he was off down the sandy road, headed for a family packing their gear into a Mercedes SUV. A girl of about nine or ten scooped him up and climbed into the vehicle, giggling as he shook the water and sand from his coat onto her.

"So what do we think about Mr. Simms?" JD asked. "Are we supposed to believe anything he said?"

"Tough to say. Guy like that, normally I'd discount just about anything he said. He's a junkie and they'll usually tell you whatever you want to hear to get police or people like us out of their faces."

"But?"

"But…I don't know. I'm used to people lying to me, just out of pure reflex. Everyone lies to the cops about everything. Criminals, victims, witnesses, lawyers, relatives, everyone. No one wants to talk to a cop. If you're having a conversation with a cop, usually your day has gone very wrong. But I didn't get the vibe from Simms that he was lying, at least not about anything that mattered. I think he was straight with us about Wyatt."

"I thought so too. I don't think he's a stupid guy. And I think he'd probably have had some indication if Wyatt was into that shit, even if they didn't hang out very much. You can usually tell when someone is hiding something, even if you don't know what it is."

"I'd like to talk to the girlfriend, Leigh," I said. "Women know stuff, even if they're not aware that they know it."

"The hell does that mean?"

"Talk to a woman who's had a guy cheat on her. Whenever it finally comes out, she'll tell you that she knew something was up six months or a year ago, she just couldn't put her finger on what was wrong."

"So let's find her."

"I don't think we'll have to. She'll probably show up at the memorial service this weekend, don't you think?" I said.

"Yeah. Not sure I want to jack her up there, though. Not real cool."

"Who said we were cool?"

"No one I can remember," JD said.

"Maybe get Simms to introduce us and see if we can talk to her later. Although, funerals and weddings and things like that are great places to get people to talk. They're emotional and say shit they normally wouldn't."

"Damn, that's cold, Tobin."

"Just facts."

After lunch, JD took off to run some errands and I found Caroline on the back deck, supine in a bikini on a chaise lounge, a paperback book veed on the ground beside the chair. She was snoring softly, her exposed belly rising and falling slowly as she snoozed. I considered my options for a moment, went back inside, grabbed two bottles of beer and went back out to the deck. I held one of the bottles a few inches over Caroline's belly and waited. The condensation began sliding down the bottle and when a lone drop finally broke free and hit her skin, Caroline was up and out of the chair within half a second.

"What?! Who? Aw, shit Danny. Such an asshole."

She grabbed up the book and threw it in my direction, missing badly. I didn't even flinch and stood sipping my beer. I held out the other one to her. She looked at me suspiciously for a minute, the way a toddler regards a rarely seen relative, and then snatched the beer from my hand.

"Mister funny man. Ha ha," she said.

"I just wanted to let you know I was home."

"Mmm. Did you two make any progress?"

"I'm not really sure. Maybe? We talked to Wyatt's old roommate, this guy Simms."

"What's he like?"

"Squirrelly is probably the best word I can think of. Probably some kind of junkie. Looks like he has about six months left, if he's lucky. But we talked to him for a bit, about Wyatt, what he was like, who he hung with, like that," I said.

"To what end?"

"Just trying to get a handle on who the guy was. And more importantly, who he wasn't."

"Meaning?"

"Well, the bit that was in the paper about Wyatt being involved with the child exploitation thing. We need to know if that's even a remote possibility before we can get anywhere else. Because if that's true, then we're done. Nothing else for us to do. But if it isn't, then we need to lock that down, because that's the whole basis of the cops' theory. And Simms shot that down right away. He said Wyatt was a good guy all the way."

"Do you think he was just defending his dead friend?" Caroline asked.

"I didn't get that feeling. He was genuinely baffled when we threw it at him. Confused by the whole idea. And when I tried to follow up a little bit, he cut us off and that was the end of it. So I'm not totally sure what to think. But I tend to come down on the side of the cops' having made a mistake, however that happened."

Caroline set her beer on the deck rail and then hoisted herself up next to it, an effortless motion that made me think about the empty house and our bed upstairs. She chewed on her thumbnail for a while and then looked up.

"Think that's a little confirmation bias on your part?" she said.

"How so?"

"Well, you guys were hired –"

"Hiring implies payment. We were asked."

"Ok, whatever. Your job is to basically prove that the cops are wrong. and her mom wants you to shoot holes in the cops' theory and prove that Wyatt wasn't what they say he was. So you go out and talk to some people, and they tell you that Wyatt was a stand-up guy, and would've never messed with anything involving kids. Therefore, the cops are wrong and you're right. Everyone can sleep easy."

"Simms is just one guy. No one person has the entire view of anyone's life, even if it's their wife or husband or son or whatever. Everyone has secrets, large or small. Simms has a specific view of Wyatt's life, and that's of a certain value to us. But we still need to talk to a bunch of other people to get the rest of the picture. When is that memorial service thing?"

"Tomorrow afternoon. Two, I think."

"Ok, we're going," I said.

"Why? I hate those things. Bunch of people reading bad poetry and throwing rose petals into a fountain."

"Need to talk to Wyatt's ex-girlfriend. Leigh. I imagine she'll be there."

"That's a good reason for you to go. Why do I need to?"

"Because you're my cover. People like you and they assume if you're with me I can't be all that bad."

"People are that dumb?" she asked.

"If they weren't, I'd be out of a job."

The next afternoon Caroline, JD, Savannah and I joined a small crowd of people as they filed into a cramped space on the ground floor of a brick building in the South End. The gallery was a few blocks from Wyatt's apartment and the floor-to-ceiling windows that fronted the street flooded the square room with sunlight. There were a couple dozen folding chairs set up in the middle of the gallery, but I wanted to see who was there, so Caroline and I found a spot along the back wall near the fire exit and watched as Wyatt's friends came in. JD and Savannah mingled, stopping often to talk with someone. I searched the crowd for faces I knew and saw one or two that I recognized from photos in Wyatt's apartment. Martin Simms was among the last to come in and he didn't look too pleased to be there. He wore the same clothes he'd had on the day before and kept his head down as he slithered through the group, moving to an empty corner near a wire sculpture of two small, black birds feeding on a faceless body. He eventually looked up to scan the room, and when I caught his eye, I saw that his eyes were red-rimmed and wet. He gave me a short nod and then looked back down at the floor.

A few minutes after two, a petite, dark-haired woman moved to the front of the room near the windows and stood silently, looking at the assembled crowd. She wore a simple black sleeveless dress and low heels. Her hair was held back in a black clip and she wore no makeup that I could see. Bright green eyes scanned the faces in front of her and she said nothing for a moment, as the people found seats and their conversations trailed off. She held a sheet of white paper folded in two and when the room was quiet, she cleared her throat and smiled brightly.

"First, let me thank all of you for coming today. It means the world to me, and I know Wyatt would be overwhelmed at the turnout. You all were his family. He loved each of you and he often said to me how lucky he felt to have such a great group of friends. I see a couple of faces here I don't recognize, so let me introduce myself. I'm Leigh Collins. He was a wonderful man and I loved him very much. As many of you did. He was so committed to his work, and I understood that and I knew that he needed to focus on it right now. But I was sure we would get married someday, even after we split up. I even thought about proposing to him once or twice." She laughed, a short, quick giggle and several people in the crowd joined in. "We all know how, um, deliberate he could be about those things. Even when we were apart, I never doubted that he loved me. Never. That feeling was with me always, and it's what kept me moving forward. Especially after he was killed."

Leigh paused and looked down, and I was sure that the tears were coming. But they didn't. Instead, she smiled again and took a deep breath.

"I can't help but think that if he were here right now he'd be disgusted with all of us, sitting inside moping around on such a beautiful day. And I have to say I feel the same way. I've had enough of the sadness and questions and days sitting inside with the shades drawn. That's not the way that Wyatt lived his life, and it's certainly not the way I intend to live the rest of mine. Grief has its place, I suppose. But I'm not interested in wallowing in it.

I'm more interested in remembering what Wyatt was about and remembering how much fun we all had together. And we had a *lot* of fun."

A man in the crowd whooped and raised a fist in the air, and others joined in, laughing, cheering.

Leigh crumpled the sheet of paper she'd been holding, which she'd never looked at, and threw it into a nearby trash can. "I had all kinds of flowery stuff I wanted to say, but I don't see the point now. Wyatt is gone and that sucks. I *hate* it. But all of us sitting around in here isn't going to change that, is it? So here's what we're going to do. Suzanne? Kevin?"

She gestured to the rear of the room and I turned to see a man and a woman emerge from a short hallway to our left. Each of them was carrying a tray laden with a bottle of tequila and stacks of shot glasses. The servers moved among the rows of chairs, handing out glasses and pouring shots, making sure that everyone was served.

When everyone was holding a glass, Leigh raised her own and looked out at the group. She swept her eyes over every one of them in turn, and I caught her gaze lingering a half second on Martin Simms, who had already drained his glass. Finally, she smiled.

"So I'd like to go around the room and let everyone have a chance to say one thing they remember about Wyatt," Leigh said.

"It can be trivial or silly or serious. Anything you want. No one has to feel obligated, but I want everyone to have the chance to speak if they'd like. I'll start. I remember the absolutely awful chicken enchiladas he made me on my birthday last year. He was in the kitchen for hours chopping and cooking and preparing everything. And they looked delicious, but the chicken was undercooked and I didn't want to say anything, so I ate it anyway. But I think I got food poisoning. I spent the whole night and half of the morning in the bathroom and Wyatt told me the next day that with all the vomiting, he was afraid that I was pregnant."

Leigh laughed and drank her tequila in one smooth, practiced move. A server refilled her glass as a tall, broad man near the front stood up.

"I only knew him for a few months, from when we worked together, but the thing I will remember about Wyatt is his generosity," the man said. "I don't think I ever paid for a lunch or a single drink when he was there. He knew I had just moved to the city from Vermont and was kind of struggling, and he just made sure I was ok. I miss that guy."

A small, well-dressed older woman stood up next. "I'm Connie Owens and Wyatt lived across the hall from me. He was a nice, polite boy. I would bother him to help me get things off high shelves or bring heavy boxes up from the basement storage sometimes. So nice, that one. But the thing I remember is his farts. Anytime he came to help me with something, he'd tell me that my cat had the worst gas and I should have her checked out or change her diet. I don't own a cat."

The crowd roared and clapped and Connie Owens drank her shot and bowed slightly at the waist before sitting down. Beside me, Caroline was giggling and I saw Martin Simms across the room, a faint smile on his lips. He stopped a passing server and got a refill of tequila and drank it quickly.

A few more people rose, speaking of Wyatt's sense of humor, his passion for his work and his friends. As the tributes wound down, I saw Savannah and JD speaking quietly off to our right, and Savannah eventually stepped away from the wall and cleared her throat.

"I'm Wyatt's sister, Savannah. Thank you all so much for coming. This is exactly what Wyatt would like to see. All of his friends together, telling lies about him and laughing. Except the thing about the farts. That's god's own truth. He was the worst. But the thing I will remember about my brother is that he *lived*. He didn't sit around talking about what he wanted to do. He went and did it. I remember when we were in high school, he decided that he was going to learn how to surf. And he just did it, in like two weeks. It was the same with his art. He had a lot of talent, but a lot of what he accomplished came from hard work. Lots of people say they want to paint or write or draw, but they never do.

Wyatt decided he was going to do something and then figured out how to get it done. Like when he wanted to learn to cook. That didn't turn out so well, apparently. But he tried. Anyway, I'm rambling, but thanks to all of you."

Savannah held her glass high. "Here's to Wyatt: a great artist, a good man and a terrible cook. Cheers!"

"Cheers!"

Caroline and I touched glasses and downed the shots of what turned out to be pretty decent tequila. If such a thing exists.

The crowd began to break up and I saw Martin Simms help himself to another shot of tequila and then slide out the front door, having spoken to no one. Caroline walked over to talk to Savannah and wrapped her in a tight hug. JD and I wandered aimlessly around the gallery for a few minutes, looking at sculptures and paintings we didn't understand. I found myself standing next to the sculpture of the black carrion birds and the faceless body. It was made of thick matte black wire that had been twisted and bent expertly. The piece had an ominous feel to it and I could easily imagine why it had been placed in a back corner of the gallery. It was not the type of thing to draw customers in from the street.

"Not my favorite piece of Wyatt's."

I turned to see Leigh Collins next to me. She smiled politely. Close up, I could see that despite her brave words and professions of being through with the mourning process, the ordeal had taken its toll. She was a pretty woman, with clear green eyes and a kind face, but there were more small wrinkles around her eyes and mouth than you'd expect for a woman her age. She held out her hand. "I'm Leigh. I don't believe we've met."

"Danny Tobin," I said, taking her hand.

She took half a step back and cocked her head to the side. "Savannah said you were big. She wasn't kidding."

"You did a nice job here. This kind of thing is never easy," I said. "But you handled it with grace."

"The tequila helped."

"That's the only time I've ever heard anyone say that tequila helped anything," I said.

"True enough." She glanced around the gallery, as if seeing it for the first time. "He loved this place. Wyatt. He said it was the only gallery he'd ever found where everyone wasn't full of shit. If he brought in a piece and they said it would sell, it sold. If something wasn't right for them, they said so and didn't just let it sit here and collect dust. That's half the game for an artist, you know. Finding someone who will tell you the truth about your work. Most people will just smile and say nice things, even if it's a pencil sketch of a half-eaten burrito."

"Burritos are delicious."

"They are, but it turns out they're not worth much on the fine art market," she said.

"Did he sell many pieces?"

"Wyatt was lucky, I guess. He had a good job, so he wasn't totally reliant on selling his art for income," she said. "But he did ok. I think he sold four or five pieces last year."

"Is that a lot? I have no idea about any of this," I said, waving my hand at the sculptures and paintings around the room.

"It's pretty good, yeah. Some of the artists Wyatt was friendly with would have covered themselves in bees and stood naked on Mass Ave to sell one painting a year. I guess I never thought about it that much, but yeah, Wyatt did well with it."

"Everyone I've talked to says he was a really talented guy. And funny. I wish I'd had the chance to meet him."

"Oh, I think the two of you might have done some damage together. If the stories I hear about you are true," she said, a note of mischief in her voice.

"Lies and innuendo. All of it," I said.

Leigh raised an eyebrow at that. "All of it?"

Tricky ground, this. I had no way of knowing which stories Savannah and JD had told her. So I punted. "I'm sure Savannah has told you that me and JD are helping the family out a little bit with Wyatt's case, just trying to see what we can find out. They don't buy the police theory on it. There's a lot of blank spaces we need to fill in and it would be great if we could sit down with you sometime and see if you can help."

"She told me you two were roaming around annoying people."

"That's our specialty," I said. "But I'm not sure we're annoying the right ones."

"So you want to see if annoying me will help?" She said it with a smile, but there was a bit of sadness in her voice. "I'm happy to sit down with you guys, but I can't tell you anything I haven't told the cops already. And that's not much. I just don't know anything useful."

"That's fine. We can add it to the file of useless stuff we've accumulated already. It's getting pretty fat. When would you have some time to talk?"

She glanced at her watch. "How about now?"

The five of us took a booth at a cramped local bar two blocks over from the gallery. The walls were done with chalkboard paint that had been covered by all kinds of graffiti, doodles, raunchy poems and the odd bit of fortune-cookie wisdom. It was a men's room writ large. On the wall above Caroline's head someone had drawn a highly detailed portrait of Bobby Orr, caught mid-air in his most-famous moment, a halo above his head and angel's wings sprouting from his Bruins' sweater.

After our waitress returned with the drinks, Savannah held her beer bottle up and said, "One more toast for Wyatt, y'all." Bottles and glasses clinked.

"So Leigh, JD and I are trying to gather as many pieces of Wyatt's life as we can and then we'll see what kind of picture it makes when we're done," I said.

"Haven't the police already done all of this? I spoke with them, I know Savannah did as well, and their mother. And many of our friends," she said.

"How long did you spend talking to them?"

She tapped a fingernail against her front teeth as she thought. "Maybe forty-five minutes. No more than an hour for sure."

"Savannah?"

"Maybe not quite that long. As long as it took me to drink a cup of coffee," she said.

"And your mom?" I asked, knowing what the answer would be.

"She was with me. We talked to them together."

"And this was Chris King and Dave Henderson you all spoke with?"

They both nodded. "Ok, so you three are the people who arguably knew Wyatt the best. His mom, his sister and his girlfriend," I said. "And the investigators spent a total of perhaps two hours speaking with you, if we're being generous. That wouldn't be out of line for an initial interview, but I would've expected them to come back to one if not all of you as they got deeper into the investigation and came up with more questions or things they wanted to run past you."

"Never happened," Leigh said, looking at Savannah, who shook her head no. "What does that mean?"

"Maybe nothing. What kind of things did they ask you?"

"Just a bunch of basic stuff, mostly things they could've gotten off my Facebook page, to be honest," Leigh said. "How long I'd known Wyatt, when we started dating, why we broke up, if he had any enemies I knew of. That was about it."

"Nothing more personal?" I asked.

She looked down at her hands. I glanced at Caroline and chin-nodded toward the bar. She and Savannah made their excuses and took two stools at the long bar across the room. Leigh looked up and her eyes were shiny and red.

"I'm sorry. I didn't want to..Savannah doesn't need to.."

"I understand."

Leigh drank what was left in her wine glass and signaled the waitress for another. When it came, she took a small sip and folded her hands on the table in front of her. "This is more than I usually drink in a month. Please don't judge me by this."

JD laughed out loud. "No one at this table is judging anyone, I promise you that."

"Thank you. To answer your question, Danny, yes, they did. Well, one of them did, the square-looking one."

"Dave Henderson," JD said, bile in his voice.

"Yes. We were at a cafe and they were both polite and sympathetic when we were all talking together. But toward the end, the other one, Chris I guess, got up to go to the bathroom. And the big one leaned across the table, it was one of those small metal ones, and says, 'How long did you know Austin liked little boys before you dropped him?' He had the most disgusting look on his face. I can't even describe it. It gave me chills. Then before I could even respond, he says, 'Did he ever try any of that shit on you?' I never said a word. I just stood up and left. And as I passed by the window of the shop where he was sitting, he smiled and waved, like we'd just had the nicest conversation. I never said anything to Savannah or anyone else about it, because I didn't know what he was talking about or where it had come from. So I kind of left it alone. I certainly didn't forget it, but I tried not to think about it."

"Then you saw the *Sunrise* story," JD said.

She nodded. "It took me three tries to read the story. It was so...wrong. It just didn't fit with anything I knew about Wyatt at all. Nothing. It's like you wake up one morning and someone tells you that the sky is yellow now and the sun is blue. It made no sense at all. I actually laughed after I'd read the whole thing. I figured it was such an absurd theory that there would be another story the next day contradicting it. But it never happened, and I kept wondering why."

"We have an idea about that," I said. "When we spoke with Henderson and King, they let it slip that they had found some evidence on the laptop that supported that theory."

She made a sour face. "What does that mean?"

I glanced at JD, who gave the tiniest shake of his head. "They didn't say. It wasn't the most cordial conversation, to be honest," I said.

"Do you believe them?"

I shrugged.

"I read that story. Whatever you guys have to say won't be worse," she said.

"Right now, we don't know what's true. We don't have enough information to make that decision. And neither one of us knew Wyatt at all," I said. "So what we have on one side is the stuff that was in the paper and what Henderson and King have told us, which isn't all that much. On the other side, we have conversations with his family and friends, all of whom paint a much different picture of Wyatt. Where the truth lies is the big question. I was a cop for a long time and I know how these things go. Sometimes the pieces fit together just so and once that happens, you usually don't spend a lot of time looking for other pieces."

Leigh shook her head. Her face was flushed and she was twisting a cocktail straw into small tight knots. "That story almost broke me. Before he was killed, Wyatt and I were talking about getting back together. We'd talked about it before, and I never really doubted that we would end up together. We just had that kind of connection. I had let myself start thinking about it and I hadn't realized how much I wanted it until he was killed. I had this huge sense of loss. I mean, not just because Wyatt was gone, but for myself. Selfishly, I realized that with him dead, I might not ever be truly happy again. I know that sounds awful, but that's how it was. He was the one for me and we missed our chance. Then, when the story came out, I had barely gotten to the point where I could deal with the fact that Wyatt was gone. I was back at work and seeing some friends here and there, and then that story just knocked me on my ass."

"Was there any part of you that wondered if some of it could be true?" JD asked.

Leigh sighed heavily and sat back in her chair. "Yeah. Goddamit. It makes me sick to say that. But yeah. How could I not? Even as well as I knew him, or thought I did, it's just human nature to start asking yourself those questions. Did I know everything he did? Of course not. No one knows everything about anyone." She took a deep swallow from her wine and looked at JD. "Are you implying that I should've known something?"

JD held up his hands. "Not at all."

"I think what we're trying to find out is whether this story is just something the cops put out there, for whatever reason, or if it's something else," I said.

Leigh held my gaze for half a minute. "What would that be?" Her voice was flat and quiet.

"I don't know. You just said that you asked yourself some of these same questions. We're doing our best here to see if there's some things that the police missed. Things that could point in another direction."

JD said: "I'd sure like to get a look at Wyatt's laptop. Twenty minutes and I betcha we clear up a lot of this shit."

"We can do that whenever you want," Leigh said. "It's just sitting in my apartment collecting dust."

"Hold on. The cops gave it back to you?" I asked.

"What do you mean? They never had it. It was at the work space he used and I went and picked it up a couple of days after he was killed."

"So whose laptop do the cops have?" JD said.

She shrugged. "Not Wyatt's."

JD laughed and smacked the top of the table hard enough to spill half of my beer. "Those shitbirds! They just took a laptop from his place and assumed it was his."

"Mmm, probably not," I said. "They would've taken any computers they found in the apartment and gone through them all pretty soon after. Figuring out who they belonged to would've come a little later, once they discovered what was on them and decided whether they cared."

"So who…"

We got JD's laptop from my Jeep and made the short walk to Leigh's apartment. It was on the third floor of a building that housed a Thai take-out joint and a Korean nail salon on the bottom floor. She let us into a small one-bedroom and went into the back and returned a minute later with the laptop. It was a recent model ThinkPad. JD took it and booted it up while he dug a serial cable out of his backpack. He connected the two machines and brought up a forensics toolkit on his own computer and went to work. A few minutes later, he closed both machines, handed Wyatt's back to Leigh.

"You have what you need?" she asked.

JD patted his laptop. "Yep. Much obliged."

Eight

I knocked on Simms's apartment door, waited two seconds and then kicked it twice, hard. The door opened a crack and I put my shoulder into it and shoved it all the way open, knocking Simms to the floor. JD and I walked in and he closed the door.

"Pizza delivery," I said.

Simms crab-walked backward, scrambling to get away from me. I followed him, forcing him farther into the living room until he banged his head into an end table. An empty forty of Schlitz wobbled for a second and then tumbled off the table, the mouth hitting Simms on the cheekbone. He yelped and blood began trickling from a tiny cut below his left eye. He moved to get up and I put my hand on his shoulder and shoved him back to the floor. My hand came back sweat-damp and I went to wipe it dry on the couch before thinking better of that and dried it on my jeans instead. Simms looked up at me through bloodshot eyes, waiting. I said nothing.

"What? What the fuck, man?" he said after a minute.

I stared down at him. JD pulled a chair over from the dining table and straddled it.

"This is my place, man. You can't fucking kick the door in and assault me. I should call the fucking cops, man." He reached for his phone on the coffee table. JD snatched it up before he could get there. It was an older flip phone model and JD opened it and began scrolling through the menu. Simms made a grab for the phone again and JD casually slapped his hand away.

"Come on, man. That's my fucking property. I don't know what you guys are doing, but this shit isn't cool, man."

"You need to upgrade your hardware, brother," JD said. "This is some Gordon Gecko shit right here." He flipped the phone over. "It doesn't even have a camera. Did you get this for your bar mitzvah or something?"

Simms turned his attention back to me. He still sat on the floor, and he pulled his knees up to his chest and rested his chin on them. "Tell me what this is," he said.

"This," I said, "is your last chance to tell us the fucking truth. That's what this is."

"Truth about what? I answered what you asked me. I don't have anything else to tell you."

I put my shoe on top of his hand and pressed it down into the hardwood floor, twisting my foot on the knuckles. He groaned and ground his teeth in pain but said nothing. I pressed down a little harder and sweat began to bead on Austin's forehead. He grabbed my leg with his other hand and tried to pry it off, so I put my other foot on his forehead and shoved him back against the table. The lamp shook, but stayed upright.

"Ask your fucking questions," he said through clenched teeth. I kept my foot on his hand.

"Whose laptop do the cops have?"

He looked bewildered. "What? Whose…" I shifted some weight to his hand and heard a soft crunch. "Unnnh, fuck! Stop. Jesus. I don't know what you mean. What laptop?"

"They took a laptop out of your old apartment after Wyatt was killed. They think it's his. It's not. So whose is it?"

He wiped some sweat from his forehead and looked down at my foot on his hand. "Mine."

"Why do they think it's Wyatt's?" JD asked.

"Because they asked me. So I said yes."

"They asked you what?" I said.

"One of the cops said, 'Did Wyatt Austin use this computer?' And I said yes. That was it."

"That's different than telling them it was his laptop though," JD said. "Did he actually use it?"

Simms shrugged, a gesture that was made somewhat more difficult with my foot still on his hand. "Maybe once or twice."

"But you let them believe it belonged to him," I said. "Why?"

He wiped his nose with his sleeve. He was sweating steadily and his filthy shirt was soaked through. He smelled of decay.

"Can I get a drink? I don't feel so good."

I nodded to JD, who went to the kitchen and came back with a High Life tallboy. Simms set the can on the floor, cracked it with his left hand and drank about half of it down. His hand shook as he set the can back on the floor.

"Better? Great. Answer my fucking question now. Why did you let the cops think that was Wyatt's laptop?"

"I didn't want to be involved."

"In what?"

Another half shrug. "Anything. I don't want to get in the middle of anything like that. I keep to myself."

"That's not the same thing as lying to the police, Martin. They tend to take that sort of thing personally. Once they find out, you're going to be right in the middle of things and it won't be a friendly conversation."

"How would they find out?" he asked, already knowing the answer.

"Because as soon as I leave here, I'm going to make a phone call and let them know. And they're going to be super fucking pissed, believe me. Super pissed. Cops hate that shit, Martin. Hate it. And Dave Henderson? That guy hates everything anyway, so this will just make his day. Give him a reason to work up a good lather."

He reached for his beer but dropped the can as he raised it to his mouth. The liquid spread out along the hardwood floor, finding the low spots and cracks. Simms looked down pitifully at the beer and then slapped the empty can across the room.

"He's an animal. He said some awful things to me. I'm not talking to him again," he said.

"Don't worry, I'm sure he'll do most of the talking. But I imagine he's going to want a better answer than you just didn't want to get involved. Tell you what. Let's practice. Pretend I'm Henderson and you need a good explanation for lying to me so I don't kick your teeth in. It'll be fun."

Simms looked miserable. "I don't know what--"

I slid my foot up to his wrist and pushed. Simms screamed and tried to scramble away but his back was to the end table and his shoes found no purchase on the wet hardwood floor. I stepped off his hand and reached down and smacked him once, twice in the face. I grabbed the front of his shirt and lifted him onto the couch. His eyes were red and unfocused and a stream of yellow snot flowed from his nose.

"Let's assume that I've done this before, ok? And let's also assume that there's some shit on that laptop that you don't want anyone to know is yours. Now, I have a pretty good idea of what that is, and it's not so good. Actually, it's pretty fucking bad, Martin. So I understand why you'd lie to the cops about the laptop, but there's another problem here. You might have noticed that the cops have decided that Wyatt's murder was related to his supposed connection to a child exploitation ring. But we all know that's bullshit, don't we? And JD and I, our job is to figure out what the real story is. Which means we need to let the cops know that they bit the wrong hook. So you see our dilemma here, Martin."

"Look, I'm sick, ok? I'm not doing good," he said.

"No shit," JD said.

Simms's eyes snapped to JD quickly and there was something hard and sharp in them. He scratched at the underside of his forearm, raising droplets of blood from a jumble of small round scabs.

"I don't think I've slept more than three hours at a time since Wyatt was killed, and when I do the nightmares are so bad that I have to wake myself up. I keep dreaming of wolves roaming the streets, tearing apart everything they find. People, animals, kids, whatever. But there's no blood on their faces. Just white foam. And their eyes are dead. Just blank. I know they're coming for me and I have to shake myself out of the dream before they get here. But every time, they get closer and closer and it's harder and harder for me to pull myself up out of the dream. I can't shake it and it's fucking wearing me out."

"The drugs probably aren't helping," I said.

"You think I'm proud of myself? Like this is what I fucking aspired to be." He snorted and wiped his nose on his sleeve again.

JD went to the fridge and handed him another tallboy. Simms nodded his thanks and hammered the beer down in two long slugs. He let out a long wet belch and threw the can in a corner of the living room where it came to rest near a long-dead ficus. A pair of daddy longlegs scampered out from behind the plant and slid under the couch. "All I want is to be left alone. I don't want to talk to anyone. Not the cops, not you two, not my fucking dad. No one."

"We'd be more than happy to leave you alone, Martin, but you fucked us up on this thing with the laptop, so we're gonna need you to come and talk to Henderson and King with us," I said. "This has to get cleared up."

He was shaking his head wearily, his chin making slow arcs across his sunken chest. "I can't. I can't go to jail. I'd be dead before lunch."

I knew he was right, but so what? The fate of Martin Simms was not high on my list of concerns.

"What's on the laptop, Martin?" JD asked.

All of the air seemed to go out of him then. His chest sagged and his head flopped back against the couch. He held his head in his hands. "I never meant to hurt anyone."

JD nodded and stood up slowly. He lifted up the chair and placed it carefully back at the table, Simms watching him all the way. He walked back and stood in front of the couch and leaned down to put his face inches from Martin's.

"You never meant to hurt anyone? You think that just because you weren't the one behind the camera that you're a harmless consumer? This shit only exists because of the demand for it from trash like you. You're as guilty as the rest of the food chain of fucking deviants that generates and spreads this stuff. You're the reason these kids are taken and abused and discarded. You. Think about that. You are responsible for the destruction of these kids' lives, their murders. That's all on your head, you piece of shit. You don't get to play dumb."

JD stepped back and walked away and I heard the front door close behind him. Simms remained on the couch, where he seemed to be sinking into the filthy cushions, becoming part of the fabric. His breathing was barely perceptible.

"This isn't going to go well for you, Martin. I'm not gonna lie to you," I said. "But it's no more than you deserve. I spent years investigating these kinds of crimes and every single person we ever arrested had an excuse. They weren't hurting anyone, it was their private collection, whatever. JD is right, if a little bit naive. Without the demand, this kind of shit wouldn't be a billion dollar business. It would still exist, but it wouldn't be that."

"I didn't know--"

"Save it. I don't give a shit. Here's what's going to happen. I'm going to give you two hours to get your shit together and then I'm going to call Henderson and King and tell them where to find you. Then you're going to tell them that's your laptop. If you don't, if you decide to lie to them again, I will make it my business to wreck your life. I will tell all of your friends and neighbors, your parents, everyone. I'll tell them what you are and what you've done. I'll take out billboards. You won't be able to get a job, eat in a restaurant or walk down the street. I'll make it so you'll wish to God you were in prison or dead. Anywhere but here. Your other option is to come clean with me and help us find out why your friend was killed. Because I'm getting the feeling here that you might have something to do with it. So there it is. My number is on the table here. Call me in two hours, either way. We understand each other?"

He lifted his hand to his face as a fresh stream of blood broke free from the cut on his cheek. He inspected the red stain on his fingers but said nothing.

JD was in the Jeep, working his way through a party size bag of Funyuns. Loudly. He had a small black laptop open on his knees and was scrolling through the Windows directory.

"Where'd that come from?"

"It stuck to my fingers on the way out of the apartment," he said.

"What are you looking for?"

"Whatever I can find. So far, not much. Looks like it's his work machine. Lot of half-finished songs, a calendar with what look like gigs, and lesson schedule. Like that. It'll take a little time to see if there's anything interesting here."

"Time we have. It's information we need."

I looked up at the apartment again and saw only stillness. I pulled out of the parking lot and headed for 93.

JD worked on the laptop while I drove. The traffic was brutal getting through the 93-Route 3 split, but it opened up once we hit Hingham. We were nearly to Plymouth when JD clapped his hands.

"Shit," he said softly.

"Got something?"

"Encrypted volume. Good size one, too."

"Secret song lyrics?"

JD said, "Yeah, probably not. Some other stuff here, too. There are some weird files and registry keys that don't look like they belong to anything. I want to get down in the weeds and see what's here."

When the call came, it wasn't from Simms.

I had called Chris King and got no answer. I left him a message with what I knew and Simms's new address. I found Brendan writing in a small leather notebook on the front porch. I dug into an all-weather storage locker that sat on the porch nearby and came out with two gloves and a baseball. He smiled and we walked out to the beach road, where we stood about thirty feet apart playing soft toss.

I said, "How long since you threw a ball?"

"Four, maybe five years." The ball came out of his hand as naturally as could be.

I backed up to about sixty feet. Brendan rolled his neck a couple times and kicked his shoes off to the side of the road. The ball hummed and smacked into the pocket of my glove. The next one was faster. The third one, faster still. Soon, he was throwing from the windup, the ball hissing through the dry air and popping the leather webbing.

Sssssss. Pop.

Sssssss. POP.

"Lemme see the change," I said and got down into a catcher's crouch.

Brendan smiled and kicked a couple of rocks out of his way and dug his right foot into the sand. The arm motion and the ball flight were identical to the fastball, but the ball seemed to hang in the air for a split second before it hit my glove. The kind of pitch that makes .300 hitters look like they're having a seizure.

"Was it twelve against Chantilly?" I said.

"Thirteen. I struck out four in the third inning. Something about a dropped third strike, as I recall."

"I caught it! It never bounced, man. I caught that ball."

"Maybe, but if you had just thrown it to first instead of arguing with the ump, I wouldn't have had to get another out."

"I was trying to help your stats," I said.

"And getting yourself tossed in the process."

"I caught it."

"Point is, if you had just done what you were supposed to do rather than having to prove that you were right, it wouldn't have mattered. You can't win an argument with a high school ump. Especially after you've brought his daughter home after one AM on a Tuesday."

I sat down in the sand. "Amy Pike. Man. She was a gymnast and she could do this thing--"

"Really, Danny? What was that?" Caroline stood on the porch, hands on hips.

I looked at Brendan. "Do tell, Daniel," he said. "What was this thing she could do?"

"Algebra. She was great at algebra."

Caroline held up my iPhone. "Call for you."

I took the phone and tried to kiss her, but she was too quick and smacked me in the side of the head before I was even close.

"Danny Tobin," I said after she had gone inside.

"It's Chris King."

"Hey Chris. What's up?"

"Got your message, so I drove over there to see what I could get from Simms."

"Any luck?"

"Not really. Tough to talk when most of your brain is splattered on the wall."

"Ah, fuck, really?"

"Really really. I knocked on the door for a couple minutes and then tried the door. He was on the couch. Well, most of him was."

"Fuck."

"You said that."

I sat down on the porch steps. "You guys still there?"

"I'm by myself. But yeah. I called the Quincy PD, let them know. But they weren't sure when they could get someone over here."

"Should I come up there?"

"Not much point. He'll still be dead. He was alive when you left here?"

"As alive as he ever looked, yeah."

King blew out his breath. "I don't need more dead people, Tobin. I need more golf and less dead people."

"You're in the wrong line of work then. Dead people tend to find their way to homicide cops," I said.

"Yeah. Look, what's this bullshit with the computers?"

"Simms told us that the laptop you guys have wasn't Wyatt's. It was his."

King was silent for a long while, the only sound on the other end of the line the traffic going by in the background. "I hate talking on the fuckin phone. Meet me up here tomorrow. Four o'clock."

I found JD at the counter, still hunched over Simms's laptop. He was muttering to himself and occasionally shoving his hand into the bag of Funyuns, which was now empty. Something he had yet to notice. I filled him in on my conversation with King.

He said, "Suicide?"

"Sounds like it."

JD pushed his hands through his hair and sighed.

"All he did was speed up the process," I said. "He was halfway out the door anyway."

"I guess. But it still doesn't feel great. Feels kinda shitty, actually."

"It fades."

He shook his head. "Did you tell King about this laptop?"

"Nope. Thought we might need to figure out what's on there first."

"I'm getting there. I don't think we're going to have any luck with that encrypted volume, though. I looked in all the obvious places and a lot of non-obvious ones and couldn't find the passphrase. I'd bet it's written down somewhere in that apartment or saved on his phone."

"That ship has sailed," I said.

"So aside from that, there's some interesting stuff going on here. I installed a packet sniffer on here and as soon as I connected to your WiFi, weird shit started happening. He's got some old malware on here that's trying to connect to command servers that aren't alive anymore, but I shut that down. Then I started seeing a bunch of packets going to an IP address that looked sort of familiar, so I looked around a little and realized it's in the IP range of a bulletproof hosting service out in Idaho that hosts a lot of badness. I need to dig through here a little more, but I'd bet he has a rootkit or something like that on here that's phoning home. And it's a pretty big volume of data. Could be keystroke logs, financial data or something else."

"Like what?"

"Not sure yet. Could be anything, really. Gimme a day or so and I'll know more."

"Do your thing," I said.

I wnet out to the back deck and sat with my feet up on the rail. The sun was just inching below the treetops along Warren Avenue and the leaves glowed. The air smelled of the encroaching autumn, of dampness and chill nights to come. Summer had always been my favorite time of year, especially as a boy. But lately I'd come to look forward to the beginning of fall, as it meant the evacuation of the tourists that overrun Plymouth from May through September. They clogged the narrow streets with RVs and tour buses and crowded into the restaurants and bars, turning downtown into a no-fly zone for any sane locals. That would end soon, and the beach would clear out and by the time the first frost arrived, I'd be daydreaming of summer's return.

As the darkness gathered I tried to process what King had told me. Simms was a lost soul and from what I'd seen he was likely a predator. I felt little in the way of guilt or sorrow for his death. But it did complicate things and raise some questions that I didn't have answers for yet. Simms had been dying a slow death, so him killing himself wouldn't have surprised anyone. But the timing was problematic, coming just after I'd badgered him into telling us about the laptop. That may have been what sent him over the edge. But he must have known that someone would figure it out at some point and come looking for him.

It just happened to be us rather than King and Henderson. But the result likely would've been the same.

Still, without Simms to say so, it would be difficult to prove that the computer the cops had was his and not Wyatt's. Especially since King and Henderson's case hung on that not being true.

My phone buzzed and I glanced at the screen to see a 617 number I didn't recognize. I punched the green button.

"Yeah?"

"Danny Tobin?" The voice was cool and low.

"Who's this?"

"My name is Louis Andino. I'm a writer with the *Sunrise*."

"Uh huh."

"Well, I'm sure you've seen my stories on the investigation into the Wyatt Austin murder."

"Is that a question?" I said.

"Ah, no. I've been covering this story, and I'm working on a follow-up piece on why the police haven't closed the case yet. I was hoping I could have a conversation with you."

"What's that got to do with me?"

"I understand that you've been looking into the case, as well."

"Where'd you hear that?"

"Here and there. Look, I think it could help us both out to sit down and talk. I've spent a lot of time looking at this case, talked to a lot of people. There's a lot of things that the cops haven't talked about."

"I'm not really in the habit of talking to reporters. Too much downside, not enough upside," I said. "You have a good day now."

I ended the call and went inside, looking for something to eat. The pickings were slim. I found a jar of peanut butter and a banana that wasn't quite dead yet, so I made a grilled peanut butter and banana sandwich and walked back out to the deck, wondering how many of these things it took to kill Elvis.

Twenty minutes later my phone buzzed again. It was Andino.

"Gonna make me drop my pants, huh? Ok, how about this: Wyatt Austin wasn't the target."

I sat forward in my chair. "And you know this how?"

"It's my job. I'm good at it. No one else has that information, so I'm trusting you not to screw me on this before I can write it."

I thought about it. Andino seemed to be plugged into the investigation in a way that maybe me and JD weren't and probably would never be. So ok.

"I have to be up that way tomorrow afternoon. I'll call you on my way and we can find a spot to meet," I said.

JD took a cab back to the yacht club and Caroline spent the rest of the evening looking at profiles of rescue dogs online while

I read. Last night, she seemed to have settled on a golden retriever. Tonight she was favoring German shepherds. Tomorrow it could be St. Bernards.

She looked up from her iPad: "I think I want a boxer. Or maybe a bull mastiff."

"I'll alert the media," I said.

Nine

The next day was a Sunday and even though I had a lot to get done, Caroline and I took the time to go for a long run. This was our Sunday ritual when all was calm, but it had been a few weeks since we'd had the time to do it.

Life was getting in the way.

We were out by 6:30 AM planning to do about twelve miles, starting at the beach and going up through town, along the waterfront, into Nelson Park and down the bike path next to the old railbed and up into North Plymouth. We popped out onto 3A and turned for home, passing by the spot where the restaurant that had served as Paolo DeSilva's meeting place had stood. It was now a discount cell phone store that catered to the hard-working Brazilian population that DeSilva had exploited and robbed for so many years.

He was dead now, murdered by the longtime friend he had betrayed, and the criminal empire he had built on the backs of his countrymen was in ashes, burned to the ground by DeSilva's own greed and arrogance. Joao Alves, DeSilva's employee and killer, had gone down with him, putting a bullet through his own head after he'd made sure DeSilva went first.

"I'm glad they're dead," Caroline said, not for the first time, as we passed the former steakhouse.

"You're not alone."

"Do you ever think about them anymore?"

"I did for a while. The first few weeks after it ended and even for a while after we took off on the boat, I'd catch myself going back and forth about it, wondering if I should've handled it differently. There were a lot of ways that it could've gone. It didn't have to end that way. But then I'd think about the girls in that truck, how DeSilva just said, screw it. Kill 'em all. And I'd remember all the other girls he'd abused over the years. The ones who thought they were coming here for decent jobs and a chance at a better life and ended up sleeping on a bare floor with ten other girls in a cold room. Those are the people I think of now. Not DeSilva or Alves. Because fuck them."

Caroline's eyes were unreadable behind her sunglasses. We ran in silence for a mile or so, and when we stopped at the light near St. Peter's downtown, she pushed the button for the walk signal and looked across the intersection at the old white church.

"You know what Brendan told me yesterday?" she said.

"Nope."

"He said you'd never seen him say Mass. Said that you went to his Ordination but that you never showed up for his first Mass the next day. He didn't sound hurt or angry, just stating a fact. Is that right?"

Technically, it was.

I hadn't been in the church that Sunday morning. I had rolled into the parking lot just as the echo of the bells calling parishioners to Mass receded. I had been up all night and my clothes were filthy and reeked of sweat and blood and wet earth. I stood in the vestibule of St. Tim's with the other sinners who didn't want to be seen in the pews and the arthritics who couldn't sit for an hour and was grateful for the overpowering scent of incense. Brendan sat in the center of the wide raised granite altar, a small private smile played on his face. I could see my father and our extended family down in the front pew. Every few minutes he'd twist around and scan the congregation.

Looking for me.

After the Gospel, Brendan rose and stepped slowly to the pulpit. He embraced the ancient priest whom he had chosen as his concelebrant, the same man who had baptized him and me and Erin so many years before. I watched as Brendan looked out at the congregation, enjoying the moment, picking out familiar faces in the pews, nodding to each of them in turn. His homily that day was about the call he had felt since childhood, the tug toward a life of service. He talked about the love and support he had always felt from our parents and he talked about how difficult the death of Erin had been for all of us. She had been the best of us, Brendan said. He spoke of the beauty of living one's life for others and of the chance for redemption that is offered to all of us.

All we need to do is take it, he said.

I left before the Mass ended and walked to my car sitting in the shade of a weeping willow tree. I stood in the late Virginia spring warmth and humidity, leaning on the car for support. My knees were weak and cicadas buzzed in my ears. I bent over and vomited in the grass next to the car. I wiped my mouth on the back of my sleeve and got in the car, the door handle slick with sweat and red blood.

I drove back to my hotel and washed the filth and death from my skin, standing under the scalding stream of water for the best part of an hour. I changed into my suit and went downstairs to the reception and made my apologies for missing the Mass. My father was more disappointed than angry, simply shaking his head when he saw me. But Brendan put his arm around me and smiled.

"Glad you made it, Danny. Long night?" he said with a chuckle.

I forced a smile. "The longest."

It had been a long twenty-four hours, actually. I had flown into Dulles from Boston the previous morning, rented a truck, and met up with a high school friend who was a Fauquier County sheriff's deputy. We met on a dirt track out in the sticks near Catharpin, where no one goes by accident. He handed me a small, heavy backpack.

"Hardware and docs in there," he said.

"Appreciate it, man. Chances he'll have any help with him?"

"Low. He doesn't seem to have any close associates. Just guys he's selling to. No one for you to worry about."

"Who is he buying from?"

"We don't know for sure, but most everyone in the metro area is supplied by Mexico these days."

"The cartels are serious," I said.

"Last time I checked, so are you," he said.

Back in the truck, I looked through the backpack and found a .45 semi auto with two clips, a small packet of photos, and a sticky note with a handwritten address on Vint Hill Road, a few miles away. I knew the area; it was a good spot. Not much around.

I drove into Manassas and found a Walmart and bought a pair of binoculars, some duct tape, a few bungees, rubber gloves. I stopped at a 7-11 nearby and got some snacks and water and then headed out 66 West to Gainesville and off onto 29 and then backroads to the address I'd been given. It took me several passes, but I eventually found the numbers on a battered white metal mailbox on Vint Hill Road. It was one of a row of a half dozen boxes in a wooden rack next to a red clay track that led off into a grove of pines fifty yards or so off the road. I drove past the mailboxes until I found a good spot and then pulled the truck onto the shoulder and tucked it under some trees.

There was mostly open land between where I'd parked and the dirt road, so I put the supplies in the backpack, grabbed the binoculars, and set off through the field. I couldn't see any houses, but I had an idea where they'd be, based on the location of the dirt road. I took a meandering route, occasionally stopping to look through the binoculars at trees in the distance, pretending to look for birds. I figured this had to be one of the few open areas like this left out here. This had all been surrounded by razor wire and guard towers when I was a kid, but a few years earlier, the government had demolished the NSA listening station that had occupied a lot of this land and sold it off in chunks. Most of it was an office park now, some had been given over to an air traffic control station, and the rest was infested by housing developments with names like Dunderstone or Bumbleton. I'd spent a lot of time on the county golf courses out here as a kid, but those had been plowed under to make room for private courses and yoga retreats.

I angled through the field in the general direction of the dirt road and then down along it until a small cluster of brick ranch houses came into view through the trees. There were three together, another two about fifty yards away, and then one off by itself, maybe a hundred yards farther on. I hoped that was the one I was looking for, but didn't think I'd be that lucky.

I wasn't.

Donald's house was in the group of three. I cut a wide circle around them and didn't see any movement in any of the houses. An old Toyota sat in front of one of them, and a newish BMW 5 series sat alongside another house. That was his place. The black metal numbers screwed into a shutter next to the front door confirmed it. I walked around aimlessly for a few minutes and then went back into the trees, found a good dry spot with a view of the house and settled in with my back against a tree.

Nothing much moved for the next couple of hours aside from a few squirrels and a blue jay in the bushes in front of one of the houses that was busy building a nest. Around mid-afternoon an older F150 came down the dirt road and pulled in next to the BMW. A large, dark-skinned guy hopped out of the driver's side carrying a small duffel bag, knocked on the door, then glanced up at what I guessed was a camera and waved. The door opened a few seconds later and the visitor handed the bag to Donald, they exchanged a few words, and then the door closed, the visitor got back in the truck and drove off. The whole thing had taken less than sixty seconds.

Over the next couple of hours, the process repeated four more times, each with a different vehicle and driver. Each of the men was alone and none of them seemed to be in any hurry or concerned about his surroundings. By the time the sun set and it started to get dark, six deliveries had taken place. A little after eight o'clock, a truck came into the drive and parked, about thirty feet away from where I sat. I took the .45 from the backpack, shouldered the pack, and crept to the edge of the treeline. When the driver's door opened I could see the man was alone, as the others had been. He was a big guy and got out carrying the requisite duffel bag. His back was to me and I walked up behind him, silent on the dirt drive, and pressed the gun into his spine and pushed him against the side of the truck.

"Not a sound," I said into his ear. "We clear?"

He nodded and held the bag out for me to take. I pushed his arm back down with my free hand and then patted him down. No weapons. I pulled his phone from his hip pocket, wallet out of his back pocket and flipped it open and read the name and address out loud to him. I then held up the phone to his face, which showed a photo of two smiling young boys in soccer uniforms.

"We're gonna walk to the door and you're gonna do exactly what you'd normally do. If anything goes wrong…"

He nodded again. I pulled him away from the truck and walked him toward the front of the house. The concrete stoop was flanked by juniper bushes and I pushed the man up onto the stoop and then crouched between the house and the bushes on the left side, out of view of the small camera mounted in the top left corner above the door.

"Knock," I said quietly.

He hesitated a second, then knocked three times quickly and looked up toward the camera. He waved. I heard the deadbolt on the door slide and as the door cracked open, I stepped up behind the man on the stoop and shoved him hard into the door, smashing it into Donald and knocking them both onto the floor in the small entryway. Donald shouted something I couldn't make out as I pushed in behind them, kicked the door shut with my heel and locked the deadbolt.

The delivery man was face down on the linoleum floor and did not try to turn over. Donald was sitting next to him, holding his face, blood seeping between his fingers. He was making a sad wheezing sound and shaking his head. He wiped his eyes on his sleeve and finally raised his head.

"Do you know who's money..." He stopped there. "Oh, fuck."

"Yeah," I said.

I held the .45 on Donald and kicked the other man in the ribs. "You good?" I asked.

"I'm ok."

"Here's what you're going to do. You're going to stand up, pick up the duffel bag, and walk to the door. Then you're going to walk out, get in your truck, and go. You're not going to look back at us. Are we clear?"

"Yeah. But what do I do with the money?"

I recited his home address to him. "Move somewhere else."

The man slowly got to his feet, grabbed the bag, and walked out the door. I heard the truck start and drive away.

"Anyone else here?" I asked Donald.

He shook his head.

"When is the next delivery due?"

"Ten minutes."

I slapped the side of his head. "When?"

"I said. Ten minutes."

I squatted down next to him and leaned in close. His breathing was still uneven and his nose was bent at a thirty degree angle. I grabbed a handful of his hair, jerked his head up and smacked his nose with my open palm. He yelped and scooted backward on the linoleum. I held onto his hair and smacked him again. And then again.

"Goddammit! Two hours, ok? Two hours! What the fuck?"

I pulled him up by his hair and shoved him into the small living room and pushed him onto a filthy loveseat that was parked in front of a brick fireplace. I stared into his eyes until he broke and dropped his chin to his chest. He heaved a deep breath.

"Danny, I loved--"

I hit him with a short jab that snapped his head back against the sofa and completed the destruction of his nose, which now took up most of his face. Blood flowed freely from it and both of his eyes were beginning to blacken. He didn't make a sound and kept his head down on his chest.

I walked into the adjacent dining area, grabbed a tall ladderback wooden chair, and set it in front of the sofa. I pulled Donald onto the chair and then used the bungees to lash him to it, with several layers of duct tape around his chest and thighs for good measure. I taped his mouth shut and then took a quick tour of the house to make sure we were alone. The house was empty.

Back in the living room, Donald was squirming against the restraints and trying to inch the chair toward the fireplace. I watched him for a couple minutes from the entryway, halfway hoping he would find a way out of the bindings. But he realized pretty quickly it was useless, and gave up. I found the TV remote on the sofa and turned it on, scanning the channels until I found one playing death metal videos. I pushed the volume up as high as it would go and then turned to Donald. His eyes were pinned and his face was crusted with blood and what little air he could get in through his ruined nose clearly wasn't enough. I tore the duct tape off his mouth and he gulped in several breaths before settling down.

He opened his mouth to speak, and then thought better of it. I went into the kitchen, found a non-heinous glass, filled it with water from the tap, and went back into the living room and held it to Donald's mouth. He gulped it down greedily. I broke the top of the glass on the hearth and then ground the jagged remnants into the top of his thigh, pushing down until I felt the glass go through his jeans and down into his leg.

He screamed and wailed and bucked against the pain. I stood on his foot and pushed down harder.

He bit down hard on his lower lip and groaned, his eyes rolling back. I pushed down harder and twisted the glass slowly back and forth. Deep red blood poured down Donald's leg and pooled on the floor and as I watched it settle into the cracks in the linoleum, I felt his body go limp. I checked his breathing: still there.

I went back into the kitchen and filled another glass with ice water and then threw it into Donald's face. He woke gasping, looked at me and then down at the glass still embedded in his thigh and fainted again. I pushed down lightly on the glass and he jumped back awake so violently he nearly tipped the chair backward. I caught the chair, set it back upright, pulled the glass from his leg, and then sat on the brick hearth facing him. The hole in his leg was jagged and purple and white and rich red blood pulsed from it every few seconds. Donald glanced down at it quickly and then turned and vomited on the floor.

I waited a minute until he was done and had composed himself enough to look at me. I waited some more. Eventually he couldn't take it.

"Is there any way out of this? Anything?" he said.

I waited.

"The guys I work for, they're gonna come looking for me as soon as I don't drop the money tomorrow. Davey, the guy who was here, he's gonna tell them what happened."

"What's he gonna tell them? That the two of you got jacked up and he somehow walked away with their money?"

He looked toward the front window. "For real, another delivery will be here in like an hour and half, something like that. The guy will see you."

"This isn't going to take that long. I'll be home in bed by then."

He licked his lips, looked around the room, down at the hole in his leg, the .45 in my hand. He was quiet for a minute. Then, "I have a safe. In the basement. There's a safe in the basement. I don't know how much is in there, probably two hundred grand at least, maybe two fifty. I give you the combination, you take the cash and walk. You were never here, I never saw you."

I nodded and stood up and picked up the broken glass. Donald started shaking and hopping in his chair.

"Danny, no, christ! Forget what I said. I wasn't thinking. Forget it."

I didn't. I dug the glass into his other leg, turning it as I went. He wailed, the death metal on the TV above my head blared, and the floor grew slick with his blood. He fainted again and while he was out I went down to the basement and found the safe. It was a big floor-standing model about four feet tall. I dug around on the nearby workbench and found a hacksaw and a pair of vise grips. I walked back upstairs to find Donald awake and white and soaked in sweat. He saw the tools in my hand and shook his head weakly.

"Donald, here's what's going to happen. You're going to tell me the combination to the safe, and if you're telling the truth about what's in there, then we can have a conversation. If you're lying, then I'm going to shoot you in the knees and leave you here. It'll probably take four or five hours for you to bleed out. Those won't be good hours."

"Danny, I'm serious. It's like I said. That thing is jammed with cash. It's yours, fucking take it."

He gave me the combination and I went down and opened the safe. He wasn't lying. It was stacked floor to ceiling with bundles of cash, all well-used and clearly not from a bank. I had no way of knowing how much was there, but Donald's estimate didn't seem outrageous. I closed and locked the safe and went back upstairs.

"It's what I told you, right? Right?"

"Yeah, you were telling the truth."

He relaxed into the chair, and some color came back into his face.

"But here's the thing, Donald: I wasn't. You could have had the Holy Grail in that safe and it wouldn't have saved you. I'm going to kill you and bury you someplace where no one will ever find you. And then I'm going to go home and never think about you again. And no one will miss you and no one will mourn you and the world will go right on turning."

As I talked, his face fell, what color had come back into it drained away and he seemed to sink into the chair. He had already lost a lot of blood and I knew he was weak, but he had a couple more hours in him. I took two of the bungees and used them as tourniquets above the wounds on his thighs, cutting off some of the blood flow. I didn't want him dying too quickly. Next, I looked around the house until I found the keys to Donald's BMW and went outside and opened the trunk. I went back inside, untied Donald, who was unconscious by then, hoisted him over my shoulder and dropped him into the trunk and closed the lid.

Back inside, I turned off the TV, gathered my bungees and backpack, and looked around to ensure nothing was left behind. I turned off the living room lights and walked out, pulling the door closed behind me.

I cruised down the dirt road to Vint Hill Road, followed that back out to 29 and headed north. Ten minutes later, I saw two granite pillars on the shoulder and pulled off onto a gravel road on the right and nosed the BMW slowly down the track among some tall grass and weeping willows. I bounced down the track for a couple hundred yards until the lights hit the redwood planks of a barn.

I cut the engine but left the lights on and got out and stood still, listening. I waited two full minutes and then walked around and popped the trunk. Donald was curled in the fetal position and the trunk stank of shit and sweat. I reached in and checked his pulse. Weak, but there. I hauled him out and hoisted him on my shoulder again and walked out past the barn and into a small open field to the right. The car's headlights backlit me as I walked and I went slowly, feeling Donald's weight more with each step. I went about fifty yards past the barn and then dropped him on the ground. He grunted.

I walked to the barn, found a shovel, and walked back out. Donald had rolled onto his back and was wheezing loudly. I jammed the shovel into the red clay next to him and squatted down. I pressed down hard on the wound in his left thigh. He groaned but didn't have the energy for more.

"Danny...Danny. I can't talk…"

"That's ok. I never wanted any information from you, or any remorse. It wouldn't have mattered anyway. You killed my sister and her baby and you've had this coming. You knew it was coming, didn't you?"

He coughed and a red bubble formed in his nostril.

"Yeah, you knew. Well, now here it is. Erin didn't know what was happening, and that's the only thing I can hold onto. She never knew. But I wanted you to know, and I wanted you to know it was me. So, I'm gonna go over here and dig a hole and then I'll be back. Don't go anywhere."

It took me about thirty minutes to dig the hole, which was only a few feet deep. Thankfully, some recent rain had loosened up the clay. I went back and found Donald on his side, moaning. I hooked him under the arms and dragged him toward the hole. He dug his heels in, but he had no energy left. I got to the edge of the hole and dropped him. He rolled on his left side and saw the grave, and then rolled onto his back, waiting.

I grabbed the shovel, walked back to the hole and pulled the .45 from my belt and looked down at Donald, his face broken, his legs torn to shreds.

"I'm ready," he said.

"So am I."

I put the .45 back in my belt and squatted down and rolled him into the hole. He landed on his back and the oblique light from the car's headlamps reflected off his eyes. I looked down at him for a minute or so, and then took the shovel and began filling the hole in. It didn't hit him for a few seconds, but once he realized what was happening, he started yelling and trying to sit up, but it was no use. I covered his legs first, and then his torso, and when I got to his head, I stopped.

"Last chance. Tell me why," I said.

He cranked his head around to look at me, his eyes wild and red. "There isn't any why." He coughed. "I got mad, and now she's dead. That's all."

"That's all," I said.

I threw the first shovelful of dirt on his face and he started to scream again. I shoveled faster, throwing more and more clay on him, listening to him cough and choke. I filled the grave in and smoothed over the top.

Then I put the shovel back in the barn, backed the BMW out of there and drove it back to where I'd left my rental truck. I parked the BMW off the road a bit, walked across the road, took out the .45, and fired three quick shots into the car's gas tank. The third one did the trick and it went up like a roman candle.

I got back in the truck and drove away, the first tendrils of the sun's light coming over the eastern horizon.

Years had passed since then, and I could still feel the sting of my father's disappointment and my own rage in the flush in my face now. The light changed and Caroline and I ran through the intersection and past St. Peter's, the lot barely half full for the seven-thirty.

"Yeah, I guess he's right," I said. "I'll get there sooner or later."

"He's your brother, Danny. You need to get your ass in a pew and show him some respect."

"I'm pretty sure the last church you were in is the one down Providence they turned into a bar."

"This isn't about me. Be a man."

I met Chris King in a Five Guys a mile down the road from Martin Simms's apartment complex. He had already ordered and was seated at a high table against the wall. I waved hello and went to the counter. When I sat down a few minutes later he had finished his double burger and was elbow deep in a brown paper bag of cajun fries.

"Fucking things are gonna kill me," he said. "Least I'll die happy."

"More than most of us can say, I guess."

He dragged a handful of fries through a puddle of ketchup on his tin foil burger wrapper and shoved them into his mouth. He looked at me as he chewed. "Definitely more than your boy Simms can say."

"Last time that guy was happy, Tom Brady still had his own hair," I said.

King lifted a small packet of papers out of his jacket pocket and laid them on the table in front of me. "Forensics report on the laptop we seized," he said.

I reached for the papers and he slapped a greasy hand on top of them. "You first, Tobin. Tell me about the computer shit."

"There's not much to it. I got to talking to Wyatt's girlfriend the other day about the investigation and I mentioned that I'd love to have an hour with Wyatt's computer. She said I could come by any time and check it out. Which I thought was a little odd since, you know, you guys were supposed to have it. So we went over to talk to Simms and he let it slip that the laptop you guys took out of their old apartment was his. Not Wyatt's."

"And he told you this why?"

"I asked really nicely. Then I stood on his wrist."

King snorted. "Subtle," he said. He balled up the paper bag and burger wrapper and threw the wad at a trash can, missing badly. "Did he tell you what was on the computer?"

"Not in so many words. But I got the general idea."

"I'll be real honest with you: it's some of the worst shit I've seen. You'll see in that report. After thirty seconds I was ready to strangle someone. Anyone. If Austin hadn't already been dead I would've killed him myself."

"It wasn't his stuff," I said.

"Yeah, I got that. So now you're telling me that the dead junkie down the road here, it was his. And I don't get to kill him either."

"Seems so."

King rubbed a hand across his face, which showed a three-day growth of beard. Dark lines rimmed his eyes. "I don't need to tell you, this fucks us up pretty good. Right in the ear. We had a solid working theory on this, likely motive, all that. Now we got jack shit."

"What you have is a reason to go back and look at the evidence again, see if anything new jumps out at you. Go back to the basics."

"I need a fucking lecture on police work from you? The guy who shot his way out of half his cases? Look, maybe we were wrong about this part, but that doesn't mean we're the JV over here. And I don't even know for sure that we were wrong. All I have is secondhand info you say you got from a guy who showed up dead a couple hours later. A junkie piece of shit. And now we're supposed to tear our case down. Does that sound like something you think I'm going to do?"

I held out my hands. "I'm just telling you what I know, man. That's it. Believe me or don't. Or tell me to fuck off. I don't care. But we're going to keep going, and we're gonna push. Wyatt's family deserves answers, not guesses."

King pushed the papers across the table.

I scanned the report, which was written in the detached, quasi-legal language that cops love so much. The description of what was on the laptop was still brutal. I scanned through a couple of sentences before I had enough. I pushed the report back to King.

"So you see where we were coming from," he said.

"Not really. I see what's on there and I know that Wyatt's dead, but even if you assume the pictures were his, which they weren't, I don't see how you connect the two right off the bat," I said. "There's thousands of assholes out there doing this, but they don't all turn up dead."

King looked out the windows at the front of the restaurant that gave onto the parking lot. He watched some cars pull in and out of slots for a while, then looked at me. "Some of them do," he said.

"Some? Meaning more than one."

"Six so far that we know about. That's just in Massachusetts. Three of them in Boston proper. There are a couple more up in Vermont that we think might be connected, but we're not sure yet."

"Six. Forgive me here, but this sounds an awful lot like you have a serial killer on your hands. But I don't recall hearing anything about that on the news or seeing it in the papers."

King shrugged. "No one cares. The bosses don't care, the media don't care. Shit, Henderson doesn't even care. The guy's not killing anyone who matters. It's a bunch of guys like Simms."

"Even junkies have families."

He stared across the table. I felt a small shiver go through me. "It's not just junkies, is it? They're all pedophiles. Someone is picking them off."

"Welcome to the party," King said.

"How long?" I asked.

"The first one we're pretty solid on was in oh-nine. The last one before Austin was end of last year. So it's been about one a year, maybe a little more."

I thought about what Louis Andino had told me on the phone, that the killer had gotten the wrong guy. "But Wyatt wasn't in that life. You must've had something to connect him to this besides what was on the computer."

"We didn't know that at the time, but yeah there's more than that. Three of the other victims were artists of one kind or another and four of the six went to the same college. Not all at the same time, but some overlap here and there. So the threads are there."

"What college?" I asked.

He looked at me. "An art school down in Georgia."

I cleared my throat. "The one Wyatt went to."

"We didn't pull this out of our asses, Tobin. We have actually done some police work here. Hard as that may be for you to recognize. Point is, Austin fit into the picture pretty well. We didn't force it. The laptop was one thing, but then his circle of friends, the art gig and the connection to the college."

"I see it. But why feed it to the media and maybe let the killer know which direction you're moving?"

"Christ, again with that? We didn't talk to the fucking press, Tobin. Did. Not. Our bosses don't even want to acknowledge that these killings might be connected, let alone have us put it out in the papers," he said. "Right now, they see this as a bunch of dead baby rapers. And who's gonna be mad about that result?"

I sat back in my chair. "Not a fucking soul."

King touched his nose.

"Unless the wrong guy gets killed," I said.

He shrugged again. "You see protesters marching down the streets? Anyone having any candlelight vigils on the Common?

We had fifty homicides in the city last year, and we're gonna roll right past that this year. No one gives a fuck about one dead body, more or less. If you're not talking about a kindergartener shot at the bus stop, the shit slides right by. Even then, it better be the cutest five-year-old in the city and his momma better be a quadriplegic war hero. Lots of people die in this city every day, in all kinds of ways. Most of them unremarkable, some fucking crazy. We had a case last month, guy was running down Boylston on a Saturday morning, tripped over the curb going into the crosswalk and got his head crushed by a taxi. Just like that. Cab driver never saw the guy, said he thought he ran over a squirrel. We're all on the way out, man. Some of us faster than others."

"Wyatt wasn't on the way out. He was on the way up. The guy had it all in front of him and he got killed for no reason. That can't stand."

He gave me a thin smile. "Don't tell me you still believe in justice."

"Only thing I believe in at this point is myself. Justice isn't my problem."

"Revenge, then?"

I said nothing. King pushed away from the table and stood. He gathered the papers, folded them neatly and slid them back into his coat pocket.

"And look where that belief has gotten you so far," he said and walked out the door.

I called Louis Andino from the parking lot and told him to meet me at John Paul II Park in Quincy. He said he knew the place and could be there in fifteen minutes. Midday traffic on the expressway was light and I was there in five. I found an empty bench and sat facing the water, watching a group of Asian men fly brightly colored kites high above the park. The kites were elaborate and the men were expert at maneuvering them, flying them in tight circles and dipping them under one another in choreographed patterns. A large green and red dragon came humming down toward my bench and I was reaching for my gun to shoot it just as it zipped skyward a few feet before it would've brained me.

"Danny Tobin?"

I turned to see a man standing next to the bench, right extended for a handshake. "You Andino?" I asked.

"Yup."

I shook his hand and waved him to the spot next to me on the bench. He was a solid guy, dressed in light khakis and a plain blue chambray shirt. He wore plain steel glasses and his brown hair was receding into a wide cul-de-sac. He carried a black messenger bag with a round red logo on it. We sat quietly and watched the kites for a couple of minutes before I spoke.

"Why do you think Wyatt Austin wasn't the intended victim?"

"It's not what I think, it's what I know."

"Tell me. Because that fucked up story you wrote sure paints a different picture."

He leaned forward, resting his elbows on his knees. "Yeah. Well, I got some information from someone I trusted and it turned out to be bad. That's one of the hazards of being a reporter. You have to rely on other people to shoot you straight, and if they don't, you come out looking like a jerk. This is one of those instances. It sucks, but it happens."

"It sucks a lot more for the people who are the collateral damage, I can tell you that," I said. "Wyatt's family has to live with everyone thinking he was involved in that shit. They have to walk around with people pointing at them and whispering. Did you ever think about maybe checking your facts with the people who knew him?"

"I talked to some of his friends and they said what friends would say. Oh he was a great guy, he was a brilliant artist, he loved his mother, and so on. But like I said, I trusted my source on this. It's a source I've relied on for a long time and I've never had a problem before."

"I haven't seen any corrections," I said.

"That's why I'm here. I want to set things right."

"How?"

"Some information exchange. I'll show you mine if you show me yours."

"You already did. But you haven't told me how you know Wyatt wasn't the right guy," I said. "Or was this another tip from your great source?"

He tipped his head. "Point taken. I'm sure you know I'm not able to reveal my sources, but this information didn't come from just one person. I've been spending the last few weeks going back over this stuff, trying to see where things got sidetracked. How did Austin end up getting killed? Who was the real target? All that stuff. I've looked back at all of my notes and the public information on it. And the truth is, it really was just the one source that led me down that path. Looking back at it all now, I can see that. So when I looked at it with fresh eyes, I saw that and I went back and checked with the source again, and it turns out the information wasn't as solid as the source thought. It was based on something that *could* have pointed to Austin and to his involvement with the child porn stuff, but mostly what it did was just point to *someone* being involved. Not necessarily him."

"Big difference."

"Yeah."

"Did you run it by the cops before you printed it?" I asked.

"I'll just say they didn't dissuade me from that line of thinking."

"Did they confirm it?"

He smiled. "C'mon, Tobin. You know better than that. The point is I didn't just make it up."

"That's funny. It's the same thing that the cops told me about that theory. Someone made that shit up, but apparently it wasn't them and it wasn't you. Convenient. So if Wyatt wasn't the target then who was?"

He said nothing.

"Ok, I'll take a stab at it. How about Martin Simms?" I said.

His eyes flashed for half a second before he caught himself. "Cops tell you that?" he asked.

"C'mon Andino, you know better than that," I said.

He laughed. "Fair enough. Yeah, that's where I landed on it."

"Why, though? How did you get there?"

"I just looked at the available evidence. There's no other scenario that really makes any sense. We know that the police have a laptop that they took out of their apartment and we know that there was a lot of really disgusting shit on there. It's not unreasonable to think that either Simms and Austin shared the computer or that it actually belonged to Simms. It's easy to make a mistake on that kind of thing. And I've done a little digging on Simms, talked to some people, looked at his history and he fits the profile for what my source suggested was true of Austin. I've been trying to get in touch with him but haven't been able to connect yet."

"You missed your chance," I said. "Simms is dead."

I watched Andino's face carefully as I delivered the news and the surprise in his eyes seemed genuine.

"What happened?" he said.

"Looks like suicide. Cops found him yesterday in his apartment."

Andino sat quietly for a long time, looking out across the park toward the river on the far side. The men with the kites had left and the park was empty but for a few power walkers making the rounds. He picked up a small rock and whipped it at a group of seagulls scavenging around a nearby trash can. They shouted in warning and flew a short distance away before reassembling near the can.

"Well, sounds like you were right. And me too," he said.

"I know I was right. He told me himself."

He gave me a sideways look. "Told you what?"

"He admitted that the laptop that the cops took out of the apartment was his. Not Austin's. So whatever is on there--and I have a pretty good idea what it is--belongs to him. He told the police that Austin used the laptop, which he apparently did once in a while. So they assumed he owned it, and Simms let them believe it. So they dig through the machine, find whatever shit they find and all of a sudden a good man is branded a child abuser. Just like that."

"When did you talk to him?"

"A couple of times. Last one was yesterday, a few hours before he died I guess."

"Why would he tell you all that?"

"I'm easy to talk to. And persuasive."

"I can imagine. Sounds to me like he was clearing the decks because he knew what he was going to do," Andino said.

I shrugged. "He was a junkie and he didn't have much longer in any case. But I think whatever conscience he might have had was getting the better of him. He and Wyatt were friends and then Wyatt was killed and Simms let the police think his friend was a monster. And now it looks like it may have been Simms's own actions that got Wyatt killed. That's a lot of weight for anyone."

"Especially someone as weak as him."

"Not a lot of sympathy for addicts, huh?"

"Listen, I've known plenty of addicts. All kinds. Some are good people, some aren't. But they're all weak. They can't control themselves and then they try to push the blame off because society tells them it's ok, you have a disease. It's not your fault. Bullshit. It *is* your fault. You have no self control. Get your shit together and stop making excuses. Be a man. At least Simms seems to have gotten that part right. He knew he was a piece of shit and he took care of it."

"That's a pretty bleak philosophy, Andino. Not everyone has the mental strength or support to get past those kinds of problems. I've seen addiction take down some pretty fucking strong guys over the years. Guys a lot tougher than you or me. It ain't an easy thing."

"Maybe not, but it's simple enough. You either give in to it or you don't."

"Well, I guess there's one less addict to piss you off now," I said. "But it doesn't necessarily clear up why someone wanted to kill him. Or why they ended up killing Wyatt instead."

"I'm sure the cops are going to look at that now that Simms is dead too," he said. "That probably didn't do them any favors in trying to close the Austin case."

I wasn't so sure how hard Henderson and King would be pushing. King hadn't sounded too eager to jump back in on this one. "I don't know about them, but I've got nothing else to do, so I'm pushing on this. Wyatt's family deserves to know what happened."

"I'm going to stick with it, as well. It might be good for both of us if we can compare notes as we go," Andino said. "As long as we're off the record, I don't have a problem with that. But if you publish one word from me, even as an anonymous source, without my say so, I'll blow your shit up."

Ten

I found Caroline in the living room, hands on hips, glaring at her painting. Her hair was in a tangle and the front of her Dropkick Murphys t-shirt was covered in paint splotches. The scenery was coming together nicely but the horse-llamas were still a little muddy. I opened my mouth to say something, but she stared at me with blank, hooded eyes and I thought better of it and went to the kitchen for a beer instead. I brought her one and stood next to her in front of the canvas. We stood silently drinking our beers for a minute or so. The refrigerator hummed and somewhere in the distance I heard a dog bark.

"Do you love me, Danny?" she said at last.

"Nearly all the time."

She nodded. "Then please never give me your honest opinion of this thing."

I kissed her on the top of the head. "Deal."

I dropped onto the couch and kicked my shoes off. "Where's Brendan?" I asked.

"He took one of your poles and walked down the beach a couple of hours ago. Said he wanted to contribute to the household. Does he know how to fish?"

"Oh yeah. He wreaked havoc on the bass ponds when we were growing up," I said. "I can't tell you how many smallmouths my mom cleaned over the years. And there isn't a lot of meat on those things. They're like fish nuggets. You need about a dozen of them for a decent meal. And when we'd be up here in the summers, me and him would walk out on the flats here at low tide and see who could get the most stripers. I don't recall ever winning."

"I hope his luck holds, because we've got a whole lot of nothing to eat here," Caroline said.

Caroline washed her paint brushes out in the back yard and then went up to shower. I finished my beer and took another one out to the front porch. I sat with my feet up on the rail and listened to the tide lapping at the rocks across the road. I was halfway through the second beer when Brendan came wandering down the road, barefoot and smiling. He climbed the stairs to the porch and dropped a small stringer of stripers at my feet like a dog returning a tennis ball covered with saliva. He leaned the long saltwater pole against the railing and sat on the cooler next to me, brushing the sand from his feet.

"Nice haul," I said. "Did you go out to the flats?"

"Yeah. It was so lovely, Danny. Just peaceful and calm. I'd forgotten how clear the water is here sometimes. Especially at this time of year. It's never clear like that in California. And the water is so cold there, you can't even put your feet in without needing medical attention."

"You ever do any fishing out there?"

"I never did for the first several years I was out there. I just couldn't justify taking the time. There's always so much work to be done. But just this year I've started going for an hour or two once a week or so and it's such a wonderful way to clear and refocus my mind. With all that's been going on I've really needed that time. It's been such a blessing. I can't say I've had much luck actually catching anything, but it's a lovely time just the same."

"Is that what you were doing today, clearing your mind?"

"It wasn't what I intended to do. I just wanted to go out and see if I could still catch a fish," he said. "But yes, I spent quite a lot of time thinking about what I want to do and what I need to do."

"And those aren't necessarily the same things?" I said.

"Are they for you?"

"Not always, no. But I can get away with doing what I want rather than what I need to do a lot easier than you can."

He smiled. "You always could."

"I notice you didn't answer my question."

He stood, clapped the sand off his hands and picked up the stringer of stripers. "Better go see about cleaning these fish," he said and walked inside.

I called JD and told him we were having stripers and new potatoes for dinner and I'd be by to pick him up in a few minutes. When I pulled into the gravel lot, he was wearing the same clothes he'd had on the day before and his shirt had acquired a fresh stain of what looked like buffalo wing sauce on the neckline.

"You know, I'm pretty sure they'd let you use the showers in the yacht club if you asked nicely," I said when he climbed into the Jeep.

"There's two on the boat. Just didn't have time to get to it today. I was up all night working on Martin's laptop."

"Any progress?"

"Some. The guy had a decent idea of how to cover his tracks online, using Tor, clearing his browser history and that sort of thing, but there were some cookies I was able to find that go back to some ugly sites, dude. Fucked up stuff."

"Kids?"

"About as bad as it gets, man. I didn't spend a lot of time looking around, but I got the general idea. These are all closed, members-only type sites, but our boy wasn't that swift at password creation so I got into a couple of them after a few hours. I wasn't going to sleep after seeing what they were, so I decided to see if I could figure out whether he had some malware on there like I thought. That's what I spent most of the night and all of today on."

"What's the verdict?' I said as we turned off Water Street onto 3A.

"There's something there for sure, and it's really, really interesting. From what I can tell so far, it seems to be modular, with each piece having a different specific task. I've been able to find four separate modules. So there's one that does keylogging and has the ability to turn the microphone and the camera on. There's another that searches a handful of directories for certain file types, like JPEGs, QuickTimes, MP4s, videos, things like that, then zips them up and sends them to a server in Idaho. Another module basically looks like it sets up a proxy service, so all of the web traffic from the machine goes through a remote server."

"DNS hijacking?"

"Pretty much."

"But if he was using Tor, that wouldn't do the attacker much good."

"No, not for Tor sessions. Those would be encrypted as they passed through his proxy, unless he's got some way to break Tor, which is rare, but it happens. But I have a feeling he was just using Tor to hit those child exploitation sites. The rest of his stuff was probably done on a regular browser. There wasn't really anything of interest there that I could see."

"That sounds like custom software. That's not anything someone pulled off a forum and reused," I said.

"Right, and it's really nice work from what I can tell. I took one of the executables and ran it through VirusTotal and got nothing."

"The thing that jumps out at me is that module that steals data. Does it pick up anything like Word docs or Excel files or PowerPoints?"

"Not that I saw. Just photos, videos and that stuff. Very picky."

"Any indications of how the stuff got on there?"

"That's tomorrow's task," he said.

At home, Brendan had the fish cleaned and filleted and Caroline was working on the potatoes. I got the grill going and JD pitched in to make a salad. I grilled the fish with just some lemon juice, salt and pepper and they made a fine dinner along with the sides. After we ate, Caroline went back to work on the painting and Brendan said he was going to read for a while before going to bed. JD and I sat down to go over his notes from working on Simms's computer.

"What would make a guy like Simms a target for this kind of thing?" I said. "He's not high on the list for the professional groups who use high-end malware like this. Not a scientist or diplomat or journalist or even anything interesting. Just a guy."

"I don't have a great answer yet but one thing I thought of is that he might not have been targeted. Sometimes what those groups do is own up one or two specific web sites that they know several of their targets use frequently and then when one of the victims hits the site, their malware tries to compromise the victim's machine."

"Right."

"So he might have been collateral damage in an attack like that. Just went to the wrong site and had a vulnerable browser or Flash version or something and got owned. If you look at the victim set of some of the pro groups, you'll usually see some weird outliers in there, like a small auto parts manufacturer that's mixed in with a bunch of non-profits or universities. So that's one possibility."

"Yeah, could be. Any others?"

"That's the best one right now. But he also could have been doing something else that we don't know about," JD said.

"Like?"

He stood up and began pacing around the living room. "Well, we know that the malware specifically looks for videos and photos. And we know that Simms was into some ugly shit."

"Ah, Jesus," I said.

"He might not have been just a consumer."

I stood and went to the window and looked at the ocean. "I hate this fucking case," I said.

Laying in bed that night, I told Caroline what JD and I had come up with.

"Do you think that's it?" she said.

"I don't know. But someone makes all of that shit. It doesn't just magically appear."

"I can't even wrap my head around what kind of person does that. They must be completely broken. How can you just…"

"Never underestimate the capacity of humans for depravity," I said. "We're the best at being the worst."

In the morning I spent some time with JD digging through some of the malware forums, looking for any information on a toolkit like the one on Simms's laptop. We found a couple of mentions of one of the executables on a UK forum, with one apparent user asking for help figuring out why the keylogger would sometimes stop working. But that was about it. While JD stayed on that, I found an online obit for Martin Simms that said he was survived by his mother, Helen, of Medford, Oregon, and a sister, Marcy, of Cohasset. I found an M. Simms in Cohasset in the white pages and called.

"I hadn't seen my brother in more than three years, Mr. Tobin, so I don't know how I could help you at all," she said after I'd identified myself as an investigator. "We were not close."

"I understand, but I'd still like to speak with you, if that's ok. You never know what will help."

She sighed. "Fine. I have some errands to do this morning, but you can come by after lunch."

She gave me the address and I said I'd see her around one.

Marcy Simms's house was on a quiet street within walking distance of Sandy Beach. It was a large rambling colonial with a three-car garage on one side and what looked like an old barn on the other. The barn had been nicely restored. A black 911 Turbo and a silver Tesla S sat in the driveway. A pair of gardeners were working in the yard, getting it ready for fall. I pressed the bell next to the front door and could hear the chimes playing "Edelweiss" deep inside the house. A minute later the door opened and a woman in her mid-thirties stood in the entryway. Marcy Simms was dressed in yoga pants and a tight-fitting workout top. She was sweating lightly and her face was flushed.

"Mr. Tobin? Please come in. You'll have to excuse me, I was just finishing up with my trainer," she said.

I stepped into the entryway and saw a man, probably in his late twenties, packing a gym bag and rolling up a couple of yoga mats. He said his goodbyes and walked out and got into the Tesla.

"Not sure I trust a car that doesn't make any noise," I said as she led me down a hall into a large, open kitchen.

"Don't trust a trainer that makes house calls, either," she said. "Please, have a seat. May I get you a drink?"

"Ice water would be great, thanks."

She brought the water in a clear Tervis tumbler. "I think this is the first time I've had anything other than a bourbon and ginger in one of these," I said.

She smiled. "Are you from one of those dreadful states down below Connecticut?"

"Virginia."

"I didn't think I heard much of a New England accent. I was raised in North Carolina, outside Charlotte. Nice to talk to a fellow heathen."

"Not many of us who are dumb enough to stay up here," I said.

"I was kidnapped here by my husband. What's your excuse?"

"My family had a summer house up here for a long time and I ended up making it my full time place a few years back. Now I'm sort of stuck. Is your husband home?"

"Not for about three years now," she said. "I don't expect him anytime soon."

"Well, don't I feel like an asshole."

"No, that would be him. No harm done."

I cleared my throat. "Well, thanks again for taking the time to talk. Like I said on the phone, I'm helping to investigate the murder of your brother's roommate, Wyatt Austin. His sister is a friend of mine. I don't know whether you've seen any of the news coverage of this…"

"I have. It's not pleasant."

"It is not. But one of the things that we're trying to figure out is whether there's any truth to the stuff that was in the paper. And, ah, we've found some things that make us think that Wyatt was killed by mistake."

"What does that have to do with my brother?"

"I think he was probably the one they meant to kill," I said.

"I assume you wouldn't be coming to me if this was idle speculation."

"No I would not. The evidence that we've found isn't necessarily conclusive. But it's pretty persuasive. It's not going to be very easy for you to hear, though."

"Mr. Tobin, I sat in the chair where you're sitting right now and listened to my husband tell me that he was going to take a few months to sail around the Caribbean to find himself. As I said, that was three years ago. Last I heard, he was in St. Bart's, living with a nineteen-year-old girl. I can certainly handle whatever it is you're going to tell me."

So I told her. She listened calmly and asked a couple of questions and generally acted as if I was giving her the extended weather forecast. I left out the bit about her brother possibly being in the business of making movies, but gave her the rest of it straight. When I was finished, she went to the refrigerator and refilled our waters and came back to the table.

"Mr. Tobin--"

"Please call me Danny. You calling me Mr. Tobin makes me itchy."

"Ok. Look, Danny. Like I told you on the phone, I was not close to my brother. We were...different people. We were only eighteen months apart, but even as children we never got along very well. Never hostile, just not close. The last time I saw him was at our summer party just before my husband left. He got very drunk and made an ugly scene when one of my neighbors tried to escort him out. He took a swing at my husband and then keyed his car on the way out. I think my brother was a very conflicted man. Who he was was not who he wanted to be."

"That's true of a lot of people."

"It certainly is," she said. "But most of them don't become child predators."

"I didn't mean--"

"Yes you did," she said. "I loved my brother, of course, but I didn't really know him. Now, I imagine you came here to ask me some rather direct questions, didn't you?"

I shifted in my chair, drank some water. "Well, your reaction has told me a lot of what I was hoping to find out, but I do have a couple of other questions."

"Please."

"How much did you know about Martin's private life?"

"Very little. I knew that he was a drug addict and a drunk. We didn't see one another often, and when we did the conversations were superficial."

"Was that an issue between you two?"

"Not really. I didn't necessarily always like the choices he made, but again, I was not going to lecture him."

"What kind of choices?"

She gave a small, tight smile. It was not pleasant. "It seems to me that you've seen the consequences of those choices, Danny."

"Marcy, thank you very much for your time and your hospitality. I know this wasn't the most pleasant visit."

She walked me to the front door, opened it and then stood on her toes and kissed me lightly on the cheek. "It was perfectly lovely to meet you, Danny, even if the conversation wasn't. And please call me Ms. Simms. It makes me sweaty if you call me Marcy."

I was sitting on the back deck of my house with Caroline, the last third of a Hendrick's gin and tonic idling in a tall glass on the table next to me. The sun was fading behind some late-afternoon clouds and we were nibbling on the remains of last night's dinner.

"She sounds like a piece of work," Caroline said.

"She was nice. Very polite."

"Pretty?"

"I mean, sort of? If you like fitness models who drive Porsches and are independently wealthy. But that's not my thing."

"Which part?"

"The Porsche. Only coke dealers and dermatologists drive Porsches."

"And fitness models, apparently."

"Well, she wasn't *that* fit…"

"Did you forget that I dusted your old ass on that swim the other day? Tell me who's fit," she said. "Tell. Me."

"You are, sweetheart."

"Goddamn right. Now, I have a couple thoughts on this conversation, if you'd like to hear them."

"Yes, babe."

"First of all, she's lying."

"About what?"

"Not sure. But she's definitely not telling you the truth about some of it."

"Why do you say that?" I said.

"A couple reasons. One, she sounds a little bit too tolerant. The way you tell it, she is all manners and southern grace and yet she completely accepted her brother being a degenerate. I don't see it. You grew up in the south. That's not exactly a common mindset down there, is it?"

"No."

"So why would she lie about that, especially now that Martin is dead? I don't know. But I think she is. Also, for someone who is so polite and well-mannered, she sure did tell you a lot about her personal life."

"I'm an excellent conversationalist," I said. "And quite handsome."

"Please try to focus."

"One thing I noticed is that we talked for probably fifteen minutes or so and she never used Martin's name. Not once. She always said 'my brother'."

Caroline snapped her fingers. "See, that's what I'm saying. Who does that? It takes a lot of mental energy to remember not to use your own brother's name. What's the point?"

"Beats me. But she said several times they weren't very close, so I didn't think much about it at the time."

"There's a difference between not close and you're dead to me. It sounds to me like she was closer to the latter. She knew more than she told you."

People knowing more than they say is an occupational hazard for cops, and I'd learned long ago to assume that everyone was holding something back. A lot of times it's mundane, irrelevant stuff, but trying to figure out when it's important is the trick. Like Caroline said, I had found it weird that Marcy Simms was so willing to discuss the intimate details of her life with me. Her husband leaving, her brother's problems. Those are the kind of things that people in her position usually go a long way around to avoid discussing.

"Maybe you should ask Brendan," Caroline said. "People tell priests all kinds of crazy shit."

"All kinds of lies, too," I said.

Eleven

Brendan had gotten friendly with the pastor at St. Peter's and had offered to say some of the early morning Masses during the week. The pastor, an elderly man brought out of retirement to tend to the shrinking flock, was grateful for the help and now Brendan was doing three or four Masses a week. I found him in the lower church, where he was hearing the confessions of a handful of parishioners. In a different time, the lower church had been used to handle overflow crowds for the Sunday morning Masses. Now it only saw use for confessions and on Christmas and Easter, when the guilt became too much for the hordes of lapsed Catholics who came back for reassurance. The lower church had exposed pipes and low ceilings and the heat was stifling, so I waited outside in the cool fall air until the last of the old men left. Brendan followed the man out and smiled at me.

"Too hot in there for you, brother?" he said.

"Nicer out here. I need a bit of help if you have a minute."

"Of course. Let's walk. It's a pleasant day and I could use some exercise. I'm afraid standing and kneeling doesn't keep me very fit."

We crossed Court Street and walked down Memorial toward the waterfront. I caught Brendan up on what I'd learned in the last couple of days, the conversations with Louis Andino and Marcy

Simms and told him the way things were pointing with Martin. He shook his head slowly.

"It seems the more people you talk to, the worse the story becomes," he said.

"It does. Every rock I turn over brings a new crop of worms."

"How can I help?"

"I don't know. I think that most of the people I've been talking to on this have been lying to me about one thing or another. Probably the only person who was honest with us was Martin, which doesn't say much for the rest of them. Let me ask you this: How do you handle it when people lie to you? Parishioners, I mean."

"Early on, it bothered me quite a bit. I figured if someone was willing to lie to a priest then they were probably willing to do many other things that were much worse. But I gradually realized that most people don't even know that they're lying half the time. They tell small lies to themselves and others all day long and never think twice about it. It's just a habit. I don't see it as malicious," he said. "I think once you understand that nearly everyone is lying about something nearly all the time, it becomes much easier to deal with people."

"That's a pretty cynical way to look at it, B."

"It's realistic. Like you, I often see people when they are at their worst. In the middle of a divorce. After the death of a loved one. During a prolonged illness. They need reassurance and help, not judgment or condemnation. But I also have the luxury of knowing that every person I speak with is a sinner, because we all are. I don't need them to tell me that."

"Yeah, but that's exactly what I need them to tell me," I said.

We stopped at Ziggy's on Water Street and bought ice cream cones and walked across to the waterfront park and sat on a bench and watched the fishing boats and ferries come in and out of the harbor for a bit. In the distance I could see the thin finger of Long Beach stretching out into the bay and my house sitting atop it.

"So ask them," Brendan said.

"Huh?"

"These people. Ask them what they've done. I find that people are so used to talking around things, not saying what they mean, that if you ask them a direct question they're often surprised enough to just answer it."

"That ain't the way they teach it in the academy," I said.

Brendan stood and stretched his back and threw the remains of his cone in a trash can. "I imagine that's true. But you don't work for the police anymore, Danny."

On the way home, I called JD to see how he was making out with Simms's laptop. He was on the boat and sounded like he'd had a lunch of pixie stix and Red Bull but said he was making a dent in the problem.

"I"m fucking on it, Tobin. I got this thing now," he said.

"Ok, but if you go into diabetic shock, don't call me."

"What? Ha, yeah. Ok. I'll call you." And he was gone.

Next, I called Louis Andino.

"Tobin. Did something happen?" he said when he answered.

"Maybe. I don't know yet. Listen, I had an interesting conversation yesterday with Martin Simms's sister."

"He has a sister?"

"Isn't it your job to know this stuff?"

"Yeah, probably."

"Anyway, I was talking to her about her brother and there's something off about her. I think it would be worth your time to talk to her. She said that she and Martin weren't close and that she hadn't seen him in a long time, but I don't think she was being totally honest."

"No one ever is. Where can I find her?"

I gave him the details and he said, "I know that area. What's she like?"

"She's...something."

When I got home, Caroline was on her way out, going to meet some friends downtown for a charity brunch. I changed into my running gear and ran down 3A into town, thinking about Marcy and her brother. I went through town and hung a left on Allerton and ran up the hill to the massive granite Forefathers Monument. I spent an hour doing repeats up and down the hill, chewing over the conversation with Marcy, wondering what it was about her that nagged at me. I couldn't find the handle to grab onto, but maybe Andino would shake something loose when he talked to her. I got home around two, sweaty and tired and no smarter.

When I got out of the shower, there was a message on my phone from JD. There was a lot of background noise and I could barely understand what he was saying, so I gave up and just called him. When he answered, the noise was still there.

"Where the hell are you?" I asked.

"In the bar at the yacht club. They're having a fiftieth anniversary party for Shirl and Jack and the band is kinda loud. Hang on, lemme walk outside real quick."

I heard him whistle and then: "Tommy! Heinekens! Be right back."

The noise fell away and he came back on the line. "Ok, sorry. Those old fuckers can throw down."

"I'm not even gonna ask why you're at someone's anniversary party. I got your message but couldn't hear what you were saying."

"I think I got it figured out with Martin's laptop. I think I know how that stuff got on there and why."

"Tell it."

"Ok, so--Hey Gina, that's like your fifth cosmo! Slow your roll!--sorry, what was I saying? Right, the laptop. So I spent last night watching where all of the traffic from the malware was going and when, but that didn't really get me anywhere. So then I was digging around in the registry and I found a few more interesting things in there, but that was a dead end too. So then--"

"Jesus man, cut to the chase."

"Right, right. Sorry. I did a job a couple years ago where I had to find a couple of guys who had stolen some financial info from the wrong people and then, um, relieved them of what they had taken. These guys operated a bunch of porn sites, expensive, members-only stuff. And I remembered that their sites didn't have normal domain names. They were just a bunch of random numbers and letters, shit that was probably generated by an algorithm. The domains would change every few days and they would email the new domains to the members. So I started typing weird numbers and letters into the address bar on Austin's machine, just trying to see what would happen," JD said.

"And?"

"And it took a while, but the autocomplete feature in the browser eventually recognized one of the combinations I tried and came up with a suggested URL that was like sixty characters long. I hit it and boom, I was right there. No password required, no nothing. Which tells me..."

"The site recognizes that computer."

"You got it. But how? Can't be the IP address. Those change all the time and most people are behind a NAT device or router anyway," JD said.

"A browser plugin or something like that?"

"Another possibility, but don't think so. I tried all of the browsers on the machine and the site immediately recognized the machine every time."

"Wait: Did you try it with a different laptop?"

"Yeah, you're on it. I tried it in a virtual machine on a Linux laptop, no luck. Just a blank screen. Tried it again on my MacBook and got the same result," he said. "So I finally just hit it with a fresh install of Windows using Edge. I get a pop-up asking me for my invitation code, which I obviously don't have. I sat there for a few minutes thinking about what to do and then I noticed a couple quick flashes on the screen. I've got that machine routing its traffic through a proxy I have and I'm watching what's going on on another laptop and all of a sudden I see the Windows machine sending all kinds of data back to their server. Machine ID, Windows version, patch levels, all of this shit. It took me a couple more hours, but what it comes down to is every time a visitor hits this site, there's some code that checks to see whether it knows the machine. If it does, everything is cool, go right on in. If it doesn't, then it installs a little piece of software in the background that performs a few more checks to see whether it's running inside a VM, things like that."

"Anti-forensics tricks," I said.

"Yup. If everything is cool with that, then the site fires off a bunch of exploits against the browser, stuff for Java, Flash, browser-specific stuff, too. The site is basically hosting an exploit kit and hitting visitors with it."

"And if one of them works, what's the result?"

"In that case, you get the jackpot: that package of goodies that's on Simms's machine," JD said. "So whoever is running this site has owned up all of his customers."

"And he has full remote control of those computers," I said.

"He sure does."

"To what end though?"

"Free content, maybe," JD said. "Remember, that malware is looking specifically for photo and video files and pulling them off these machines."

"Yeah, and even if someone notices what's going on, who are they going to complain to?"

"And, maybe it gives this guy some leverage for blackmail or whatever down the road if he wants to go that route," JD said.

I considered that for a minute. "Nice work, man. Real nice."

"Thanks. Listen, they're getting ready to do the toast for Shirl and Jack. I gotta get back inside."

"Give them my best. Whoever they are."

That night I sat up late, looking through my case notes and all of the bits and pieces we'd collected in the last few weeks. This case, more than most, seemed to have a lot of pieces that almost fit, but not quite. I thought about the talk I'd had with Brendan and the discussion with Marcy Simms about her brother and her relationship with him, and that was one of the pieces that didn't fit.

Given the circumstances, it was understandable for her to be eager to distance herself from her brother and his actions. But that's not the way that her protestations came across. She seemed more frustrated with him for being a junkie and a drunk than for being involved in a child sex ring. It was more like an inconvenience for her than anything else.

The other thing I needed to figure out was why the guy behind this site that JD had uncovered was keeping tabs on his customers. I knew that it was common for sites like that to be restricted to direct acquaintances and others who were vouched for by a known member. A lot of times these were people who knew each other in real life. You couldn't just stumble onto the site and pay the monthly fee. That was how the owner ended up in jail or beaten to death in a parking lot.

So security was a must, but what was the point of spying on customers?

The most likely scenario I could come up with was paranoia about law enforcement. Having a presence on every user's machine would give the owner visibility into their actions and some level of assurance that none of them was a cop. That's what the anti-forensics techniques were about, so having the malware on the machines just took it to another level. But it still seemed like a long way to go.

Then again, this guy didn't seem to take many chances.

In the morning, I made a quick breakfast of chorizo and feta omelettes with sliced cantaloupe on the side. As I was cleaning up I got a call from Louis Andino.

"What did you think?" I asked.

"She's a handful," he said. "You weren't kidding."

"Have any luck talking to her?"

"A little. She was on her way out, so she didn't have much time to talk. She also seemed a little pissed that I showed up at her house unannounced."

"Did you tell her I put you onto her?"

"I'm not a moron, Tobin. Do you have any time later today? I wanted to check some stuff with you."

"Sure, if you're ok coming down here. There's a place called Speedwell on Main Street. Meet me there around one."

"See you then."

"What was that?" Caroline asked.

"That reporter from the *Sunrise*. He went out and talked to Marcy Simms and wants to meet later to talk. Want to come?"

"Sure."

Caroline was standing in the living room working on her painting and she stopped mid-brush stroke, with her hand poised above the canvas. "Keep it up, old man, and you'll find out a few things about me you might not like," she said.

I walked over and looked at the painting, which was still very much a work in progress. It was definitely looking more like something an artist had done, however, and less like a group project from the Art Institute of Myopia. The llamas or horses or whatever they were supposed to be were much more defined and recognizable as living things and the trees in the distance were taking on sharpness and life. Caroline was working on a figure in the meadow, near a fence in the foreground. It was too soon to tell whether it was man, woman, or child, and I wasn't about to hazard a guess.

I opened my mouth to speak and she said, "Don't."

We got to Speedwell a little before one and I spotted Andino sitting at the far end of the bar, his messenger bag slung over the back of his stool. All of the bar seats were taken and the stools on the counter opposite it were full too. We weaved through the crowd and I introduced Caroline to Andino.

"Place always like this?" he asked.

"It's jammed almost all the time, especially in the summer. Lemme see if I can grab us a table."

I spotted the owner, Jordan, coming out of the kitchen and waved him down. "Any chance of grabbing a high top for three?" I asked.

He scanned the room and said, "Gimme two minutes. I gotcha."

Andino had given Caroline his seat at the bar and he was standing behind her, finishing his beer. I squeezed in next to Caroline and got the attention of the bartender, Nicole.

"Danny, what's it gonna be?"

"Two Fiddleheads and another Bud."

"You got it. Mug 97?"

"That's it."

Nicole went off to get our drinks and the woman sitting on the stool behind me pressed her elbow into my back, letting me know

I was in her space. I turned and apologized and said I'd only be a minute.

"If you wanted a spot at the bar, you should've gotten here earlier. Life lesson for you," she said.

I smiled sweetly, paid for the beers when Nicole brought them. Jordan tapped me on the shoulder and said our table was all set and as we left the bar area, the woman next to me stood up to greet a friend who was coming to take the empty spot. As she went to sit back down, Caroline hooked her foot inside one of the legs of the stool and moved it just far enough so that the woman missed it entirely and dropped into a heap on the concrete floor with a thud. Her glass of rum punch teetered on the edge of the oak bar and then toppled over into her lap. Caroline never broke stride and when we got to the high top in the back corner, the woman and her friend were vainly trying to blot the red punch out of the woman's white shorts.

"Remind me not to make her mad," Andino said when we sat down.

"Yeah, that's a good policy. So tell me about your chat with Marcy."

"Well, I told her I had done some digging on her brother's murder and eventually turned up her name," he said. "I asked her about her relationship with her brother, how much she knew about his life, his friends. She gave me the same lines she gave you, how they weren't close, she didn't know much about his life the last few years. So I asked her some softballs instead, to see where she'd go. I asked how often she'd seen him in the last couple years, and she said not too much, but she had gone to his apartment the weekend before he died."

"See, that's not at all what she told me. She said it had been several years since she'd seen him."

"So that's one," Andino said. "I also asked how long she'd lived in Cohasset, how she liked it. Not much there, but she mentioned that she had moved here from Texas. I lived there for a while, so we talked about that, how little we missed it, stuff like that."

"Man, she's got all kinds of bullshit. She told me she'd come here from North Carolina. Did you tell her you had lived in Texas, or did she say it first?"

"I told her. She asked where my accent was from."

"You barely have an accent," Caroline said. "I would not have pegged you as being from Texas at all."

"I appreciate that. Weird, though. You're right."

"That's two. Anything else?"

"Lemme look at my notes real quick." He pulled out his notebook and read for a minute, then said: "Nah, I don't think so. She was polite and mostly pleasant. I don't know what the deal is, though. Something's not right there."

"If she's going to lie to one of you, there's no reason she wouldn't lie to both of you. She isn't real interested in people knowing much about her. That much seems pretty clear," Caroline said.

"Yeah. I'm going to write something on this. My editors are looking for a follow-up, and I think a look at the victims and their families would be a good angle. No one has really covered that part of it. Do you want to go on the record at all?"

I thought about that for a minute. "You can attribute this to me: Investigating murders is difficult under the best of circumstances and it's a lot more difficult when people lie to you. You'd think that victims' families would want to help, but it turns out that's not always the case. I don't understand it, but I guess people have their own agendas."

"Going right after it."

"I like the direct approach," I said.

"That's a fact," Caroline said. She looked at Andino with curiosity. "Why are you so interested in this story? I mean lots of people get murdered every day. All over the place. Nobody pays much attention to most of them. Why do you care?"

"It's my job."

"Ok, sure."

Andino smiled. "Not buying that?"

"Maybe part of it. It's his job, too," she said, nodding at me. "But he doesn't take jobs he's not interested in."

"Well, technically this isn't a job..." I said.

"Pipe down. Buy you see what I'm getting at, Louis?"

"I think for me, this one is interesting for a few reasons. It's a good story, I'm sorry to say for your friends' sake. Two roommates, both dead in violent fashion within a few days of each other. The police running around in circles, getting nowhere. The possibility of a serial killer. And then you add in the child exploitation angle, and it's a rich vein to mine."

"Have you had any experience with stories like this? With kids?" Caroline asked.

Andino blinked and took a long sip of his Bud. "I have."

"I checked out your archives online. I didn't see anything like this in there," I said.

"Didn't say it was a story I covered. I just said I have some experience with it."

I nodded and Caroline looked down at her hands on the table. "I'm so sorry. I didn't..." she said.

"No need. No reason you would know. I decided a long time ago not to let it define me."

Caroline excused herself to go to the ladies' room and squeezed Andino's shoulder on the way by.

I started to say something and Andino held up his hand. "Tobin, it's fine. Don't sweat it. And please don't let her feel bad about asking. It was a logical question."

"Ok. So, Marcy. I'm inclined to push her and see what happens. I don't think she's the type to sit idly by while things are happening."

"Me neither. So let's give her a little shove."

"Let's."

"I'll probably have this out in the next couple days, so be on the lookout."

"Yeah. Alright, thanks. Stay in touch."

"Right," he picked up his messenger bag and was gone.

Caroline came back to the table a minute later. "I'm an idiot."

"No way you could have known, babe. He made a point of telling me you shouldn't worry about it. I think he's put it behind him."

She shook her head. "I don't think he has."

Twelve

Two days later, I woke to my phone buzzing on the nightstand. Caroline was still asleep, so I stepped out onto the deck.

"Yeah."

"What the fuck are you trying to prove, man?" It was Chris King.

"It's seven in the morning, Chris. I couldn't have done anything that bad yet. I haven't even taken a crap."

"You took a giant crap in the paper this morning, funny man."

"The story's out?"

"Oh, it's out. Thanks for the heads up on that, by the way," King said. "What are you doing talking to that guy?"

"You jealous? I know he's your guy."

He sighed. "I never talked to him, Tobin. You know this. Quit fucking around."

I decided to try something. "That's not the way he told it. He made it sound like you guys had talked several times."

"I don't give a shit how he made it sound. I've met that guy exactly zero times and talked to him on the phone once, and that was only long enough to tell him to get lost. You don't believe me, let me get in the same room with him and we'll work it out."

"Ok, look. I'm trying to kick something loose on this," I said. "I went out to see Martin's sister the other day to see what she knew about him. I thought maybe she could give me some pointers to other people who could help."

"And?"

"And she spent most of the conversation lying to me, and I don't know why."

"Yes you do. Because you're a cop and everyone's instinct is to lie to cops."

"I'm not a cop anymore."

He snorted. "You think that matters to someone like her? You look, talk, and act like police, so to her you're police. What do you think she was lying about?"

"That's the thing. Nothing that matters. Where she grew up, what kind of jobs she's held, dumb shit. I wasn't asking her if she killed her brother."

"Maybe you should have," King said.

"What else is in Andino's story? Does he make me sound smart?"

"He's a reporter. All he cares about is making himself sound smart. It's mostly just a rehash of the case, some color on Martin and some barely shaded shots at us for not solving Austin's murder. Those come from you too?"

"I would've put my name on that," I said.

"I bet. Just so you know, we went to see Marcy too and didn't see anything interesting."

"Nothing?"

"Well, those legs..."

"Anything I don't know?"

"Don't think so. She was very polite and gracious."

"She talk about her husband at all?" I asked.

"Only to mention that he was out of town on business. She said he was in San Diego or San Jose. Somewhere out west," King said. "I said we'd like to talk with him when he got back, and she said she wasn't sure when that would be, but she'd let me know."

Another lie.

"How about from now on you let me know if you're planning to shit on us in the media?" King said. "Is that too much to ask?"

"I can probably handle that."

"So where are you at on this whole thing at this point?"

"I feel like we're in a cul-de-sac, just driving around in circles. I'm pretty sure that Austin was not involved in any of this and he was just collateral damage. That much seems clear."

King sighed. "Yeah."

"And Simms looks like he was in it up to his neck. What I don't know is what his role was. I've got some stuff that makes me think he was just a grunt, but some other things point a different direction. So who knows?"

"I think I'm supposed to know," King said.

"What's next for you?"

"I'm going back over the files from the other cases I told you about the other day. See if there's anything in there that will point us in the right direction. Because right now we're pretty much nowhere."

"Anything on those that you can share with me? Names and dates at least?"

"I don't see why not. That stuff is public record if you know where to look. I'll email it to you later."

"Thanks."

"Stay out of the papers, Tobin."

King's email arrived an hour later and it had more than just the promised names and dates of death. There were names of investigating officers in each jurisdiction and a small summary of each case. It wasn't hard to see why King thought they were tied together. Like he had said earlier, there was some overlap in the college years of some of the victims, some of them had worked together at various times, and others had grown up in the same towns. They were all men, between twenty-seven and thirty-two when they were killed.

The thing that really tied them together, though, was the way they had been murdered. Each of the men had been killed with a single gunshot to the head. In all but one case, the entrance wound was in the front; the outlier was shot in the left temple. All of the victims had been found in their homes, and all of the cases remained unsolved. Police had arrested a local truck driver in one of the Boston killings, but he had been released quickly when he showed records proving he was in Mississippi at the time of the murder.

There were digital forensics reports on three of the victims' computers, and one of them had an encrypted volume just like the one taken from Austin's apartment. The police got nowhere with that and neither of the other two victims had anything unusual on their machines. All in all, the files showed a group of murders that likely were connected, but with virtually nothing in the way of motive. There was something there, but there were plenty of holes, too.

I spent a little time looking back at the pieces Andino had written in the last few years, and didn't see anything that I'd missed. He had mainly covered the police beat at most of his stops and seemed to have good sources everywhere he went. Most police departments, big or small, have a love-hate relationship with the media. They know they need the press for certain things, and in order to keep things civil they have to slide reporters information from time to time, too. Andino seemed to know how to play the game as well as anyone. The stuff he'd written in California and Utah and Texas clearly relied on some pretty deep connections inside the local departments. He had written some nice stuff actually, including a good series on some of the murders in Massachusetts that King was tracking. He definitely knew his stuff.

That afternoon I met JD at the yacht club and we settled into the salon on the *Buffer Overflow* to go over the files.

"Ok, so I see what you're saying," he said when he was finished. "Lots of connections between these guys, killed the same way. But how does that help us with Wyatt?"

"I'm not sure it does yet. But he overlapped with two of these guys in college, and that place is small so they probably were at least acquaintances. If you found out that three of the guys you went to college with had all been killed the same way, wouldn't you think something was up?"

"Yeah. I just don't know if this gets us any closer to getting Wyatt's name out of the mud and figuring out who killed him."

"What did you think of the encrypted volume on the other guy's laptop?" I asked.

"Nothing, really. He was a lawyer, so it could easily have been client files. Half the population uses encryption now, thanks to Snowden. Most of them use it badly, but they're trying."

"Could be client files. Or it could be photos and videos," I said.

"Or it could be the recipe for Kentucky Fried Chicken. The thing is that most of these child exploitation rings don't send photos around anymore. They're all stored on hosting services. There's no point in individuals keeping personal collections of this shit when it's all accessible anytime from their phones. And most of those phones are encrypted by default now, so if the cops kick down your door, there's nothing to find. This is one of the reasons the FBI's argument about encryption killing so many of these investigations is such bullshit. They know that encrypted comms are not the problem. The hosting providers are. You get to them and you get the bad guys."

"That doesn't make our man Martin look real smart."

JD sat forward. "I've been thinking about that. We only know a few things about him. We know he was a really talented musician who was stuck giving lessons to kids who didn't give a shit. We know he and Wyatt were friends but not super close. And we know that something happened a couple of years ago that sent him down a pretty dark alley. We can be reasonably sure about a few other things. We think he was involved in this child exploitation ring in a big way, possibly as a producer. And it's also pretty likely that he was the original target of whoever killed Wyatt. That's about it. Did I miss anything?"

"His personal hygiene habits were highly questionable."

"That's being kind. But he didn't seem like a stupid guy. By the time we met him, he was a fucking mess, but I never got the sense he was anyone's fool."

"No. He was kind of beaten down by life and exhausted, but stupid is not one of the words I'd use to describe him," I said.

"So then why would he have a laptop stuffed with exploitation material? Like I said, there's no reason for him or anyone else to store that stuff now. It's a liability."

"Not to stereotype here, but people who have an appetite for that kind of garbage aren't necessarily rational," I said.

"Sure, but let's take it to the next step. We think that Martin was probably involved in producing some of the photos and videos, right? But from what his sister and his friends tell us and from what we saw, he was in no kind of mental shape to handle that kind of thing. He could barely order a pizza. So could he be running some kind of mini empire?"

"Not by himself, no. But these things usually aren't one-man operations."

"So who's the second shooter?" JD asked.

"We agree it wasn't Wyatt."

"Right."

"Then I'd start right here," I said and patted the files.

We spent the rest of the afternoon and evening going through the files, separately at first and then together. On second reading nothing new jumped out at me. By the third or fourth time through, I began to see some patterns. Several of the victims were successful by all outward appearances. Aside from the lawyer, there were two executives from financial companies in Boston, a guy who owned a software company, and another who helped run an art museum. Several of the men had spent time at the same college, and while a couple of them were New England natives, they all had moved to the Boston area within a year or two of graduation. All of them had lived in the city for a while and then had moved to surrounding towns.

But the thing that stood out most was that none of them had children. Four of the men were married when they were killed, one was divorced, and the other had never been married.

"Neither one of us has kids either," JD said.

"No, but how many married couples do you know who don't? One or two?"

"I don't know that many married people, but yeah, not a lot I guess."

"It's a little weird, that's all," I said. "And weirdness is what we look for when we don't have much else."

JD walked into the galley and came back with two Dale's Pale Ales, handed me one and then pointed at the files spread out on the table in front of us. "If you had to pick one out of that bunch, who would it be?"

"The real estate guy. What's his name, Richmond?"

JD smiled. "Greg Richmond. Why?"

"The notes from the interviews King and his team did are just odd. They couldn't really identify any close friends of his. Even his ex-wife couldn't come up with more than one or two people he talked to regularly. The guy sold houses for a living and somehow didn't really know anyone. Tough way to make money. And, one of the women King interviewed who had bought a house from him said he was 'creepy'. That's not usually something you hear about a guy who was murdered. People normally go out of their way to say nice things about dead folks. Especially murder victims."

"He's my pick too," JD said. "But for a different reason."

"Which is?"

"He's from Florida."

"So let's go talk to some of Richmond's non-friends," I said. "The good thing about people who don't like someone is that they'll usually tell you stuff that their friends won't."

"I'm gonna pass. I need to spend some more time on this malware stuff tomorrow. I feel like I'm close, but I know I'm missing something obvious."

"And you don't want to miss any anniversary parties."

Greg Richmond had owned a modest white colonial in Hanover, but he had lived in an apartment in Boston and his ex-wife had stayed in the house. It was a block off the main drag, on about half an acre near a little league baseball complex and within shouting distance of three churches. I parked a couple houses down and walked up. The side door opened as I was walking up the driveway and a woman came down the steps toward a newish Range Rover. She froze on the bottom step when she saw me.

"What?" she said. She was a petite redhead, probably around thirty-five. She was dressed as if she was going for a run or maybe to a spin class.

"I'm an investigator working on some recent murders and I was hoping to ask you a few questions if you have a minute."

"What kind of investigator?"

"The private kind."

She pulled the door all the way closed and walked down the driveway past me. "No thanks."

"Mrs. Richmond, I'm--"

She whirled around to face me. "That is *not* my name. Never was."

"I apologize." I held out my hand. "I'm Danny Tobin."

She hesitated, then shook my hand. "Melissa Sandford. I don't know anything about any murders."

"Well, you know about one."

"Not really. We weren't married when he was killed. I spoke with the police at the time, but there wasn't much I could say. I have no idea who killed him. I'm sorry."

"I understand. But I'd still like to talk for a few minutes if you don't mind," I said.

"I was just going out for a run."

"Can I join?"

She looked at my outfit: jeans, t-shirt and hiking boots. "Might be a little tough for you," she said.

"I have gear in my Jeep. Gimme three minutes."

"I'll give you one."

We ran back up to the main road and made a left and settled into a comfortable pace while I made some small talk about training and races for a few minutes. Then I explained our case to her: Wyatt's murder, Simms's suicide, the media mess, the other killings King was working.

"And Greg's murder is one of those," she said.

"That's right. We believe that they're all connected and that they're also related to Wyatt's murder. Which is why I wanted to talk to you. What can you tell me about his friends?"

"That he didn't have any. Not real ones, anyway."

"Never?"

"Not that I know of. If we went to a party or a dinner with people, it was my friends or people from my job."

"Didn't you find that weird?"

"Of course I did. Who doesn't have friends? But he was a weird guy anyway," she said. "That wasn't nearly the strangest thing about him."

"What was?"

"Hmm. I guess maybe the Taylor Swift collection."

"I'm sorry?"

"He collected Taylor Swift stuff. Like shirts, posters, tickets, pillows, diaries, whatever. Everything. He was obsessed with her. I'm not sure he even liked her music, or knew what it sounded like. He just had a thing for her."

"Like, in a sexual way?" I asked.

She laughed. "Sex was the furthest thing from that guy's mind. At least as far as I ever saw. This was more like the way some guys are totally into Star Trek or comic books."

"That's fuckin weird."

"Like I said."

"Not to be indelicate here, but how did you end up with him if you knew he was a little, ah, off?" I asked.

"You've been delicate so far?"

"Hard to believe, I know."

"Not really," she said and then sighed. "Oldest story in the world. Boy meets girl. Boy and girl get drunk. Girl gets pregnant. Girl marries idiot."

"You were young?"

"I was twenty, he was twenty-two. I'm not sure I see how any of this is helping you. The police didn't get anywhere on this. They looked at all the evidence and talked to everyone. So I don't know how you're going to do any better."

"Because I'm not the police," I said. "I don't give a shit about evidence. I care about finding out what happened."

She gave a short laugh. "And those are two different things?"

"Can be. Cops need to build a case that can hold up in court. I'm trying to figure out what the most likely scenario is. Can you think of why someone would want to kill Greg?"

"I'll tell you what I told the police: I thought about killing him out of sheer boredom a hundred times. But why someone else would want to do it, I have no idea," Sandford said. "He was good at his job and he was nice enough I guess, but there was nothing there. He was like a cardboard cutout of a person."

"If he didn't have any real friends, what about enemies? Maybe someone who got screwed on a real estate deal?"

She was quiet for a few moments. "I guess that's possible, but I wouldn't know about it. He didn't talk to me about his business. We didn't talk about much of anything, really."

"He ran his own firm?"

"He had a partner, she still runs the agency. Greg mostly handled the stuff from here up to about Braintree and she took care of everything from here down to the Cape. They did well. His partner, Marcy, is a piece of work. But she knows how to sell, that's for sure."

Marcy.

Not the most common name. But it could be a coincidence. Could be.

We looped around a park and headed back to her house. Had to wait at an intersection for a black Grand Cherokee busting a red light. We had been gone about forty minutes, good for maybe five miles, and when we walked up her driveway, Melissa Sandford stopped next to her Range Rover.

"Thanks for the run," I said. "Good workout."

"Nice try. You're not even sweating."

"It's cool out here."

"Uh huh. Listen, I didn't particularly like Greg and I never loved him, but he didn't deserve to be murdered. I hope you find whoever did it. I really do."

"I will."

"And what then?" she asked.

"We'll see. I need to find him first," I said. "Oh, what was your husband's partner's name again?"

"Marcy Simms. Do you want her number?"
"I think I can find her."

Thirteen

I called JD on the way home.

"Are you fucking kidding me?" he said.

"I am not."

"Christ. Who are these people?"

"I think we're starting to find that out. Listen, I want you to get whatever you can about Marcy. She was lying to me and she lied to Andino and Chris King, too. I want some more information before I go talk to her again."

"Can do."

"I don't like people lying to me, especially when I don't know why they're lying."

"If you knew why she was lying, she wouldn't have had to lie," JD said.

"Cut that logic shit out. I'm trying to think. So I'm gonna head home and sit on the deck and drink some beer and talk to Caroline and see what I can come up with. There's a lot of weirdness going on. Call me later."

I went home and sat on the deck and drank some beer and talked to Caroline. We came up with exactly nothing except an agreement to make mac and cheese with bacon in the crock pot for dinner. So I did that, which felt like an accomplishment. After dinner Caroline went to work on her painting and I went upstairs to the small desk off our bedroom. Caroline had tired of me wadding up paper and throwing it on the floor when I was working on things like this, so I had painted a four-by-four square of wall above the desk with that weird paint that's like a chalkboard, which let me scrawl and doodle all over the place without getting yelled at. Currently, the wall displayed a drawing of a stick figure man being hit in the nuts with a football thrown by another stick figure.

Thanks, JD.

I drew a box around the illustration and wrote DO NOT ERASE above it, and then drew a makeshift diagram to illustrate the relationships and connections among all of the players. I had figured out over the years that it was easier for me to make connections and analyze information if it was laid out in front of me, rather than just rattling around in my brain.

Caroline said that made me a visual learner.

Looking at it from the outside, the people involved in the case mostly seemed to be disconnected and without much in common. Wyatt Austin was an artist and designer from a good family with plenty of friends and a happy life and reasonable expectations that life would continue; he went to college in Atlanta and moved to Boston and had a nice girlfriend. Martin Simms was a gifted musician stuck teaching piano and guitar to rich kids rather than writing and performing his own music; he was also a drug addict and ultimately a suicide victim. Marcy Simms was...what? A trophy wife without a husband; Greg Richmond's business partner; a serial liar. Richmond was a deeply weird guy, but probably otherwise harmless; divorced, no kids; lots of bizarre hobbies. And there were the other murder victims that Chris King--and I--figured were killed by the same person who killed Wyatt and Greg Richmond.

Some definite connections among those victims and Wyatt, but how did they all attract the attention of a serial killer?

I spent half an hour trying to put together an idea on that, gave up and called Chris King.

"Same place I ended up," he said. "It's why I haven't gotten anywhere with the bosses on it. They wanted to know what the common thread was, and I didn't have a good answer. Still don't."

"I'm looking at these guys, and I see a bunch of dudes who may have known each other or crossed paths years ago. Or maybe not. All killed in a similar way, but the murders are spread out over a long period of time, longer than you'd expect with an active serial killer."

"That's about the size of it. The time frame is what bugs me the most."

"How long ago did you guys get onto this?"

"Maybe eighteen months ago. Right after the real estate guy was killed, what's his name?"

"Greg Richmond. I talked to his ex-wife today for a while."

I told King about the conclusion that JD and I came to about Richmond being the most likely candidate to have worked with Martin and why. I also filled him in on my conversation with Melissa Sandford.

"Taylor Swift?" he said.

"Could've been Justin Bieber, I guess. But still, weird as shit."

"I had the same thought at the time, about him not having any friends. It's not unique, but it jumped out at me. The ex-wife seemed normal enough. Couldn't figure out why she was with him to begin with."

"Got pregnant," I said. "They got married, but she lost the baby about five months in. They were never close, but she said the miscarriage soured things even more. Richmond couldn't get past it."

"Yeah, I knew that, but most people don't stick it out after that. No real reason to stay together if the kid isn't in the picture," King said.

"Here's another fun fact: Greg Richmond's partner in the real estate firm was your girl Marcy Simms."

"Knew that too."

"I figured you probably did."

"Listen, I wanted to see what you came up with from those files, without me poisoning the well. Or your brain."

"You ever talk to Marcy about it?"

"Only about Richmond, when we were investigating his murder. Austin obviously wasn't in the picture at that point, and neither was her brother," King said.

"Wanna take a ride down here tomorrow and have a talk with her?"

"Who's gonna say no to that invitation?"

"I think her trainer leaves around one..."

"See you there."

It was past eleven o'clock later that night, which was at least an hour past her normal bedtime, but Caroline was still painting. She did not look happy about it.

"No *Real Housewives of Atlanta* tonight?" I said.

"Tanya isn't on tonight's episode, so I'm out. Plus, I need to finish this stupid thing. Whatsherface is getting awful damn pushy about it."

I stood next to her and watched as she made some tiny brushstrokes that soon turned into a tiny bird perched on top of a split-rail fence. The horse-llamas had now become about three-quarters horsey and the figure in the foreground was recognizable as a woman. She wore tall riding boots and was looking over her shoulder at the viewer. Invitingly, I thought.

"Jesus, Danny. Not every woman is trying to sleep with you," Caroline said.

"Well, they're not all as smart as you."

"That's the goddamn truth. Remember that."

"I have to run back up to Cohasset in the morning," I said.

She gave me the side eye. Hard. "To see little miss hot pants?"

"Show some respect, please. Her name is Marcy. And yes. It's very important. For the work. That I'm doing. On the case."

"I'm free in the morning. Maybe I'll chaperone," she said.

"I don't know if--" She cut me off with a glance. "Sure, babe. Sounds good."

Chris King was sitting in his car outside Marcy's house when we pulled up a few minutes past one the next day. Marcy's Porsche sat in the driveway. King got out of his car and walked over to my Jeep. I introduced him to Caroline and explained that I wanted to get her read on Marcy.

"You're Scott Nelson's daughter?"

"I sure am."

"He's a good cop. Good man, too."

"Nice of you to say. Thanks."

"Do we have a plan here?" he asked.

"I want to push her hard on Richmond, see what she knew about him and why she didn't talk to us about him before. See if we can get her a little upset."

"I'm game, but she's smart. I wouldn't expect her to spill a bunch of feelings on the table."

"Let's see," Caroline said.

Marcy Simms was not pleased to see us. Or more specifically, me. She conveyed that emotion by pointing a finger at me and saying: "Fuck off."

"Easy," I said, holding out my hands. "We just need to talk for a few minutes."

"Last time we talked, you took a shit on me in the paper. I had to hear about it from that bitch Sally Crawford at the yacht club. She couldn't wait to tell me. So, no thanks. I'm done talking to you guys."

"I didn't say anything to that reporter that wasn't true. You were not a lot of help to me or Chris, and all we're trying to do is find out who killed your brother's friend. We're not out here for fun. And we can't get shit done if people don't help us."

"This doesn't have anything to do with me anymore," she said. "I told you I didn't know anything about Wyatt or what he did and I also told you I wasn't close with my brother, so I can't help you on that end either."

"Yeah you told us a lot of stuff, but not all of it matches up," King said. "You told me one thing and Tobin another. And some things you didn't tell us at all."

"Like the fact that Greg Richmond was your business partner," I said.

"Why does that matter? You never asked me about him. Either one of you."

"It matters because he was killed in exactly the same way Wyatt Austin was killed, and there are a couple of connections between them," I said. "Including you."

She cocked her head and leaned against the doorjamb. "So now I'm a suspect?"

"No one said that," I said.

"You're not even a cop. I don't care what you say. What about you, detective?"

King shrugged. "Everyone's a suspect until they're not. I find it interesting that you're getting defensive right off the bat, when we just wanted to ask you a couple things about Richmond."

"So ask."

"Could we step inside?" I said.

Marcy looked at Caroline, as if noticing her for the first time. "Who are you?"

"Caroline Nelson. I'm with Danny."

"How nice for you. Fine, let's go inside."

We sat on stools around an Aruba-sized granite island in the kitchen. Marcy leaned against the sink, her arms folded.

"How well did you know Greg?" King asked.

"As well as anyone, I guess. We were business partners. Co-workers. We were there to make money, and that's what we did. I didn't get to know him real well until later on, but he was a good man."

"How long did you two work together?" I asked.

"Mmmm, about seven years, I think. He came on as an agent and then bought into the firm about three years later," she said. "After he died, things really started to go downhill. He had become sort of the anchor."

"Was he good?"

"At selling? Yeah, he was. You can't survive in real estate if you can't sell, and Greg was really good. Which is weird, because he wasn't the most social guy. At all. But he related to our clients really well."

"Ok. Let's go back to the beginning. How did Richmond end up at your firm?" King said.

"He applied, like anyone else."

"From Georgia?" King asked.

"I guess. I don't really remember. To be honest, I wasn't that involved in the daily operations of the agency. I have a lot of other things going on."

Caroline: "I bet."

"I'm sorry?" Marcy said.

"I'm just confused. I mean, this is a real estate agency that you own. Or own part of. And you're not clear where your business partner came from or why," Caroline said. "That seems odd to me. If I owned a business, I'd know what was up at all times."

Marcy gave a tight smile. "That's great. How old are you? Twenty-four? I couldn't give a good goddamn what you would or wouldn't do with your hypothetical business. I own an actual, real life business. And those things come with real life problems and consequences. I'm not just running around putting signs in people's yards. People depend on me to run this agency and do it well. They have families. This is not a joke to me."

"You sure? Because it seems like you're not all that interested in helping these guys out," Caroline said. "And they're the ones who are trying to figure out what happened to your partner and your brother's friend. But don't let them get in your way."

Marcy pushed herself off the counter and stepped across to face me and Caroline.

"You think I'm happy that Greg was murdered? I went to the police station. I sat with his wife. I saw the pictures. I saw little pieces of his skull stuck in the couch cushions. I saw the pink stains and bits of brain on the wall behind him. You think that's a good time? Does that sound like fun to you?"

I laid my hand on Caroline's arm under the countertop and squeezed. Not gently. She pried my fingers off her forearm and placed my hand back in my lap. Not gently.

"I'm a cop's daughter. I know what crime scenes look like," Caroline said. "I know what grief looks like, what it feels like. And this isn't it. You're not it. You might be upset that your partner is gone, but it's only because his death hurt your business. Not because you're sad that a human being is dead."

Marcy turned and got a glass from a cabinet above the sink, filled it with water from a tap on the front of the refrigerator, and took a long drink. She set the glass down carefully on the counter and began spinning it slowly in her hands, a quarter turn at a time. After several full rotations of the glass, she looked up.

"You stupid, stupid bitch."

I rose halfway off my stool, but it was Caroline's turn to pull me back down. I sat but she kept her hand carved into my thigh. In my peripheral vision I saw King shift in his seat and bring his hand down under the counter.

Caroline said nothing, just waited. In another room, a clock ticked. Outside the kitchen sliding glass door an unseen mourning dove cooed.

After half a minute, Marcy Simms said: "You don't know a thing about me or Greg. Or probably anything else." Her voice was quiet and calm. "He was my partner, in every sense of the word. We ran a successful business together. We worked very closely for several years. And…"

King: "And?"

Marcy said nothing. Her face was blank. I looked over at Caroline, who was watching Marcy intently. Caroline kept her eyes on the other woman but smiled slightly.

"And what?" Caroline said quietly. "What else?"

Marcy reached into a drawer in the island and King and I both moved our hands to our hips, but she brought out nothing but a framed picture. She held it in front of her for several seconds and then laid it on the counter. King and I leaned forward to have a look, but Caroline just glanced at it and then went back to watching Marcy. The photo was of a young girl, maybe four years old, at the beach. She was squatting on her heels and dangling a small crab by the claw in one hand, a smile of pure joy and delight on her face. She wore a pink bucket hat and a clump of bright white sand clung to the tip of her nose, and the sun reflected off flat blue water behind her.

"And her," Marcy Simms said.

King: "Your daughter. And Richmond's."

Marcy half-sobbed, half-snorted. "Fucking outstanding work, detective. Stellar."

"How old is she, Marcy?" I asked. "She looks about three or four here."

"She was four and a half when that was taken."

"Which was when?"

"About three and half years ago. She would be just about eight now."

"Would...?" King said.

"How long has she been gone?" I asked.

Marcy took a tissue from her pocket, wiped her eyes, blew her nose. Walked into the butler's pantry off the kitchen, came back with a fifth of Jameson and four crystal tumblers with seashells etched into the sides. Poured two fingers into each one, handed them around, put hers back in one long, practiced drink. King and I followed suit. Caroline watched Marcy and slid her glass over to me.

Marcy refilled the glasses, and drank half of hers. "Three years and one month. She's been gone for three years and a month," she said.

I did the math. "I'm very sorry. Do you mind telling us what happened?"

She finished the rest of the Jameson. I took the bottle and poured another couple ounces in her glass. She picked it up, put it back down, walked over to the windows in the sitting area that afforded an obscene view of Cohasset harbor and the Atlantic beyond. The back lawn sloped gently down toward the water about a hundred yards away. A boathouse squatted where the deep green of the grass gave way to the even deeper blue of the sea. Marcy tapped the window.

"Just on the other side of that big oak out there, the one on the left, was a sandbox. Tim, my husband, built it for Wendy. He and his brother did it in a weekend. It's really nice, six feet square. She loved it so much. We'd spend hours out there, digging, building, burying. Whatever. She was such an outdoorsy kid."

Caroline walked over with Marcy's glass. Marcy nodded her thanks and took a sip.

"It's not that close to the water, but there's not really any barriers between there and the shore, so we never took the chance. We always stayed with her when she was out there. So Wendy and I were in there on a Sunday morning, trying to build a stable for her little ponies. Tim was down in the boathouse. He'd just bought a new boat--well, not new, but new to him. It was some old wooden speed boat-type thing. Chris something? I know shit about boats."

"A Chris-Craft?" I asked.

"Sounds right. It was very nice looking, all polished wood, but Tim said the engine needed a lot of work. So he was down there doing God knows what. I remember it was a super windy day. There's a bunch of rocks down at the edge of the water there and the surf was crashing pretty hard. Wendy and I were playing and I heard this awful sound, like metal dragging against stone. I wasn't sure whether it was from the water or what, so I didn't really do anything. Then I heard it again and something else."

"Like?" I said.

"I still don't know. But it was probably Tim yelling. I couldn't tell for sure with the wind and the waves and all, but I told Wendy to sit still and I ran down to the boathouse. You can see it's only like twenty yards. I was there in a second. When I looked inside, Tim was pressed underneath the back of the boat, trying to get it back onto the mounts. I guess it had slid off somehow and he had caught one corner of it and was yelling at me to come help him."

"He didn't have it up on a hoist?" I asked.

"He did, but I guess it wasn't cranked up high enough, so when it slid down, it kind of came down on him."

I could picture it, him in there mucking around with the engine, wandering back and forth, bumps one of the supports and all of a sudden he's got half a launch leaning on him. Or at least a quarter. Marcy comes in, he screams for help…

"Ok, so you run in to help."

"I could see that the boat was still on the hoist so even if he let it go, it wasn't really going to do any damage. It would've just swung free for a second, maybe knocked over the other supports. But I was standing in the doorway looking up the hill at Wendy, only half paying attention to Tim. She was just standing in the sandbox looking at me, smiling. Oh God, her smile."

She looked at her glass, drank the rest of the Jameson, put the glass down on a side table and opened a door onto the back deck and walked out. Caroline followed. I looked back at King and held my hands up, as if to say, what now? He waved me ahead.

Caroline and I trailed Marcy down the lawn, around a koi pond the size of a middle school gym, past a planting bed full of red, yellow, coral, and white roses, and finally past the giant oak to the area where the sandbox must have been. She paused for a second, then walked down to the boathouse. We followed.

Marcy stood on the wooden deck behind the building and looked out at the sea. The water was relatively calm, with just a few small ripples.

"I yelled back to Wendy to stay put and then went in here. I tried to help Tim move the boat, but even the two of us weren't strong enough to do it. He wasn't hurt; he was worried about damaging the boat. He kept yelling at me that it was made of teak and there was no replacing those boards. We wrestled with it for a minute or two and then I just told him he'd have to suck it up and fix the goddamn boat and let go. I ran up the hill to check on

Wendy and she was gone. I ran all around the yard looking for her, screaming her name. Nothing."

Marcy walked around the rear of the boathouse to the corner of the deck, where the water came right up to a group of jagged black rocks. She pointed to a small, calm pool formed by four or five tall rocks.

"She was right there, floating face up, eyes open, like she was lying in a hammock looking for animals in the clouds. She loved the water so much. It couldn't have been more than two minutes, tops. I just...I didn't..."

She sat on one of the black rocks, her feet dangling above the blue water where her daughter had drowned. She began to cry softly. Caroline touched my arm and chin-nodded me toward the house.

I found King still sitting at the counter, pouring whiskey into his glass. He motioned to me with the bottle and I nodded. We drank in silence for several minutes and then I repeated what Marcy had told us.

"No wonder she's a fucking handful," he said. "Can you imagine?"

I could. But I said: "No, I can not. Nor do I want to."

"Fuck."

"Fuck all that."

"Where are they?" King asked.

"Down by the boathouse. Caroline told me to run along. If there's anything else to get out of Marcy, she'll get it."

He nodded into his glass. "This is one majorly fucked up family, man. For real. Her with the dead kid and the husband who runs off a month later."

"Percentage he knew the kid wasn't his?" I said.

"Zero point zero zero. That is not a woman who admits her flaws easily."

"So what do you figure? She and the husband want kids but can't make it work for whatever reason. She looks around for a likely candidate, finds Richmond and then tells old Timmy it's a Christmas miracle, she's pregnant."

"Sounds about right."

"Nothing right about it," I said.

By the time Caroline and Marcy came back in, the light was fading outside and King and I had worked our way through most of the bottle of Jameson. Marcy walked past us, through the kitchen and into the back bedroom. Caroline followed long enough to say a few words and close the door. She came and stood next to me at the island, took my glass and had a long sip.

"Fuck," she said.

"That seems to be the general consensus," King said.

I told her what King and I had pieced together and she said we had it pretty much right. "What'd we miss?" I asked.

"The thing with Greg Richmond. It wasn't a deliberate effort by her to go find someone to get her pregnant," Caroline said. "She said that once it became clear that she and Tim weren't going to have kids, he kept his distance. They weren't hostile to each other, but they weren't close either. Just kind of went through the motions. The relationship with Richmond just sort of developed, she said, one of those things that happens when you work closely with someone, I guess. Anyway, when she got pregnant, they decided to just let Tim think it was his."

"Easiest thing to do," King said.

"What about Richmond's wife, Melissa? Did she know?" I asked.

"Yeah."

"That explains some things," I said.

"I'm not sure when she found out or how, but Marcy said she definitely knew. So, Melissa loses her baby, is never able to have another one, then finds out her husband gets someone else pregnant. Fuck."

"That's usually what causes it," King said.

I took a sip of whiskey to hide my smile and looked at Caroline, who side-eyed King for a solid ten seconds.

"Jerks," she said finally. "All of you. Fucking jerks."
"That's usually--"
"Don't."

Fourteen

When we got home, Brendan was in the kitchen cooking and JD was on the couch, two laptops on the table in front of him. He was pounding the keys on one while glancing occasionally at the other. Never saw us come in. Caroline went upstairs to shower and I went to the kitchen to see what Brendan was up to. He popped the top on a Gentile Brewing IPA and handed it to me. I leaned against the counter and had a long drink and he went back to chopping vegetables and throwing them into a sizzling wok.

"What's for dinner, hon?" I asked.

"Chicken stir fry with green peppers, mushrooms, and chiles. Jasmine rice on the side. You're on your own for dessert."

"Sounds good."

Brendan turned away from the stove and looked at me. "Have you eaten anything today? You look a little rough."

"Does Jameson count?"

He went to the fridge and came back with a tub of hot salsa and dropped it on the counter in front of me, along with some tortilla chips. "Eat, dummy."

I ate. And talked. And then talked some more. And ate some more.

When I was done talking, Brendan turned off the range, moved the stir fry to a serving dish and took everything to the table.

Caroline and I ate like jackals while Brendan and JD took a more measured approach, using utensils and teeth. After our second helpings, Caroline filled them in on some of the details she'd gotten from Marcy.

"In all honesty, I'm surprised she is still alive," Brendan said. "I've counseled many people in her situation, both men and women who have gone through loss and marital trauma, but I can't recall anyone who has endured what she has. I really can't."

"You think she's a suicide risk?" JD said.

"Oh, I think she would've already done it if that was in her nature."

"She's no quitter," Caroline said.

"I wouldn't blame her," I said.

"No one would," Brendan said.

He caught the raised eyebrow from Caroline. "Free will is the foundation of humanity," he said.

"She's had a pretty rough go, that's for sure," Caroline said. "But lots of people hit tough stretches and come out fine on the other side."

"You think she's one of them?" Brendan asked.

Caroline thought about that for a few seconds, then shook her head. "I don't know if she's on the other side yet, but she's definitely not ok."

Later, JD and I sat in the living room to talk about what we'd both learned about Marcy.

"Ok, so she's a bit of a wingnut," JD said, opening his laptop.

"I'm aware."

"No, I mean like she's had a few different lives, from what I can tell. She was born in Wellesley, she and her brother both. Family seems to have had some pretty decent money. Dad was an investor and was one of the first guys in on DEC."

"Damn."

"Right. Got his money out before that all went to shit. Marcy was into gymnastics and horses up through high school, seemed to be a fairly normal kid. Then the old man made a couple big bets on Webvan and Kozmo. Those did not go especially well."

"Oof. Not Pets dot com?"

"He missed that one somehow. But the other two cleaned him out. He had to sell the house in Wellesley and moved the family to New York, upstate somewhere. Place called, what is it, Oneonta? Something of a step down, I'd guess. So this was the spring of Marcy's senior year of high school. She was accepted at Brown and UVA, but wound up at SUNY-Binghamton when the money dried up. She did well there, came out with a degree in marketing and business and moved to the city. Spent about six years there, working for a couple of PR firms, then left for San Francisco. There isn't much out there on what she was doing for the next couple of years, but then she shows up again as the wine director at a restaurant in North Beach. Does that for about three years and then there's another blank spot for like eighteen months before she surfaces here."

"That's a lot of movement for sure, but I don't know that it's especially unusual. People seem to move around more now than they used to."

"Yup, but it's the periods where there's no data on where she was or what she was doing that are interesting to me," JD said. "It's really hard to do that. There are records of everything and everyone, but not her."

"Also, none of what you said lines up with what she told me about where she'd lived and what she'd done. And it's different from what she told Chris King, too," I said. "She's lying to everyone."

"I called the restaurant she worked at in San Francisco, pretended I was checking references for a job she was applying for. The manager wasn't there at the time Marcy was, but he put the owner on the phone, who said she'd been recommended to him by a friend in the wine industry and that she was a big favorite of their customers. He said when she left, she told him she was moving back home to Minnesota to take care of her mom, who was dying."

"Was she?"

"If so, it's very slowly and not in Minnesota. Her parents still live in New York as far as I can tell and are both still alive," he said.

"She's really something," I said.

"You sound a little impressed."

"Maybe a little. Who has the time and energy to keep up with all of those lies?"

"Not me. And what's the point of it?" JD asked.

"Could be anything. Maybe she had a rough time in college, had a guy that was stalking her or something and she needed to get clear. Or maybe her childhood wasn't as idyllic as it looks on paper and she's been trying to move away from it. Or she just likes to reinvent herself every few years and start fresh. I don't know. But I've seen plenty of versions of all of those. Lots of people live lives that don't match up with what the rest of us think is typical or normal."

"Like people who live on boats."

"As an example. If I had to guess I'd put her somewhere in the category of running from a bad relationship or other traumatic event."

"I don't know, man. That girl does not seem like someone who runs. From anything. I mean she's living in the same house where her daughter died. That's hard core," JD said. "I can't really see her pulling up stakes and moving across the country because some guy gave her a hard time, you know?"

I slouched back in my chair. "So what then?"

We kicked it around for a few more minutes, getting nowhere. Caroline wandered downstairs and into the kitchen looking for dessert. She came back with a small stack of Oreos and sat on my lap and looked at the notes spread on the table.

"Making any progress?" she asked.

"I don't know. It's hard to tell. JD found some interesting stuff on Marcy but I don't know what any of it means, especially in context with what we learned about her today," I said.

"Tell me," Caroline said.

JD gave her the short version of Marcy's travels and skin-shedding and I told her I thought Marcy was probably running from something and that JD didn't agree.

"I don't agree with you either, Danny. It's not like I know her that well, or at all really. But she didn't show me any signs that she was the type to bail out if things got tough for her. Look what happened with her daughter. It doesn't get a lot worse than that, and that's probably harder on the woman than the man in that situation."

"And her husband was the one who took off," I said.

"And she stuck. I'm not saying it's out of the question that she ran from something at some point, I just don't think it's the most likely scenario."

"Maybe not. But I'd bet a lot of American dollars that she has something back there that she doesn't want anyone to see," I said.

"Don't we all," Caroline said.

"Not me. My life is an open book," JD said.

Caroline stood and patted JD on the head as she walked toward the stairs. "And what a book it is."

"I think I want to go talk to Melissa Sandford again," I said. "She knew about the thing between her husband and Marcy and stayed married to him for a while. And it wasn't even a real marriage to begin with, so why bother at that point?"

"Inertia?"

"I guess. Man, this case would be a lot simpler if I understood women even a little bit."

"So would life," JD said.

We talked through it some more and agreed we would go see Melissa in the morning. JD said he was going to work on the last bit of the malware issue with Austin's laptop that night, which meant he'd probably be at it all night. Savannah was planning to spend the day seeing some of the sights in Plymouth.

"Try to at least remember to shower in the morning," I said as he was packing up to leave.

"No promises."

Caroline was laying in bed watching TV when I went up. "Anything good?"

"Eh, some movie with Patrick Dempsey and that girl."

"So, no," I said.

"Very much no."

"What are you up to tomorrow?"

"Ah, just painting and hanging around here I guess. What's up?"

"JD and I are going to go up to Hanover to see Melissa Sandford again. I want to check a few things out with her about Marcy and her ex-husband. Shouldn't take too long. Was thinking maybe we could go to the range in the afternoon. It's been a while."

She stretched and yawned. "Sure, but no pouting this time."

"You slightly outshot me."

"Like hell."

Before going to sleep, I called Melissa and she said she would be home until about eleven the next morning and could talk for a few minutes.

"I really don't know what else I can tell you though," she said. "Just want to see why some of the things Marcy told us don't really line up with what you said."

"Because she's a fucking liar, that's why."

Caroline and I were up by seven and ran for an hour through the back roads of Plymouth and we made plans to meet at a range in West Plymouth after lunch. I left the beach before nine and found JD waiting in the parking lot at the yacht club, chatting with a woman who looked to be in her early seventies. She patted him on the arm and gave him a quick kiss on the cheek as I pulled up. He climbed in the Jeep and I headed for the highway.

"Savannah know about your new girlfriend?" I asked.

"That's my girl Shirl, from the party the other night. She's a hot ticket."

"So you said. Listen: I was thinking last night about the thing with the malware. We know that when it gets onto a machine it starts looking for photo and video files, right? So what if we set up some files for it to find that have some of our own code in them?"

"We can do that, but to what end?"

"Intelligence gathering. I want to get some information about who's on the other end of that stuff. We need to find a way to get to this guy, either directly or by drawing him out. I was thinking that if you can create a couple of files disguised as photos that are actually executables and embed some code that would give us a line into what we're dealing with here."

"I'd have to think about that some, but off the top of my head I'd say it's possible. I've used a couple of techniques for disguising files like that before. I'd just need to figure out what we want it to do and all that. But the bigger issue would be how we get the executable to run once he has it. I have some ideas, but I'd need to test them out."

"Give it some thought."

A few minutes after we hit Route 3, I took a call from Louis Andino. "Just checking in," he said. "Anything moving on your end?"

"Maybe. I'm heading up to Hanover to see the ex-wife of a guy who was killed before Austin. Might be connected."

"Who's the dead guy?"

I told him what we knew or thought we knew about Greg Richmond, Marcy Simms, and Melissa Sandford. I left out the bit about Marcy's dead daughter; I didn't think that was my story to tell.

"Can I use any of this?" Andino asked when I was finished.

I thought about it for a minute. "Not yet. I want to talk to Sandford again and see what I can get from her. But some of that stuff you can probably confirm through public records.

Richmond's murder was in the papers, and the divorce and so on."

"I'll hold off until I hear back from you. Call me later today?"

"If there's anything to tell."

Melissa Sandford was in the front yard, trimming low branches from a large Japanese maple tree when we pulled up. I introduced JD and Melissa led us up onto the front porch.

"After I talked with you last time, I went to see Marcy. I'd talked to her before, but didn't know about the relationship she had with your husband. She told us a lot about the relationship and we talked about your husband's murder. I got the impression that you knew about their relationship for quite a while before the divorce."

"A few months, I guess."

"How did you find out?"

"I knew something was going on for a few weeks and I eventually got up the nerve to ask him one night, and he admitted it. Said that Melissa understood him better than I did, that they had a real connection."

She spat the last word as if it burned her tongue. "So why stay with him after that?" I asked.

"Convenience. Familiarity, I guess. Unwinding a marriage, even one that doesn't involve kids, is a pain in the ass and I guess

I wasn't in a great hurry to start that process," she said. "We both knew the marriage was over, it was just a matter of getting around to making it official. Greg didn't spend a lot of time here, even before the affair, so it wasn't much of a difference really. We had separate lives and I have plenty of friends, so it was fine. At least for a while."

"What changed?" JD said.

"I guess I just got tired of playing house and I told him he needed to find another place to live."

"What is Marcy's husband like?" I asked.

"I never met him. He was never really around from what I could tell. He traveled a lot for work I guess. Marcy didn't talk about him much."

"Were you and Marcy ever friendly? I mean, before she…"

"Started screwing my husband? No, I never cared for her at all. She's very taken with herself and doesn't have a lot of time for anyone else. I always found her cold and petty."

"Did that change when her daughter was born? I asked.

Melissa looked from me to JD and back again. Confused. "What do you mean? She doesn't have any children."

I took a deep breath. "Uh, she did, actually. She had a daughter with Greg. The girl died when she was almost five years old."

Melissa's mouth hung open and she shook her head back and forth. She stood up and walked to the end of the porch and back. "No, there's no way. She was never pregnant."

I looked at JD, who shrugged. "You're sure?"

"I saw her at least once a month, even after the divorce. No way she was ever pregnant. You've seen her. She would be showing after about half an hour with that body. No way."

"Ah Christ," I said. "You're really sure? I mean, she told us a pretty brutal story about this girl. She said she drowned on their property while she and her husband were a few feet away. Said it was the beginning of the end of her marriage. That, and the affair with your husband."

"Wait a minute. How old did she tell you this girl was?"

I explained the full story Marcy had told us, including the bit about Wendy supposedly being Greg and Marcy's daughter. She was stoic through most of it, but the pain was evident on her face by the time I was finished.

"Look, I don't know who the girl in the picture was, but I can tell you that woman and Greg never had a baby. I can't believe what a manipulative bitch she is. Jesus."

"I know this is tough for you, Melissa, but how can you be sure? Half the stories on Dateline are about guys who have secret families in another state," I said.

"I'm a hundred percent sure. Greg had a vasectomy about a year after I miscarried. He said he couldn't deal with that kind of situation again and didn't want to take any chances. I was there. He was cut, believe me," she said. "I paid the bill."

I already knew Marcy was lying to me about her background, and to everyone else, for that matter. But that hardly made her unique. People lied about their past all the time. What she was selling us about her daughter was something else. Inventing that kind of story, possibly on the spot, takes a kind of deviousness that most people don't possess.

"That was a pretty convincing performance she gave us. I'm used to dealing with liars and I bought every bit of her story."

"She's pretty and smart and manipulative, so you believed her," Melissa said.

"I don't know. My girlfriend was there and she was convinced. And she's not predisposed to like or trust most other women."

"I don't know what to tell you. But if Marcy had a child, it wasn't from Greg and she did a hell of a job of hiding it."

"Do you know what Marcy's husband's last name is? I notice she doesn't use it," JD said.

"Thorne," she said.

We talked for a few more minutes and then Melissa said she had to get ready for a doctor's appointment. As we wound through the back streets of Hanover toward the highway, JD pulled out his laptop and began typing furiously. I called Caroline and told her we were on the way to the range, but I needed to drop JD off at the yacht club first and then I'd meet her.

"No, I'm coming with you," JD said.

"You are?"

"What, I can't blow up some shit too?"

I pulled the Jeep onto Route 3 and headed south, thinking about Melissa Sandford and Marcy Simms and why Marcy would have pushed that story on us about her daughter. She was obviously a severely troubled person and very smart. A dangerous combination.

"Dude, Melissa was right. There's no birth or death records for anyone named Wendy Simms in Massachusetts in the last ten years," JD said.

"What about the husband's last name? Thorne."

"Nope. No Wendy Thorn, T-H-O-R-N or T-H-O-R-N-E."

"Ok, let's think about this. She's told fifty different stories about where she's from and where she's lived and what she's done. She doesn't seem to have much in the way of friends, and her reaction to her brother's death wasn't really overwhelming."

"I'm not sure we really know anything at all about her for sure," JD said.

"I know one thing: We're about to get up in her shit."

It was just past noon when we got to the range. It was a private club on a dirt road, hidden in an old pine forest and surrounded by cranberry bogs. Caroline was already there and had brought sandwiches and drinks. We sat in the small lounge and talked as we ate. I told her what Melissa had said, and what JD had found, or not found, about Marcy's fictional daughter. Caroline listened quietly, finished her sandwich, balled up the foil wrapper in her hand and stood.

"Do they have a female silhouette in here?" she asked.

We went in and found three lanes together. I brought my Sig 9 mm and Caroline was shooting with the Colt .38 super auto her dad had gotten her for college graduation. JD rented an army .45 at the counter and we each went through a couple of magazines to warm up before deciding on a closest to the pin contest. Three shots each at our own targets, whoever had the tightest group in the ten ring won. Ten bucks each per round.

I was the only one who had ever fired a shot in anger, but Caroline was a better pure shooter than I was. JD had grown up hunting deer and turkeys, and he didn't often shoot with a pistol, but he was a good shot. Caroline took the first round and I got the next two before JD took one to make it interesting. We only had a few minutes left on our time, so we bet the pot on the last round. I put two within a millimeter of each other and then choked on the third shot, jerking it into the eight ring. JD bunched his three right at the top of the ten ring, with hardly any daylight between them.

"I'm impressed that you guys can see that far," Caroline said.

She stepped to the line and fired three shots in quick succession. Pop pop pop. I could tell from the end of the lane that she'd won, and when the target zipped up to us, her shots looked more like one large hole than a group. She took off her glasses and scooped the money off the shelf.

"Don't feel bad, boys. I've done worse to better," she said.

Afterward, we went back to the lounge and allowed Caroline to buy the first round of beers. While she was at the bar, I went over to say hello to a Plymouth cop I'd worked with a couple times when I was a trooper.

"Hear you're giving the Boston cops hell," he said.

"Trying. They're dragging their feet on it. No one cares," I said.

"Only matters if there's enough media heat to make the bosses uncomfortable. No ink, no stink," he said.

"Might have to make our own stink on this one."

"Keep your head down, Danny."

We drank our beers and let Caroline gloat for a while and then tried to figure out what to do next. Caroline wanted to drive up to Cohasset and shoot Marcy, which, although very satisfying, was probably counterproductive.

"It could just be in the foot. Or maybe the knee," she said.

"Can't say I disagree," JD said.

"No one is shooting her. At least not yet," I said.

"Ok, but if anyone gets to, it's me," Caroline said.

"Yes, honey. Now, can we try to focus? JD, I'd like you to keep going on the stuff you were working on. We need to get that nailed down. I want some visibility into her shit. In the meantime, I'm going to circle back with Chris King and see where they're at now. I also want to see what else he can find on Marcy. She fooled him too, so he's gonna be plenty mad."

"How much do you think Marcy's pathological lying has to do with her family?" Caroline said.

"I don't follow."

"Well, it seems like she lived a pretty charmed life until her dad's investments went bad. She lived in a safe, happy bubble and then things kind of fell apart. The life she had imagined for herself was gone and she ended up at a second-tier college and then had to start building her own life," Caroline said. "So she does that bit by bit and decides that she isn't going to let people know where she came from and what she'd lost. A clean slate.

And it goes from there. And then she has some success, finds a good husband, and at some point discovers that her brother is involved in a child exploitation ring. So she keeps the lies going, to keep her life going."

JD said: "I can see it, except the bit with her brother. I don't know why she would protect him once she found out what he was doing. That's fucked."

"Do we know that she was protecting him," I asked.

"She told you straight up that she knew what he was when you went there the first time, right?"

"Yeah."

"Then she was protecting him. Implicitly if not explicitly."

"Seems so. But why? She told me she didn't particularly care for him, even before she figured out what he was doing. So what's the point?"

Caroline stopped mid-sip. Looked from me to JD and back again. "What if it's her? Not him. What if it's Marcy?"

"You mean what if she was involved with it?" JD asked.

"No, not involved. What if it was *her*?"

"That would mean…" I said.

"Oh my God," JD said.

Fifteen

Things started to move.

I called Chris King as JD and I drove back to the beach. "Listen, I might have something for you."

I told him about the conversation with Melissa Sandford, what JD had found online, and our suspicions about Marcy. He listened for a couple minutes, then was quiet.

"You there?" I asked.

"Just thinking. I'm in the office for about an hour more, so I'll do some more digging on Marcy and see what I can find. What are you doing?"

"We're gonna do the same, but from a different angle."

"Tobin…"

"Call you later."

Next, I called Melissa, and got no answer. I waited five minutes and tried again with the same result.

JD spent the drive home on his laptop. As we pulled onto the beach road, he closed the laptop and shook his head.

"What?" I said.

"Can't believe I missed it. It's all there. All the moving around, the lies about where she's lived and what she's done. All of it. We should've seen it."

"People lie for a lot of different reasons, and it's not always the ones you'd think. We didn't have a good reason to think she was involved with this," I said. "Plenty of women do the same kind of thing if they're running from abusive relationships."

"Still."

I pulled into my driveway and cut the engine. "Let's focus on what we can do now," I said. "I want to confirm that she's involved in this as soon as possible and then shut her shit down. One way or the other."

"How?" JD said.

"I have a couple ideas, but I need to think them through a little more. I want to see what King comes up with, too. He can talk to the cops in California and New York and wherever else she's been and get stuff we can't. Till then, I want to put some pressure on Marcy and see what she does."

"What if she closes up shop and takes off for Mexico?"

"That's why we're gonna watch her. If she bolts, I want to know about it. If she farts, I want to know about it."

"Women like her don't fart. And I'm not sitting in the woods all night watching her house," he said.

"Me neither."

"So who then?"

"Dax."

"Can you get in touch with him?" JD asked.

"Yeah. He'll be here tomorrow."

JD shifted in his seat and wiped his hands on his shorts. "Why didn't you tell me? I need to know this stuff. I mean, shit."

"Take it easy. You haven't seen him in a long time. From what I hear he's a different guy."

"Different is one word for it."

"You know what I mean."

"Are we planning to feed her to the sharks? If not, what the fuck is Dax coming for?"

"Moral support."

"Moral. Yeah."

"Listen, Dax is going to handle that end of it. What I need from you is a picture of her infrastructure. Find her network, her cloud service, her cold storage, and figure out what it all looks like. I want to know the scope of what we're dealing with, and I don't want to be surprised by her flipping a switch and setting it all on fire when we get close."

"Yeah, I'm on it. But, Dax?"

We found Caroline in the kitchen. She was chopping jalapenos and red bell peppers and tossing them into a sizzling cast iron skillet. The pepper hissed and popped as they hit the pan. A few chicken breasts were under the broiler.

"It's her, right?" she asked, as we came through the screen door.

"Think so," I said.

"You *think* so? It's her, Danny."

"We're in the same place. The thing we need to figure out now is how to handle it."

"No, you don't. Tie up what you have, give it to Chris King. You're not a cop anymore."

"I'm aware. What I meant was, how do we tell Chris what we have and why we have it? Most of what I have is from people who will never testify. Or even talk to the cops. Melissa Sandford would tell King to go fuck himself."

"Who cares? Not your problem. You tell King what you know, and then it's his responsibility."

"It doesn't really work like that. Even if I gave him a giant notebook with a detailed confession he'd still need to go back and talk to all of those witnesses and get the same statements. It's stupid, but that's how it is."

She turned and leaned against the counter and wiped her hands on a dish towel. "Danny, you got into this to help Savannah and figure out who killed her brother. Not to go chasing after some cunt who's running a child exploitation ring. That's not your job. Let King handle it."

"Probably more like an empire, from what we've seen. There's a lot of people involved and I don't even want to think about how many kids have been forced into this. Marcy Simms is probably the one who's running it. You said it yourself. I'm not letting her skate."

"I'm not asking you to. I'm asking you to let the cops do their job. If you don't trust King, then let's call my dad. He can handle it, or find someone who can," she said.

"Not yet. I want to watch her for a bit and maybe put some pressure on her and see what she does. I don't think she knows we're on her. There's no reason she should."

Caroline shook her head as she stirred the veggies. "You're thinking about it the wrong way, Danny. She's not the one who matters. It's the kids. Like you said, who knows how many of them have been tortured by these people? We'll probably never know, but the longer you let her breathe free air, the longer those kids are victimized. Think about that."

I went to the fridge and dug around until I came up with a can of Second Wind Juggernot. I popped the top, took a long drink as I leaned against the counter and watched her cook.

"It's a good point," I said after a minute. "But we need to balance that against the need to have her sewn up. If I go to King or your dad with this stuff, it needs to be rock solid. It can't be a bunch of bullshit conjecture and gut feelings. That won't fly."

"If?"

"I'm just saying, you never know how things will turn out. She could see us coming and head for Alaska, or--"

"Or…"

"Who knows? She's smart. She's changed identities and lives more times than JD has changed his underwear this year. She could burn the whole thing down and walk away and that would be that."

"That can't happen, Danny. Can. Not.."

I put my arms around her waist and pulled her to me. "Listen, babe. Marcy Simms is done, one way or another. What's happened to all of those kids in the past is out of our control, but she isn't. JD is crawling all over her network right now, so it's only a matter of time before he's in there. Once that happens, we will have her. The best case scenario for her will be to walk into the sea and not look back."

When the food was done, we took our plates out on the back deck, where we found JD and Savannah, who had come down after playing tourist for the day. The sun was just dipping down below the trees on Warren Avenue, throwing pink and orange and yellow streaks against the low clouds. Caroline put plates in front of Savannah and JD and he scooped a handful of the peppers into his mouth while still typing. A second later, the hot oil and jalapeno hit him and he howled and snatched the beer from my hand and powered the rest of it down.

"Jesus, Caro. What'd I ever do to you?" he said.

"I thought I was being nice by bringing you some food," she said. "I guess I should've brought what, Cheetos and Code Red? Isn't that what you people like?"

JD was already back on his keyboard. "You people? Hackers have feelings too. We just hide them under our black hoodies."

"You've never worn a hoodie in your life," I said.

"Because I'm too smart to live anywhere the temperature drops below eighty," he said.

"Getting anywhere?" Savannah asked.

"Made a little progress."

"Like what?" Caroline asked.

"Well, if I was in her business, I wouldn't have a damn thing on my own network. Nothing. It would all be on a hosting provider somewhere with redundant backups far away, like Latvia. The feds have a much harder time intimidating a mob-owned hosting company than an individual. She's not dumb, as we've established, so I figured she has something along those lines set up. But she needs a way to access all of it."

"And that's where we can get her," I said.

"That's right. But we need to get into her house again. Or I do, at the very least. Getting into her laptop will be a lot easier than owning up the hosting provider."

"So let's take a drive tomorrow," I said. "Dax should be here by noon, we can get him briefed and then head up there. How much time do you need?"

"About as much time as it would plausibly take me to drop the kids off at the pool," he said.

"So an hour," Caroline said.

"After these peppers you fed me, more like thirty seconds."

"You girls want to come? You don't have to," I said.

"My only thing is I need to keep myself from punching her in the throat."

After dinner I called King back to see if he'd gotten anywhere.

"I think you've got something," he said, exhaustion in his voice.

"Tell me."

"Talked to a guy out in San Francisco. As soon as I mentioned her name he was all ears. Apparently she was working as a daycare supervisor for a while out in the East Bay somewhere. The parents and kids loved her, but toward the end of her time there a little girl from the daycare disappeared. Six years old. They were on a field trip, walking around some park and the girl just vanished. Marcy was supposed to go on the trip but she called in sick that day and then never came back to work."

"And the girl?"

"Nothing."

"How did they connect it to Marcy?"

"Her co-workers said she and this girl were very close. Marcy went out of her way to make sure the girl was taken care of, always chose her for activities. The other staff members said Marcy talked about how much she'd like to have a daughter like her. The girl's name was, ah, Sophie Carter. Her parents sued the day care facility and ended up settling out of court. The guy I talked to was very interested to find out that Marcy had surfaced and had a whole lot of questions for me about this case."

"Hey, thanks man. I appreciate the help."

"Tobin. What are you guys gonna do?"

"Not sure yet. But when I figure it out, you'll be the last to know."

What we did was go to bed. Not all together. And not all of us. Savannah took the spare room upstairs and JD stayed downstairs working and said he'd sleep on the couch. If he slept, which was doubtful. Even when he had nothing going on, JD rarely slept more than three or four hours a night, and when he was deep into a project, he could go two or three days without closing his eyes.

And so when Caroline and I came downstairs in the morning, it was no surprise to see JD standing at the kitchen counter, his laptop in front of him and the remnants of last night's dinner on a plate next to it. He glanced up as we came into the kitchen and didn't seem to register who we were and went back to his machine. A minute later he looked back up.

"Hey guys. Sleep good?"

"Sure," I said. "You?"

"No thanks."

"Right. Hey, we're gonna go for a short run and then let's go through the details of what we need to do with Marcy today," I said. "Dax should be here by noon."

He nodded and kept typing. Which was a good sign.

We ran down the beach road and out onto 3A, heading north into town. The morning was cool and bright, with none of the humidity that had hung around all summer. We took it easy through the hills on the way to Jabez Corner and then picked it up a little as we moved into downtown Plymouth. The sun was just coming up over the horizon as we ran through Stephen's Field and I could see the light reflecting off the windows of our house in the distance.

"What do you guys plan to do once JD does whatever he's doing on her network?" Caroline asked.

"Depends. Maybe nothing."

"You don't do nothing."

"I need to find out if she's connected to Wyatt's murder, and the others."

"And if she is?"

I said nothing.

"That's not your decision to make, Danny, and you know it. If you guys can tie her to the murders, then you clue King in and let him handle it from there. All Savannah asked you to do is find out what happened to Wyatt. That's where it ends."

"We've been through this. The things we're doing aren't necessarily admissible in court, so telling King about it would just put us and him in a bad spot. We need to see where this takes us and then we'll decide. But Marcy's time is about to be up."

We went back and forth on that for a while and got nowhere.

"Where are you at on the new dog idea?" I said.

"I think we should get a rescue dog. I can't really settle on a breed, so why not just go see what the shelters have? You ok with that?"

"Sure. I like rescuing things."

"Yeah you do."

The public parking lot was mostly empty when we got back to the beach, aside from the vehicles of a few stray fishermen who were strung out along the low tide line surfcasting. As we got within a hundred yards of the house, Caroline shoved me sideways and took off at a dead sprint. I tripped and went down on one knee in the sand and swore. Jesus she hated losing. I got back to my feet and looked up to see her forty yards away already. No chance. I trotted after her and saw her look back and smile as she approached a black pickup parked along the rocks. The driver's door opened and a huge man emerged, silhouetted by the sun behind him. He stepped into the road toward Caroline, who was still looking over her shoulder at me.

I went into a full sprint. "Caroline. Caro! Stop!"

She swung her head forward and dug her feet in, stopping a yard short of the man now blocking her way. I was ten yards behind her when a cloud slid in front of the sun and the man's face came into focus.

"Dax. Christ. I almost shot you."

He looked at my running gear and empty hands. "With your dick?"

"You know what I mean."

"Sure. You're gonna introduce me here?"

Caroline stuck out her hand. "Caroline. I'm with him."

Dax laughed and took her hand. "Lucky you."

JD was still in the kitchen, standing at the counter. He glanced up as we walked in, went back to his laptop, then did a double-take when he saw Dax behind us. He stood and walked past me and Caroline. Dax eyed him for a second, then wrapped him in a bear hug and lifted JD off his feet.

We sat on the upstairs deck facing the ocean and watched a couple of sailboats make lazy circles offshore.

"Thanks for bringing me across the fucking ocean just to see some more sand, Tobin," Dax said.

"Hey, don't blame me. I didn't know where you were. I just sent the message and here you are."

"Where *were* you?" JD said.

"Here and there. Wherever the action is. And the money."

"Mom know you're here?" JD asked.

Dax shook his head. "Wasn't sure how long this would take, so I didn't want to tell her and then not be able to go see her."

"You better hope she doesn't find out."

"You better hope you don't tell her," Dax said, then looked at me. "So what *are* we doing?"

"Just need you to keep an eye on someone for a few days while we do some things. Easy duty."

"Isn't watching people what *you* do?"

"Well…" I filled him in on the case so far, Marcy Simms, Greg Richmond and the other murders that King thought were connected to Wyatt's, and what we were planning to do.

"Doesn't sound too hard. I could use a break, anyway," he said.

JD laughed and I said, "You haven't met Marcy yet. She's nothing but hard."

Dax yawned and stretched. "We'll see."

Savannah walked out onto the deck and JD introduced her. Dax stood and hugged her. "So you're the one."

Savannah laughed. "I am?"

"That's the way I hear it."

She smiled and Dax put his hand on her shoulder. "Don't worry. We got this."

Sixteen

Before we left, I pulled Dax aside while Caroline, Savannah and JD were getting ready.

"Listen, I'm not sure how this is going to go. You need to be on your toes," I said.

He looked confused. "Tobin, I assumed you wouldn't bring me all the way over here just to babysit some mark. I've run into plenty of women who were ready and willing to tear my throat out. Several of them tried."

"And you're still here."

"And they're not."

"One other thing: I have a feeling that she's got some help somewhere. I don't make her as the type to actually do any killing. She's cold and smart. But a killer…I don't see it."

"You guys handle it in the house and I'll take care of it outside. You won't have any surprises."

"Let's get you some tools, though."

We went inside and up to the master bedroom, where I'd installed a small gun safe in the floor a few years earlier. I slid aside the throw rug, lifted up the D ring and unlocked it. The safe held mine and Caroline's handguns, along with a few others that didn't have any serial numbers. Dax grabbed a cold Glock 22 from the safe, checked it, nodded. I gave him two clips.

"Anything bigger?" he asked.

I took him out back to a stainless steel box about the size of a large coffin that sat under the deck. It was anchored to a concrete pad on all four corners and had a fingerprint biometric lock on it, which JD told me was a piece of shit. But it had held up so far. I opened the box, and Dax leaned in and then smiled.

"There we go."

The box currently held fifteen long guns, some I'd bought, some I'd acquired in various other ways.

"Help yourself," I said.

Dax spent about ten minutes looking through the inventory and eventually settled on a scoped Remington 700 that I'd had for quite a while. It had seen some shit. He gave it a once-over, checked the action.

"Let's go."

We ate a quick lunch and then Caroline, Savannah, JD, and I piled into the Jeep for the drive up to Marcy's house in Cohasset. Dax followed in his truck. When we got close to the house, Dax pulled off into a turnaround as I'd told him to. He'd wait there until we came out and then move the truck to a better spot closer to the house and settle in. I pulled into Marcy's driveway and put the Jeep nose-to-nose with her 911, just in case she got the urge to leave with a quickness.

As we walked up to the front porch, the door opened and Marcy stood in the entryway. She was wearing black yoga pants and a pink form-fitting Nike long sleeve top. Her hair was carefully mussed. She looked the three of us over, glanced over our shoulders, and then fixed a smile on her face.

"Oh hey. Danny, how are you?"

"Yeah good, Marcy. Do you have a minute? I had a couple of things I wanted to run by you. I hope we're not interrupting anything."

She gave a half-glance over her shoulder and then opened the door wide. "Not at all. Come on in."

We filed into the entry and Marcy led us into the kitchen. She gave Caroline a quick hug and I introduced Savannah. "I was just about to have a glass of wine. Would anyone else care for some?"

Caroline glanced at me and I shrugged. "Sure. It's past noon, right?"

Marcy went to a small wet bar set up in an alcove on the side of the kitchen, looked over several bottles of wine, and selected one. She took a churchkey from a drawer and removed the foil wrap and uncorked the bottle with practiced ease. She poured four glasses of a deep red wine.

"Oh, that's good," Savannah said after a sip. "What is it?"

"It's a cab, maybe from California? I'm afraid I don't know much about wine. I just know what I like," Marcy said.

We drank the wine for a few minutes and made small talk about the weather and the Sox and then Marcy said, "So what did you need to talk about, Danny?"

"Well, I've been thinking about some of the things we talked about and I wondered if maybe you could walk us through some of it again. I know it's difficult, but I think it might help us get a better handle on some of this."

She took a careful sip of her wine. "Sure. It can't hurt any more than it already does."

Marcy led us out to the back deck, where there was a sunken fire pit and an outdoor bar. We sat in low comfortable chairs around the fire pit and faced the boat house, the dock, and the ocean beyond it. The sandbox area was just out of sight down the slope.

"Savannah, my condolences on your brother. It's a truly awful thing to lose someone so close to you," Marcy said.

"Thank you. I'm sorry that we have that in common."

Marcy nodded. "I'm afraid my brother just didn't have the strength to get past his demons. I'm confident the police will find the person responsible for your brother's death."

"I'm not. My money is on these guys."

Marcy, sitting opposite me, fixed me with a look and waited.

"I know all of this is hard for you to talk about, but--"

"It's fine. Ask me what you want."

"So, between what you told all of us and what you and Caroline talked about separately, I think we have a decent idea of what you've been through. And I honestly don't mean to keep reopening old wounds, but I'm just a little unclear on some of the details of your relationship with Greg and how that all played out. Things got a little intense when we talked about it last time, so if you wouldn't mind just telling us again how he came to work for your firm and how you two became involved, it would really help."

She closed her eyes for a few seconds then sat forward in her chair and looked out toward the boat house. "Like I told you before, I really don't recall exactly how Greg joined us. I think it may have been through a friend's recommendation, but I'm not positive. It was a long time ago. Real estate isn't like other businesses. Agents are kind of like independent contractors who latch on with one firm or another and there tends to be a lot of turnover, so someone coming in or leaving doesn't register much. He was just someone else walking through the door I guess."

"And as far as the relationship?" I asked. "How did that come about?"

"I mean, how does any relationship start? I couldn't pinpoint a day or a conversation, but we became friendly over the course of his first few months with the firm. I helped him with a couple of sales down here, people I knew. We had a few lunches together, dinners after a late night in the office, that kind of thing. After Greg was with us for a couple of years, maybe three, I'm not sure, my original partner got sick and needed to leave. He ended up dying a couple months later. So I needed someone else to come in as a partner and Greg had the money to invest and was interested, so that was that."

"Does real estate pay that well?" Caroline said.

"It can. But it wasn't his money. His wife has some kind of family money from I don't even know what. I didn't ask. He came in as a forty percent partner and I kept control of the business. After that, we were obviously spending more time together, talking about all sorts of things, our careers, our ambitions, our marriages. Neither one of us was particularly happy in our marriage but I think his was worse than mine. Have you met his wife? Ok, then you can see why. She's completely self-absorbed, arrogant, and entitled. If she hadn't gotten herself knocked up, Greg never would have married her and…"

Her voice trailed off and she took a sip of her wine to buy herself some time. As she did, I nodded slightly at JD, who stood.

"Do you mind if I use your bathroom?" he asked Marcy.

"Certainly. If you go in through the kitchen and then left, there's one off the study there," she said.

JD walked into the house and I began counting in my head. Marcy sighed and said, "I don't see how this is going to help you guys find whoever killed Greg and those other people. It doesn't have anything to do with me."

"We're just looking for any kind of common thread, anything we can pull on that might start unraveling," I said. "Did Greg ever tell you much about his time in Georgia or his friends down there?"

"Not really. I knew that he went to school down there and started work in Atlanta, but that's about it."

"So if I gave you some names of people he might have known in Atlanta, do you think you'd know any of them?"

"I doubt it, but who knows."

I took my time getting my notes app open on my phone, still silently counting the time JD had been gone. I read off several of the names of the other victims we had associated with Wyatt Austin's killer. I didn't see any indication she recognized any of them and she said she didn't. I made up a couple of other names to kill some more time and she shook her head at those, too. I ran through my mental list of stuff I could plausibly ask her and was coming up dry when Savannah stepped in.

"How long have you been in this house? It's such a great spot."

Marcy folded her hands in her lap and looked around the yard. The entire property was spectacular, even by Cohasset standards, and the rear portion of it was large enough for a small subdivision. The deck where we were sitting was two thousand square feet all day and there was a stone patio of equal size below that that led out onto the deep green lawn, perfectly landscaped and with the town-meeting-approved ratio of old growth oaks and maples to younger evergreens. The lawn was roughly the size of the town I grew up in and the boat house could've housed a family of four comfortably, even with the boat in it. It was the kind of property that was conceived and executed specifically to make other rich white people jealous.

It was weaponized wealth.

"How long? I'm not even sure, to be honest," Marcy said at last. "Tim had come here house hunting after we got married and he found this place. I guess it's probably been five or seven years anyway. It's not really my taste, but it's fine I suppose. I'd rather be in Monterey or Hilton Head, but here I am."

My phone hummed in my pocket with a text message just as Marcy finished her wine and stood up and my stomach dropped.

"Would anyone else care for some more wine?" she asked.

I stammered: "Ah, um, well…"

"Beat you to it." It was JD walking across the deck with the wine bottle in his hand. He refilled Marcy's glass and topped off the rest of us. He winked at me and then sat back down. As my pulse rate recovered, I looked at my phone and saw a text from JD that was just two lines of thumbs-up emojis.

Marcy nodded her thanks to JD and took a long sip of her wine. "Tell me Caroline, how did Danny get lucky enough to land you?"

"Well, like you said before, who can really say how these things start? He came into my bar a few times and we had some nice conversations and it kind of went from there, I guess."

"You two have some things in common, don't you? I understand your father is a police officer, Caroline."

I'd never mentioned that to Marcy. Caroline shifted in her seat. "He is."

"That must have been a part of it, no?"

"I don't have any unresolved daddy issues, if that's where you're going."

"Oh, we all do, honey. Every girl wants to make her daddy proud and most of us spend our lives thinking we're not good enough and trying to overachieve to prove our worth. So we make choices that aren't in our best interests and then wonder why things go sideways. It's an old, sad song."

"Maybe so, but I'm not old and I'm sure as hell not sad," Caroline said, some grit creeping into her voice.

"I guess you're not. But youth doesn't last and happiness is an illusion."

"It's funny you think so. To me, happiness is a conscious decision and youth does last. Unless someone takes it away from you."

A hard, heartless smile from Marcy. "And how would that happen? Youth has an expiration date."

Caroline, sitting forward in her chair now. "You say that like it's a fact. It's not. I know people in their seventies who are younger than any of us. It's about how you think, how you live, how you interact with other people. It's not a function of your age. It can last for decades or it can get snatched away when you need it the most. I guess you never know until it happens. Some people never have the chance to be young at all."

Marcy fixed a half smile on her face and looked at Caroline for what seemed like an hour but was likely thirty seconds. "Say it."

Caroline, leaning back, smirking. Me, locking eyes with Marcy, hand on the Glock under my shirt. Savannah hands clenched on the arms of her chair. JD, unsure, looking from me to Caroline to Marcy and back again. No one spoke.

"Say it."

Caroline, leaning forward again. "You say it. You fucking say it."

Marcy, stock still. Then, a small sip of wine, a small smirk. Caroline stood without a word and walked out into the yard and down toward the oak tree on the way to the boat house. I could see the Chris-Craft bobbing gently. She circled the oak, looking carefully at the ground, scuffing her feet on the grass here and there. She made a show of it, bending down to examine the grass, picking up handfuls of dirt, and then walked slowly back up to the deck and sat down. Marcy watching her all the while.

"You must give me the name of your landscaper, Marcy. I don't see any trace of that fancy sandbox out there. It's like it was never there at all," Caroline said.

Marcy, coiled in her chair: "Say it."

I laid my hand on Caroline's arm and she threw it back in my lap. And we waited. The air closed in, the clouds hung low. And we waited.

After thirty minutes or thirty seconds, Caroline said,. "Time to go."

And so we went. Marcy walked us back through the house and out into the driveway without a word. She stood on the front porch as we got into the Jeep, arms folded across her chest, eyes on Caroline. I hit the ignition and put it into gear and Caroline grabbed my hand on the shifter.

Quietly, to me: "No."

"What?"

"She can't, this can't…"

"Don't worry."

She squeezed my hand tight. "Danny. Do you understand me?"

"I do."

Seventeen

I pulled up next to Dax's truck and found him slouched in his seat, a Gamecocks hat pulled low.

"How'd that go?" he asked without moving.

"I don't think we'll be getting an invitation to her next garden party, but we accomplished what we came to do," I said.

"JD work his magic?"

"I think we're good. We'll find out when we get back to the house.."

"You see anything while we were in there?" I asked.

"Nothing. Counted seven Range Rovers and four Teslas in, what, an hour? A lot of overcompensation going on here."

"You good for the night? Need anything?"

"All set. I'll hit you up if anything happens. What do you want me to do if she decides to leave?"

"Go with her. If she takes off, it could be for good."

"Roger that. See y'all in the morning then."

Caroline was quiet on the way home, so JD filled me in on what he'd done on his bathroom break. He had found a small high-end Windows laptop in a walk-in closet off the bedroom. It was locked, of course, so he had inserted a USB drive that automatically installed a small rootkit and keylogger that would record and send logs of the keystrokes on the machine back to one of JD's servers every thirty seconds when the laptop was active.

"What do you expect?" I asked him.

"With a little luck, she'll be spooked and head right for it and start taking things apart. That will save me some trouble. But if she doesn't, then I will."

When we got home, Brendan was sitting on the front porch reading my worn and faded paperback copy of *Hell to Pay*. Caroline was ahead of us and gave him a kiss on the cheek and a small hug and walked inside. Brendan gave me a questioning look and I shook my head and dropped into the chair next to him. Savannah hoisted herself onto the porch railing and looked out at the sea.

"That woman is an absolute piece of work. If she ever had feelings, she swallowed them a long time ago," I said.

"Savannah, what did you think?" Brendan asked.

"She's made of granite. Danny's right. She puts up a nice, sweet, polite front, but that's all it is. I bet she doesn't have one real friend. I don't know if she killed Wyatt, but it wouldn't shock me. Hell, I wouldn't be surprised if she killed her own brother."

"There is some historical precedent for that," Brendan said.

Inside, I heard a whoop and JD came running out onto the porch.

"Got her," he said.

As JD had thought, Marcy had gone right to her laptop and logged in to the admin console for the site. JD's keylogger snagged her credentials and sent them back to his server. The credentials were for a hosting provider in Romania that was well-known for hosting badness and providing cover for cybercrime groups and exploitation rings. High level shitheels. About a half an hour after the credentials came through, we saw the keylog dump showing that Marcy had logged out of the console. Five minutes later, JD logged in. He dug around in the directories for a few minutes, getting the lay of the land.

"There must be two dozen individual sites here. It's pretty much set up like I thought. She has a domain generation algorithm that's generating new domains for each of the sites every three days, and the IP addresses for the domains are rotating on a random schedule. Hard to pin down for any length of time, and I'd think that if any of them was taken down, it wouldn't matter much. She would just pop it back up on another virtual host real quick and move on."

"Those hosting companies are pretty much immune to law enforcement action," I said. "I worked a few of those cases and takedown orders and cease and desists go nowhere. Local law enforcement does not care and those companies basically just refuse to respond to legal processes and if something does get to them, they just shut the doors and open up under a different name."

"We don't need to worry about that. She's never getting back in here and I'm gonna burn this all to the ground."

"Does she have a customer database in there somewhere? Emails, usernames, anything?" I asked.

After a few minutes he shook his head. "She probably has that stored offline somewhere. It wouldn't make sense to have it in the same setup as the operational system."

"Think about how many of these operations are out there, man. Hundreds? Thousands? This is just one, and probably a pretty small one. So we tear this down and what, someone else just steps in to fill the void. We take her down and she hires an army of lawyers and drags it out for years and maybe pleads out. Is there even any point?"

"Yes." It was Caroline from across the room, still painting. "The kids are the point."

"Babe, I know. I'm just saying--"

"Danny."

"I know."

"Ohhh shit," JD said.

"What?"

"Hang on a sec. Lemme make sure." A couple more minutes of typing. "We got her fucking bank accounts too."

"She hit those too after we left?"

"Looks like it, yeah. I think she's starting to pull up stakes."

"Ok, I'm gonna call Dax and let him know and then let's figure out what we need to do. Don't try to log in to her bank accounts yet. If she has two-factor set up or some logging system we don't want her getting a notification."

"Thanks, dad."

"What bank is it?" I asked.

"Not sure but the IP address is in a block that's in Aruba."

I called Dax and let him know what we'd found and that Marcy might be on the move sooner than later. He had found a good spot that gave him a view of both the front of the house and the boat house in case she got creative. Next, I called Louis Andino. I had promised to let him know if he could use any of the stuff I had told him earlier about Marcy, Greg Richmond, and that whole situation and I wanted to make sure he hadn't jumped the gun.

He answered on the first ring. "Tobin. What's the word?"

"Listen, some things are happening on my end and I think if you use any of the things we talked about before about Marcy and Richmond it might spook some people. And we need everyone to stay un-spooked for the time being."

"Ah shit."

"Did you already write something? Tell me you didn't."

"I wrote the bones of the story but haven't put on the meat yet. I was hoping to push something online maybe tomorrow or the next day on this."

"Ok look: I'm gonna tell you a couple things but this shit does NOT go anywhere near publication until I give you the go ahead. Good?"

"Sure."

"I think we have a big piece of this figured out and we're in the process right now of making sure we're right about that."

Andino sucked in his breath. "Which piece?"

"I can't tell you that exactly, but our visit with Marcy today helped nail it down. We have a good idea of what her involvement level is and what she's done. We have a couple of things in motion that will confirm that and also ensure that she's done with this."

"I need something more specific than that, Tobin."

"You're aware of what the motive behind Wyatt Austin's murder is, yeah?"

"Of course."

"Well, that had nothing to do with him. He wasn't involved at all. It's Marcy and her brother who have been running this thing. From the beginning. Long before Austin ever met them or she ever moved here."

"And you know this how?"

"Because I'm better at my job than you are at yours."

A short silence. "Scale of one to ten, how sure are you?"

"Sure enough that I need you to shut the fuck up about it until I say otherwise."

More silence. "Fine, but if you're wrong, you're a dead man."

"I'll call you when."

Brendan had come in from the porch while I was talking to Andino and was sitting on the couch watching Caroline paint, something I was always being told that I wasn't allowed to do.

"At least someone is taking an interest in my work," Caroline called over her shoulder, not quietly.

I walked over and looked at the progress she'd made. It was coming together nicely, with the animals now totally identifiable as horses. The woman in the foreground looked to be complete, her features in sharp contrast to the landscape around her, eyes bright and focused on the viewer. Her gaze drew my attention and unnerved me at the same time. She looked familiar but I'd never met the woman who Caroline was doing the picture for, and this was supposed to be her. I didn't like it.

"Llamas are looking good, Caro," I said.

"Eat shit."

I went upstairs to take a shower and when I came back down, Brendan was heading out to drive JD and Savannah back to the yacht club.

"Don't fuck with her stuff tonight," I said to JD. "We need to keep her on the line."

"Yup. We're gonna go drink about five beers with the boaty people and then sleep the sleep of the righteous."

That night I sat outside on the small deck off our bedroom and looked over my notes while Caroline worked on her painting. The lights of downtown Plymouth were visible off in the distance and I could hear the mournful horns of the Captain John tour boats as they left the harbor for their twilight cruises. They would go out around the jetty, past Saquish and out into the Atlantic proper where, if they had a notion, they'd be able to motor right up to Marcy Simms's back yard. I sat with my notes and pictured Marcy in her house, trying to figure out what went wrong and how we got on to her. If everything went right, it wouldn't matter. We'd have her sewn up.

But she was only half of the equation. The other half was still unknown, and that was what really worried me. We still had no real handle on who had killed Wyatt Austin and Greg Richmond and the others. The number of people who would be motivated to kill members of a child exploitation ring was not small, and I didn't really have any sense that Marcy was the one. Too much exposure for her. So that narrowed the suspect pool down to...everyone but her.

Not ideal.

I heard the slider open and Caroline walked out onto the deck, a can of Mayflower New World in each hand. She handed me one and sank into the seat next to me. We sat with our feet up on the railing watching the last of the light fade from the western sky.

"The painting is really looking good, babe. Jokes aside."

"Thanks. I just want to be done with it and move on to something else. I have a couple ideas for a mural I'd like to do downstairs on the wall behind the couch."

"Is one of them me as a satyr standing on the beach with the waves crashing in the background as mermaids feed me grapes and oysters?"

"Do I talk in my sleep?"

"It's not the first time someone has had the idea. It's kind of embarrassing but it comes with the territory, I guess."

"What a trooper you are."

"Was."

"So, what do you think Marcy is going to do? Think she's going to pull the ripcord?"

"I'm counting on it. She would be crazy to stay. Not that she isn't crazy, obviously. But she's also smart and I think she knows that it's game over. I was really hoping she would do something today but we didn't get that lucky."

"I really wanted to drag her down to the water by her hair and hold her under until she turned blue. That twat. How does she sleep? How does she get up every day and not stick her head in the oven?"

"People can rationalize just about anything and after long enough, even the worst shit can seem routine. I think she sees this as a job. It's just a way to make money. She's not the one actually exploiting the kids, so it's ok in her mind."

"I'm gonna ask you a question and it's ok if you don't want to answer it but I need to ask."

"I'll answer anything you ask."

"Is she going to come out of this alive?"

"That's up to her."

"Really?"

"We're going into this with the hope that we can put her into a position where she has no choice but to give it up."

"Hope is not a plan."

"I'm pretty good at improvising, and I think we have the advantage on her right now. We know more about her than she does about us and she doesn't know what we know. Right now she realizes that we've caught onto her lies about her daughter and maybe she thinks we know some of the other stuff she's told us about her background isn't true either. But I don't think she realizes what we know about her operation. If we confront her with that and lay all of our cards on the table, she might fold."

"I can't believe she'd put in all of that effort and then just throw her hands up at the first sign of a little trouble."

"We are not a little trouble."

"You know what I mean. And don't you think she has her own plan? Someone with her level of intelligence and conniving and preparation would have to have a contingency plan set up if something goes wrong."

"I'm positive that she does and I think that's what she's doing right now, starting to put that in motion. But she thinks she's smarter than we are, which might lead to her making a mistake."

"To be fair, she probably is smarter than you."

"We're about to find out," I said.

After Caroline went to bed, I stayed outside looking over my notes and thinking about what I knew and what I still couldn't figure out. I knew Marcy Simms was operating a long-running child exploitation business and that she was a highly accomplished liar and con artist. I knew she had spent most of her adult life trying to outrun her past, and had been pretty successful at it. I knew she was a control freak who kept a tight grip on every detail of her life. I knew that her brother had killed himself after getting caught up in her business. And I knew that Wyatt Austin had been killed, possibly because he was thought to be associated with the Simms's operation.

The list of things I didn't know was shorter but more important: Who killed Wyatt and how was that person connected to Marcy, if at all?

Marcy herself didn't make much sense as the killer, at least based on what we knew about her. From all outward appearances, she had a very comfortable life with a successful real estate business, and she also had a highly lucrative side business. Why risk all of that? Plus, like I'd told Dax, I didn't make her as a killer. But I'd been wrong about this kind of stuff before, and who really knew what anyone else was capable of.

Martin was another possibility, but there were a number of mitigating factors. One, he was friends with Wyatt and didn't seem to have any real reason to kill him. Two, even though he had killed himself, I didn't think he had the nerve to kill Wyatt, let alone several people. He was a pretty mild guy from what I saw, and Marcy's descriptions of him supported that. He didn't fit the bill, either.

So that left...everyone else on the planet.

Eighteen

I woke up with an elbow in the ribs. And then a poke in the eye. And then a kick in the dick.

"Answer your phone or I'm throwing it in the ocean."

Caroline dropped my phone onto my chest and rolled over. I looked at the screen and saw Dax's name. The clock said 7:42.

"Tell me."

"She's getting ready to move."

"How soon?"

"Within an hour. Maybe less. She's made four trips to the boat in the last half hour, carrying a decent load of stuff each time. I can't see what, but she's packing up to go for sure. She pulled the Porsche into the garage. What do you want me to do?"

"Hang tight for now and keep your eye on her. I'll get back to you in ten."

I walked outside and called JD. He answered immediately.

"She's about to move," I said.

"Too late. I've got everything I need."

"I'll pick you up in fifteen minutes. Be ready."

"I'm staying here. I have a few things I need to monitor and then it's lights out for all these shitbirds."

"What's the plan?" I asked.

"Later."

"Keep Savannah there and calm. I'll be in touch."

I went back inside and told Caroline what was going on.

She got out of bed and paced around the small bedroom, running her hands through her hair and biting her lip. She walked out to the deck, sat down, stood up, sat down, stood up, came inside and punched me in the chest. Hard.

"Let's fucking go," she said.

"Caro, this isn't a situation for you."

"Say that again."

I didn't say it again. Instead, I moved aside the throw rug, opened the floor safe and took out my Glock and Caroline's .38 and we got dressed.

I called Dax on the way downstairs. I could hear the ocean in the background. "What's she doing?"

"She's fucking leaving. Like now. She's got the boat packed and she's buttoning up the house right now, man."

"Where are you?"

"In the trees near the barn."

"Strapped?"

"Affirmative."

"Ok. Look, we're thirty-five minutes out at best. I'm not exactly sure what to tell you, but she cannot get on that boat and leave. That can't happen. We're getting in the Jeep now and flying, but it's a haul."

"Got it. I'll hit you when I know what's up. Don't call me for now. I'm gonna need to be quiet."

"Stay low."

"Mmm, shit, hang on a sec."

The line went silent for thirty seconds and then he came back.

"Car just pulled up the road here. Parked about twenty yards from the driveway. Lone male getting out, coming this way, up the driveway."

I waited.

I waited some more.

"He knocked on the front door, and now he's heading around back."

"Can you describe him?" I asked.

"Medium build, sturdy, dark hair. Carrying a messenger bag, wearing jeans and hiking boots I think."

"Is the bag black with a red logo on it?"

"Yup."

Goddmanit. "That's our guy. Let me know if he goes with Marcy."

"And then what?"

"You don't let him."

"Roger that."

"Keep an AirPod in so we can communicate. I may not be able to call."

Brendan was sitting at the counter in the kitchen, spinning a St. Christopher medal like a top. "It's that time?" he asked, not looking up.

"It looks like it," I said.

Caroline came down the stairs behind me, dressed for a beach day but carrying a backpack that I knew held our weapons, extra clips, and a few other goodies. She grabbed four bottles of water from the fridge, put them into the backpack, kissed Brendan on the cheek, and walked out the door.

Brendan stopped spinning the medal and looked at me.

"Danny."

"I know."

He stood and faced me and grabbed my shoulders. "Danny. I don't know the details of what you're doing, but there is justice and there is retribution. I'm not sure which one you're after, but the only thing I care about is that all of you come back home."

I pulled him close and then stood back. "Love you, brother."

Caroline was in the driver's seat of the Jeep when I walked out. I stopped short, then walked to the passenger's side and got in. She shoved it into reverse, spun onto the beach road and then slammed it into second and pushed the accelerator to the floor.

We hit 3A running and Caroline pushed it hard all the way to the highway and then stood on it. It was too loud to call, so I texted Dax to let him know we were twenty minutes out, then JD to tell him the situation. He didn't reply right away, so I wasn't sure what to expect, but I knew he was on it.

Dax replied: She's getting on the boat. Moving NOW.

Fuck.

I called JD. He answered before the first ring ended. "Danny she's fucking done."

"Listen listen. JD, I need you to get the boat moving and head north right now. She's about to make a run for it. Like, now."

"Oh shit, ok. Where are you?"

"On 3 headed up. Just passed exit six."

"Hop off on seven and come back down here. We'll get to her faster on the boat. Meet me here."

I looked at Caroline and she nodded and steered the Jeep onto the ramp. "On the way."

We pulled into the Plymouth Yacht Club lot in a hurry and Caroline stuck the Jeep in a visitor spot and we sprinted for the docks down behind the club. JD was on the stern of the *Buffer Overflow*, pulling the lines in and making ready. Caroline threw the backpack aboard, went around to the bow and pulled the last lines in, and then we went aboard.

"What are we doing?" JD asked as we eased out of the slip.

"Good. We're doing good," I said.

We went out around Saquish and Gurnet Light and then JD pushed the twin MTU motors hard, due north. As soon as we cleared the light, I texted Dax to give him the new plan. I knew he wouldn't reply, but I wanted him to know where we were if things went south.

The sun was high and bright as we came around Gurnet Light, and I could see half a dozen other boats already moving out to sea. It would be a fine day for fishing or cruising or just sitting out on Brown's Bank and drinking cold beer and playing cornhole. Some of my favorite things. But we wouldn't be doing any of those.

I went into the cabin and found JD at the controls. "How long?"

"We'll be in her backyard in ten minutes."

"Make it eight."

Back on deck, Caroline was sitting on a padded bench on the stern, watching a group of seagulls dip and dive through our wake. I sat down and we watched the birds and the water and listened to the roar of the motors for a minute. Caroline was leaning back, her face tilted up to the sun, a small smile on her face. Without any context, you might have thought she was on her way to Nantucket for a holiday weekend. She looked content.

The sea was calm and JD was pushing the *BO* hard. We passed Brant Rock and Humarock and Scituate Light and when we came around Minot Beach I felt JD power the motors down. The boat slowed and Caroline sat up and handed me the backpack. She stretched and cracked her neck and looked in at Cohasset Harbor. It was calm and I didn't see any boats coming out.

JD stuck his head out of the cabin: "Am I going in or waiting here?"

I went into the cabin and grabbed the binoculars. I found Marcy's house and scanned down until I saw the boathouse and the dock. We were at an angle, but I could see that the Chris-Craft was still in there. I scanned up to the lawn and saw three figures walking down from the house to the water. It looked like Marcy and a man walking in front, with Dax behind them. We were probably five hundred yards out, but I could tell that the two people in front were walking carefully and that Dax had the rifle held low on them. He was checking the woods on either side and looking back toward the house.

"Let's go in," I said. "It'll be easier to handle this there than out here."

JD maneuvered us in toward the boathouse on an angle, allowing them to see us while also giving us a chance to move in quickly if we needed to. I texted Dax again: Keep them on the dock. Got eyes on you, just raise a hand to ack.

A few seconds later, I saw Dax raise his left hand quickly and then yank both of the people ahead of him to a stop and sit them on the grass a few yards short of the dock and boathouse. The man turned around to say something and Dax shoved a boot in his back. JD maneuvered the *Buffer Overflow* in on the vacant side of the dock, opposite the boathouse, turning it so it was facing back out to sea.

"Stay here and stay ready," I said to JD.

"Yup."

Out on the deck, I saw that Caroline was already on the dock and walking up to the lawn. The backpack was on the bench and I pulled my Glock out and noticed that Caroline's gun was gone. I ticked the Glock into my waistband and hopped onto the dock and caught up with Caroline.

"Just follow my lead. I want to get her to talk and get something we can hand over to your dad or King."

"You know she's not going to say shit, Danny. And who's that with her?"

We walked off the dock and up the lawn. In the shade of the massive live oak, in the spot where a sandbox could have been, Marcy Simms sat, her knees pulled up to her chest. Her wrists were zip tied in front of her and a small trickle of blood crept down from a gash above her left eyebrow. Next to her sat Lous Andino, his messenger bag still slung across his chest. His hands were zip tied as well, but he was a little worse for wear than Marcy. His mouth was a bloody mess and I could see a decent sized cut on his scalp, hair matted with blood. Marcy stared straight ahead, deadeyed. Andino looked down at the ground.

Dax handed me a weathered 9 mm pistol. "That's his," he said, nodding at Andino.

"He just handed it over?"

"Well, when I got into the house, he was standing over her in the entryway, screaming, holding the gun in her face. And then he wasn't."

"Yeah. Did you catch any of what he was saying?"

"Something about how she was the last one."

"And what did she say?"

"Shoot me. She said, shoot me."

Caroline squatted down in front of Marcy and took the .38 from her pocket. She tapped it against Marcy's knee. "Morning, sunshine. Wanna go for a little cruise?"

Marcy cleared her throat and hocked up what sounded like a massive loogie, but before she got it out, Dax kicked her in the ribs and she inhaled sharply, nearly choking. Caroline listened to her cough for a few seconds and then, when she had recovered, slapped her once, then twice, across the face, and stood up.

Marcy was about to say something and Dax kicked her again, this time on the other side. She yelped and rolled onto her side and stayed there. I went and stood over her and put my face an inch away from hers.

"This is probably the best part of what could be a really long day. If you're the stupid bitch that I hope you are, you'll keep talking shit to us and me and Dax will spend as much time as it takes to find out what we want to know, and then I'll let Dax take you into that barn of yours, shoot you in the stomach and light it on fire. So here's what we're going to do. We're going to go for a nice little ride on JD's very expensive boat and have a chat. He does not take kindly to people bleeding on that boat, so this won't be a long ride, one way or the other. You answer our questions, and we will come back and call the police and you'll go to jail for the rest of your life. Or, and I honest to God hope this is what you choose, you act like your stupid self. In which case, gun, stomach, barn, fire. We clear?"

Marcy didn't answer, so I put my foot on her ribs and pushed. "Mmmmm, fuck. Clear, we're clear."

"Dax?"

He handed Caroline the rifle, yanked Marcy off the ground and threw her over his shoulder in one smooth motion and carried her down the dock to the boat. Then I turned my attention to Louis Andino. He was stone faced and was staring straight ahead, rocking back and forth on his butt.

"Who is this?" Caroline asked.

"This, love, is Louis Andino. The star crime reporter for the *Sunrise*. He's a really good reporter, actually. Has some great sources and some really good instincts. He knows where the stories are and how to get them. Actually, it turns out he creates some of the stories himself. Isn't that right, Louis?"

No reply.

I kicked him in the crotch.

"Right, Louis?"

He moaned.

Caroline: "What do you mean?"

"Do you want me to tell it, Louis? Or can you catch your breath long enough to do it?"

Andino spat a gob of blood onto the grass and rolled onto his back. He tried to sit up, but I had to help him. Once he was upright, he looked at me and Caroline, out at the boat and the ocean beyond it. He shook his head and dropped his chin to his chest.

"Figures," I said.

I yanked Andino up by the wrists and walked him down the dock. Caroline went ahead of us, climbed aboard, set her .38 and the rifle on the bench, and helped me pull Andino onto the boat. I shoved him onto the deck and sat him against the bench across from Marcy. Dax was standing against the glass door to the salon, watching. JD came out of the door as we came aboard and stood with Dax.

"Who's this motherfucker?" he asked, pointing at Andino.

I kicked Andino again. "Speak, shitheel."

"Fuck off."

I grabbed a handful of his hair and bounced his head off the deck and pulled him upright again. He sagged back against the bench but said nothing. He stared at Marcy instead. She seemed to be just as interested in who Andino was as Caroline and JD were.

"Tell you what. Let's get moving and then we'll all talk this through. JD, how about we head out toward Stellwagen?"

He nodded and went back inside. Caroline went in with him.

I stayed outside and sat on the bench next to Andino. Dax sat on the bench near Marcy. Andino kept his eyes on Marcy and she kept hers on him. She was not about to look away. The only people on the boat who knew who Andino was were me and JD, but everyone knew who and what Marcy was. We sat and waited in silence and I watched the sea go by. I had nothing to say, but I was hoping that Marcy or Andino would get bored or frustrated or desperate and start talking. My money was on Andino. Marcy was too hard and too smart. There was no upside for her.

"Tobin." It was Marcy.

I watched a whaler head out toward the bank.

"Tobin."

I took my sunglasses off and looked at her, my gun held loosely by my side.

"What?"

"Danny, what do you make in a year? A hundred grand? One fifty tops? Doing shit work for other people. I make that before lunch. Every day. It just comes to me, out of the ether. It just shows up. That house back there, that's my fucking summer home. I have houses I've never even been to. My accountants buy them. I have a ranch in Wyoming that's apparently the size of Rhode Island. I've never seen it. This is what's happening out there. This business is as big as Netflix. And I'm no one. No. One. Not even in the top ten. Most of the big players are in

Ukraine or Russia or Thailand. Say the word and the ranch is yours. Or the house in Hilton Head, or Aruba. Or even the Cohasset place. It's a dump but it's yours. You pick."

I went into the salon, spoke to Caroline for a minute, and walked back out and sat next to Andino again. I looked at Marcy and Dax and then down at Andino.

"Louis, are you ready to tell everyone why you're here?"

He spit on the deck. "Fuck off."

I sighed and motioned to Dax. He walked over and we picked Andino up and held him over the side of the boat and dipped his head into the water a couple of times. We were doing a solid twelve knots and his face skipped off the surface of the water and he yelped like a wounded dog. We hefted him back up and dropped him on the deck.

"And so?" I asked.

"Fuck--"

Dax put his boot on Andino's crotch and pressed.

"Unnnh--"

Dax shifted his weight.

Andino slid down the deck and laid on his back. Dax knelt next to him, pulled a Buck knife from his belt, flipped it open and pressed it against Andino's thigh. Andino froze and nodded at me.

I heard the salon door slide open and Caroline walked out.

"Louis, you have one chance to tell this. We know most of it, so if you tell it wrong, you die slowly today. Tell it right, you might die in prison fifty years from now."

He sat back up against the bench and pulled his knees up to his chest. He looked at me, then Dax, then finally at Marcy. He pointed at her with his zip-tied hands.

"She said she's no one, that there's hundreds like her. There may be a lot of others, but there's no one like her. She *is* the one. She's not one of many. She's it."

"How do you know?" I asked.

Andino gave a short laugh. "Because I've killed all of the others."

Marcy straightened up and her eyes snapped to Andino. "You what? Who?"

He laughed again. "You fucking know. You know exactly who. You could name them as easily as I could. The Texas group, the Utah cult, the families in NorCal. The guys up here. All of them. I got them all. Did you think you were just smarter than everyone else? That you had a better business model? You're this successful because you're the last one standing right now."

He spat on the deck.

"Tell you what Tobin, I don't have much money, but you cut me loose and give me one minute with her, you won't have to worry about either one of us ever again. Just one minute."

I looked at Marcy Simms. "The first day I met you I could tell you were garbage. But I figured you were a trophy wife who fucked her way to the middle, so I didn't think that much about it. Make a little money here and there, sleep with the right people, go to the right parties. Ta da. Nouveau riche garbage. But garbage with the right car in the driveway of the right house in the right town in the right state. Not that upstate New York craphole, right? You're too good for that."

Marcy sat on the deck, her eyes flat.

"And then once you found out you couldn't have kids, that you were an embarrassment to your husband, you decided to take your anger out on everyone else. To destroy their lives and their kids' lives, and the lives of everyone they knew. Sound about right?"

Marcy raised her head and looked at me, Caroline, Andino. She put a small, sad smile on her face. She sat up quickly and Dax pushed his .45 into the back of her head and she froze and then put her hands out in front of her, palms up.

"That's a pretty good story."

"I thought so."

She scooted back up the bench a bit. "Funny part is, you thought this was some ideological thing. Do I seem like an idealist to you?"

I didn't answer.

She scooted back up some more, adjusting her back. "The last fucking thing I am is an idealist. I'm a capitalist. I grew up wealthy and when my dad pissed that money away and I ended up at a shitty state college with the peasants, I made some decisions. I decided I would find a way to get back to where I belonged. I would find the right people, I would work hard and I would take every chance I had to move up and out. And I decided I would never be poor again, no matter what."

"So it was purely business?" Caroline asked.

"What else would it be? I met some people in California and they were making a pile of money doing low quality video stuff. Even before the internet really took off. So I saw the way things were going, I had an opportunity to exploit it, and I took it. This is a product like anything else. There's a demand for it and I knew how to create the supply. I was owed a good life and I decided to take it."

Andino snorted. "You know I was one of those kids, right? Like, this isn't an abstract thing? There are actual humans on the other side of those cameras."

Marcy shrugged. "And?"

I grabbed Andino's shoulder, expecting him to move, but he didn't. When he spoke, he sounded sad and resigned. "You're so much worse than I thought you'd be. Jesus. Do you wanna know what a monster you are? I found that guy in Utah who had eleven daughters with four different women. He had built a makeshift studio in his barn and would bring in his brothers and uncles and cousins to do the video work. I spent three months watching them and I learned their schedule. And one Sunday, when I knew all of the girls were in the house making dinner, and all the men were in the barn getting ready for the next day, I went in with two friends and we locked the doors and we burned the barn down. We doused it in gasoline and blocked every exit and we lit it up. Then we sat on the hood of my truck and listened to them scream. Somehow, one of them managed to make it out of the barn and came running toward the driveway where we were. His back was on fire and he was screaming like nothing I'd ever heard. It was horrific. I stood there and listened to it. I let him howl. It took, I don't know, three minutes, for him to finally die. That was a brutal three minutes. And honestly, I think that's too good for you, Marcy. If these guys would let me, I'd take you apart with my bare hands, piece by piece."

Marcy blinked and sat quietly for a minute or so. Then she straightened up and shifted her weight and looked at Andino. "Is this the part where I feel bad for you? I sure hope not, because I don't give a fuck. Not one. We're both going to die out here. It doesn't matter what my motives were, or what your sad little childhood sob story is. No one fucking cares."

Caroline stared at Marcy for what felt like an hour, then walked over to her, bent down, and looked at her from an inch away. "You're right about that. No one gives a shit about you and they'll never find out what happened to you. You weren't owed shit. No one is. But you destroyed the lives of thousands of kids just to make up for your daddy's mistakes? What a sad little life you must have had. And guess what. Now it's over."

"I bet your daddy the cop would be so proud," Marcy said.

Caroline pivoted and punched Marcy in the face. Then she picked Marcy up by her arms and sat her on the bench and pressed hard on the cut above her eyebrow, drawing a fresh flow of blood. Marcy didn't flinch and kept her eyes on Caroline's. The blood made its way into Marcy's eye and she had to blink and started shaking her head.

Caroline grabbed Marcy's chin and pointed to Dax. "You see him? What does he look like to you?"

Marcy shook her head, trying to clear her eyes. "Violence. He looks like violence."

"And that's what he is. But I'm the one you need to worry about. Not him."

I went back into the cabin with Caroline, leaving Dax outside with Andino and Marcy. JD said we were ten minutes out from Stellwagen Bank.

"What then?" he asked.

"Then we end this bullshit and go home," I said.

"Look man, I know we have to do what we have to do out here, but there's a couple of things we need to think about. Like, how much does Chris King know about all of this?"

"He knows most of what we know, but not all of it. Enough to make things uncomfortable for us, yeah. But he doesn't know about Andino."

"Why not?" Caroline asked.

"Well, he knows that there's a person who killed Wyatt and several other people, but he doesn't know that it's Andino. I didn't have that info last time we talked. And he doesn't know about the stuff that Andino told us just now about the other killings out west. So as far as he knows, Marcy could be the whole package."

"So why don't we give him that package?" JD said.

I looked at Caroline. She shook her head. "No. She doesn't get off that easily."

"Babe, easy is me throwing her in the ocean. Easy is Dax shooting her in the head. Handing her to the police as a serial murderer and head of a child exploitation empire is not easy. She'll get life in prison and the odds are she won't make it more than six months inside. Word gets around."

"What's the worst possible outcome for her?" Caroline asked.

"That."

"Then let's figure it out. I want the maximum amount of suffering for her."

So we figured it out. I called Chris King and gave him a little bit of information and he agreed to meet us back at Marcy's house at four. And then we had to talk about Andino. There was no good way to discuss it, but it came down to a binary choice.

It was Caroline who made the decision.

Nineteen

JD cut the engines and slowed the boat to a dead stop and motioned me up to the controls. "We sure?" he asked.

"We are."

"Danny…"

"I know."

"So we head back to Cohasset and hand her over to King?"

"That's it."

"What prevents her from telling this story?"

"Nothing. But who would believe her? King has information about her that will put her away for life. And you have everything else. And none of that exonerates her."

JD nodded, looked over his shoulder and started the engines. I grabbed Caroline's hand and pulled her close. "Are we sure?" I asked. "This has some risk that we don't have to carry."

She squeezed my hand hard. "I'm sure. Are you?"

I took a deep breath, looked out at Andino and Marcy on the deck, looked at my friends in the cabin, thought about what the decision we were making might mean. I squeezed Caroline's hand, looked at her and nodded.

"Let's fucking go," I said.

She nodded, tears in her eyes, and walked over to the helm and sat in the chair next to JD and put her head on his shoulder. JD brought the big engines up to speed and we made a wide turn and headed back toward Plymouth. I dropped onto the couch in the salon and closed my eyes. There was a dull ache in the back of my head and I could feel a deep fatigue in my bones. I was exhausted by the investigation, but also by trying to get into the minds of people like Marcy Simms and Louis Andino. Those were not healthy places to spend time and it was taking its toll.

On me and Caroline, both.

I walked back outside and found both Andino and Marcy slumped on the deck and Dax sitting on the bench facing aft, watching them. I sat next to Dax and looked out at the vortex behind the boat.

"What are we doing?" he asked. We were out of earshot of Marcy and Andino and the big twin two thousand horsepower motors ensured no one could hear us anyway.

"Going back."

"The way I understood it, there would be two fewer people on the boat when we came back."

"Things changed. We're going to let the cops have her."

"How? We're just going to roll up and say, Ah shit, we decided not to kill this one. She's all yours."

"Not in so many words, but sort of. I know the Boston cop that's investigating Wyatt's murder and the other ones connected to it. I told him a little bit about what we've got on Marcy and he knows that JD has the forensic evidence to bury Marcy. So we're giving it to him. She eats it all."

Dax looked out at the sea for a bit, then at Marcy, then at me. "Fine by me."

He nodded at Andino, who was staring at Marcy. "And him?"

I looked away, watched a group of gulls dive at a school of baitfish on the surface.

"Tobin."

"Yeah. He walks."

Dax looked at me for a few seconds and then chuckled. "That's some shit. Damn, son."

"Yeah."

"Y'all really came all the way out here on this big fuckin' boat with these two turds and we're going to bring them back in? Can I just shoot her a little bit? Like, in the foot or something? I flew a long way to get here, Tobin."

"Tell you what. When this is all done, you're coming with us on the next vacation. On me."

"Ok, but I'd still like to shoot her a little."

"Me too, man. Me too."

I left Dax with Andino and Marcy and went back inside. Caroline was asleep on the couch in the salon, snoring softly. I found JD at the topside controls, his feet up on the console, a blank look on his face.

"So tell me about Marcy's network," I said. "When I called this morning you said you had her."

He dropped his feet to the deck and leaned forward, checked the GPS chart, nodded to himself. "That seems like a hundred years ago."

"It sure does."

"Ok. So. After I got to her laptop that day, she hit the admin panel for her sites and then her bank accounts. I got her credentials for all of those, along with quite a bit of other stuff. But the most important part is I figured out the mechanism she was using to push updates to her customers and collect their stuff. It was pretty basic, but clean and effective. It would send an update to the known list of machines every seventy-two hours, giving them the most recent site addresses and checking for any new photo or video files on those machines. The client side code would run the anti-forensics tricks to see if it was running in a virtual machine or a sandbox and all that. Nothing spectacular, but it worked."

"No way in hell she wrote that," I said.

"Oh no. I'm sure it was contract work. Easy enough to find someone to do that these days. Anyway, I reverse engineered the update mechanism and was able to enumerate how many machines were in her list."

"I'm not sure I want to know."

"North of twenty thousand. Almost twenty-one."

"Jesus."

"Andino was not lying about her operation. She's the apex predator right now, it looks like. And she's supplying other people farther down the food chain with videos, pictures, access to kids and money laundering services. Andino was right, man. She's it."

I walked to the back of the flying bridge and looked down at Marcy Simms and Lous Andino sitting on the deck. I could see Dax, his legs stretched out, ankles crossed, his .45 resting on his thigh. If I whistled and gave the sign, Dax would shoot them both and throw them in the Atlantic and then come in for a beer.

"So what do we do?"

"Do? It's done, man. I hijacked the update mechanism and pushed a ransomware binary to every one of those machines about an hour ago. They're all locked and encrypted. Every single one of those people is completely fucked. I can ID every one of those machines and the binary is a unique build, so the only people who have that specific variant are her customers. There's no two ways about it. If anyone raises their hand and calls law enforcement about it..."

"Holy shit, man. Oh my god. And the money?"

"Oh, that?"

I kicked him in the shin. "I know it doesn't matter to you, but I'm guessing it's real money."

"Is eight figures real?"

"Tell me."

"Just the cash in the accounts that I have access to right now is a little more than forty million. I'm sure there's more accounts and some Bitcoin wallets I can't get to, but it's a lot, man. Plus all that real estate she talked about. It's an empire. Like Andino said."

I considered the amount of damage that Marcy Simms must have done in the last few years in order to make that much money and it made my heart race. She had built a worldwide business on the pain and misery of thousands of kids and she'd never thought twice about the consequences. As she said, it was just a business. Money was money, regardless of how you made it.

"We're taking that money," I said. "It's not going to the IRS."

"Fine by me. But where's it going?"

"I've got some ideas."

We motored into Cohasset just after three-thirty and after we tied the *Buffer Overflow* up, we took Andino and Marcy up the lawn to the fire pit and sat them in chairs. I handed Andino's pistol back to Dax and he went to move his truck out of sight while Caroline and I stayed by the fire pit. It was quiet for a few minutes and then Marcy couldn't help herself.

"Lost your nerve huh, Danny?"

Caroline laughed and I saw Andino shake his head.

"Couldn't do it, could you? I've heard a lot of talk about what a tough guy you are. How dangerous you are. And you had us out in the middle of the ocean and you choked. So now what, genius? You think you've got it all figured out? You don't know the half of it. It's so much bigger than you think, and you'll never find it."

It was my turn, a deep and satisfying laugh. "Marcy, we have all of it. Every single bit. We have your bank accounts, we have your network, we have your customers. We have you sitting right here. We have everything we need, and goading me isn't going to work. If we wanted to kill you, Dax would have tossed you off the boat an hour ago in small pieces. We decided it would be better for us, and so much worse for you, to go another way."

My phone buzzed and I saw it was Chris King. "Hey man. We're here."

"I'm about thirty minutes out. Had to make a quick stop."

"No problem. We'll be here."

"Caroline, can you try not to kill her for a few minutes? I need to have a chat with Louis."

"No promises," she said.

"Do your best."

I pulled Andino out of the chair and walked him up to the house and into the kitchen. Dax was standing inside, the .45 in his right hand and a pair of metal shears on the granite island in front of him.

"Hi kids."

Andino slumped at the sight of Dax and I pulled him up and dropped him onto a stool at the counter. He tried to meet Dax's gaze but gave up after a few seconds. "Get on with it," he said.

I nodded to Dax, and he picked up the shears, grabbed Andino's wrists, and cut the zip ties. They came off with a loud snap and Andino jerked backward, as if it had been a gunshot. I put my hands on his shoulders and pressed him down onto the stool and Dax trained the .45 on him.

"So here it is, Louis," I said. "You killed Wyatt and from what you told us, it sounds like probably thirty or forty other people. Is that about right?"

He shrugged. "Maybe. It's a lot."

I looked at Dax, who shook his head.

"Ok, well none of us is innocent in this room. Here's what we're going to do, and this is non-negotiable. I'm going to say this once and if you don't like it, then JD has the boat ready."

He nodded.

"You're going to get in your car and drive out of here. I don't care where you go, but it needs to be far away and you need to disappear. Not for a month or a year, but for good. If I ever hear your name again or hear about something that sounds like you, I will find you and I'll bring Dax and then you'll wish to god we had ended this today. If you ever get in trouble with the cops or decide you need to speak our names to someone, think about that long and hard. Think about who you are and who we are."

He sat quietly for a time. Then he stood and looked around the kitchen and out the back door at Marcy sitting by the fire pit with Caroline standing over her.

"There's another side to that coin. Don't let me see your shadow behind me. I know where to find you. All of you. And I know what you've done and what you're about to do, so keep that in mind."

I nodded. "Now, fuck off and never let me hear your name again."

Dax walked Andino out to his car. He would follow Andino to his apartment, watch him pack, and then follow him out of the state in whichever direction he chose to go. There was no way to know whether Andino would keep his mouth shut, but if he didn't, he knew it was all over for him, too. We were both putting our faith in the other's desire not to go to prison for life. Mutually assured destruction.

I went back out to the fire pit and sat down. Caroline was sitting across from Marcy, her gun in her lap. "Is he gone?"

"Yup."

"Your turn," Caroline said and yanked Marcy out of her chair and walked her toward the house. Marcy squirmed and twisted, but Caroline kept pushing her toward the house. When we got inside, Caroline pushed her into a chair at the table and I sat on a stool at the island, facing her.

"So what? You're going to kill me in my own house?"

Caroline handed me the gun, kissed me, and walked back outside, down the lawn, onto the dock and went back aboard the boat. I waited. Marcy shifted in her seat, glancing nervously at the gun. After a minute, my phone buzzed and Chris King was on the other end.

"I'm in the driveway."

"Coming out."

I pulled Marcy out of the chair, grabbed the meat shears off the counter, and walked her to the door. "I'm going to cut these off of you and open the door. If you do anything stupid, you get shot. Understand?"

She nodded.

I cut the zip ties off, put them in my pocket along with the shears, and opened the door. Chris King was standing on the porch. A Cohasset town cop stood behind him, a piece of paper in his hands

"Marcy Simms, I have a search warrant for these premises. Please read it and sign it," the Cohasset officer said. "The warrant includes any and all electronic devices, computers, and digital storage devices."

He handed her the warrant and a pen, which she took in silence. She glanced at the warrant, signed it, and handed it back. "Most of the time when we serve search warrants, people ask us what it's about," King said.

She stayed silent.

King and the Cohasset officer came in and got to work. I had told King where to find Marcy's laptop and what he would find on it. JD had remotely unlocked it after we'd come back to the house. King spent some time wandering around and opening drawers before finding the laptop and the 9 mm that Dax had planted in Marcy's room. King brought them both out to the kitchen and sat at the island and began looking through the laptop. Marcy watched in silence and after a few minutes, King closed the laptop and looked at her.

"Would you like to talk?"

"I'd like to call my attorney."

"That's fine. We have more than enough probable cause to arrest you right now. So go ahead and make that call."

Half an hour later, Marcy Simms was in the back of the Cohasset cruiser and her lawyer was standing in the driveway talking to King. I went back out to the boat to avoid any uncomfortable questions from the lawyer and King came out after he'd finished up. We were all sitting in the salon when he came in. King dropped onto a couch and sighed deeply. "You got any bourbon on this tub?"

"Sure. Pappy Fifteen good enough?" JD said.

King laughed. "Goddamn I'm in the wrong line of work. Yeah, I can choke that down."

JD went to the bar and poured a generous three fingers of Pappy in a plastic tumbler with the Gamecocks logo on it and brought it over to King. "Jesus, man. You have a two million dollar boat and plastic cups?"

"Four million. But my friends tend to get a little rowdy, so crystal doesn't make much sense with our crowd."

"So I've heard." He sipped the bourbon and closed his eyes for a few seconds. "Tobin, I have to ask you: Are we going to find any surprises when we dig into all of this? I mean, stuff that's going to poke some holes in this case against her."

"You're good. You've got plenty on that laptop alone."

"The child exploitation thing looks like a win, but I'm trying to sew up these killings. I'm homicide, remember?"

"The motive is all there. Your victims were her competitors. The rest of it I can't help you with."

"When I get her in an interrogation room, is she going to tell me a story I don't want to hear about today?"

"We went for a nice day cruise. If she says anything different, I don't know what to tell you."

"This is such a shitshow. All I want is for this to be over."

"That's what we all want," I said.

King drank the last of his bourbon and stood up. "I truly hope you didn't fuck me on this, Tobin. For your sake, and mine."

After King left, Caroline and I took the Jeep back to Plymouth and JD took the *Buffer Overflow* back to the yacht club. We picked him up there and headed home. As we came down the beach road and pulled into the driveway, Savannah came down the front stairs and climbed into the back of the Jeep and embraced JD before he could get out. She held his face in her hands and tears stained her cheeks.

"You're ok. You're all ok," she said.

"We're good."

"Dax?"

"He'll be here soon. He had a couple things to do, but he's good."

She leaned into the front and hugged Caroline and me and held on for a long time. "Thank you. Thank you."

Inside, Brendan was waiting, a broad smile on his face. Caroline dropped her backpack and wrapped him in a long hug. Brendan held her tight, whispered something to her and then walked over to me. He took my hands, turned them over, examining them. Nodded to himself and then pulled me close.

"You did your job today," he said. "You all came back."

I smiled and my eyes got a little sweaty.

"That's all that matters, Danny."

Brendan and Savannah made hand pressed burgers on the grill with bacon and cheddar and a pasta salad. We ate like wolves and afterward, we walked across the beach road, climbed over the dunes, and sat our asses in the sand and watched the tide roll out and drank wine from plastic cups. The sun was just dipping below the trees behind us and the water was the yellow-orange of an October oak leaf.

Twenty

We spent the next few days hanging around the house and the beach, doing a whole lot of nothing. The Boston news stations had short items about a prominent South Shore real estate broker who had been arrested and charged with running a major child exploitation ring. They reported that the investigation was ongoing and that the FBI had been called in to assist. The *Globe* had a weekend feature on Marcy Simms that connected her to Greg Richmond, mentioned her brother's suicide, and included some quotes from an anonymous law enforcement source who confirmed that they had taken a gun out of her house that was the same caliber as the one that was used to kill Wyatt Austin, and hinting that Marcy may face murder charges down the road, too. A few of the better tech sites--Dark Reading, Decipher, Wired-- had pieces about a widespread ransomware attack that hit thousands of people around the world. Security experts quoted in the stories said they had never seen the strain of ransomware before and were confounded by the fact that there was no actual ransom demand. The infected machines were just bricked. There were also a couple of stories about an anonymous donation to Boston Children's Hospital, which the TV news people said was one of the largest in the hospital's history.

JD and Savannah had taken the boat over to Nantucket for a while to unwind and Brendan had continued helping out at St. Peter's. Caroline took a couple of days to finish her painting, which had come out beautifully and contained exactly zero llamas, and on a warm Saturday in August we drove up to Hingham to deliver it. The woman who had commissioned it was overwhelmed and promised to give Caroline's name to all of her friends. Judging by the size of her house and the Tiffany diamond on her finger, those were bound to be some good people to know.

"If you get in with the Hingham ladies who lunch, I may not have to work at all," I said on the way home.

"And that would be different how?"

We had the roof off the Jeep and took the long way home, meandering down 3A, catching glimpses of the ocean as we made our way south and savoring the warm salt breeze. In Kingston, I pulled into a small gravel lot in front of a nondescript brick building.

"What's this?" Caroline said.

"I think I found our new dog. Come on."

We walked around the back and found a man loading food into dishes in a small warren of chain-link kennels. There were a dozen or so dogs of who knows what mix of breeds, and when the man saw us coming he put the food bag down and came over.

"You the one who called?" he asked.

"Yup, Danny Tobin. This is Caroline."

He shook our hands. "I'm Jim. Follow me and let's see if he's the right one for you."

We went down the row of kennels and he stopped and unlocked the door to one at the far end. We couldn't see the dog, but a few seconds later Jim walked out with a shaggy little brown and white ball of energy on the end of his leash. Caroline gasped and squeezed my arm and then dropped onto the dirt and began scratching the dog under the chin. In five seconds, he was on his back and Caroline was rubbing his belly.

"Oh my God, Danny. He's adorable. What is he?"

"He's an Australian shepherd," Jim said. "We've had him for about three weeks. We think he's about six months old, maybe a little less."

"Does he have a name?"

"Not yet. We don't really like to name them if they don't come in with one already. Just in case, well, you know."

The dog had now climbed onto Caroline's lap and I knew that was the end of that. We went inside and did the paperwork and a few minutes later we were on the way home, the dog in Caroline's lap, his head hanging out the open window.

At home, Brendan was sitting in the living room reading and his bags were piled near the front door. The dog bounded into the house, sniffed at Brendan for a bit and then tore off to explore the rest of the place with Caroline trying to keep up.

"Heading home?" I asked Brendan.

"Heading out, but not home. I've decided to stay here at St. Peter's, at least for the time being. The pastor plans to retire by the end of the year and I've had some good talks with the diocese about taking over."

"That's great, man. So you're feeling better about the direction you want to take?"

"I am. Being here with all of you seeing how much you all love each other and look after each other reenergized me. It reminded me that there is plenty of goodness in the world, even if it's not always so easy to find. We need more of that and I feel like I can still help."

"If you can't, I don't know who can," I said.

"Thanks, and thank you for giving me this time. I do have one more request, though, if it's not too much to ask…"

Later that afternoon, Caroline and I drove into town, parked the Jeep in the small lot next to St. Peter's and walked up the worn granite stairs and into the dark vestibule. I moved to a pew on the back row, but Caroline took my hand and walked me up the aisle and steered me into the front pew. We sat down just as Brendan walked out of the small door to the right of the altar. The small congregation stood and Brendan bowed and took his place. He looked out at the congregation and looked at each of the thirty or so parishioners in turn, finally finding Caroline and me. He smiled and raised his arms.

"Thank you all for coming."

Epilogue

A month later, on the Friday of Labor Day weekend, JD eased the *Buffer Overflow* into a narrow cove in Orleans, maneuvering carefully around Hopkins Island and skirting some smaller boats and a couple on paddleboards who gave us a wide berth. He cut the motors and we coasted up to a long oak dock that stuck out into the cove like a red carpet. JD and I unloaded the gear while Savannah and Caroline walked up the dock with the dog and onto the wide, gently sloping lawn. Halfway up the hill, we lost sight of the girls. JD and I hauled the bags up the hill and the granite stairs that led to the patio surrounding the infinity pool. We dropped the bags on the pool deck.

"Not bad, Danny. Not bad," JD said.

"You found the money. All I did was spend it."

A small guest house sat to the right of the pool and the massive main house loomed above, all white clapboard New England. At the outdoor bar on the far side of the pool I saw Caroline, Savannah, and Dax waiting. Dax was crouched over, scratching the dog behind the ear. I put my arm around JD's shoulder and we walked over to the bar. Dax punched JD in the chest and gave me a hug that nearly broke a rib.

"Any time, boys," he said. "I'm three deep. Who's the fuzzy new guy?"

Caroline picked the dog up in her arms. "This is Nate," she said.

Dax smiled and scratched Nate under the chin and Caroline put him down to let him explore. "Nate dog."

"Who let you have another dog?" Dax said. "Isn't there some kind of background check?"

JD laughed and Caroline and Savannah tried to hide smiles. "I hate you people so much."

Dax handed each of us a beer and we all walked down to the pool and sat on the stairs, dangling our feet in the heated water. An inflatable swan turned in circles in the deep end and Nate barreled past us and leapt into the pool. He paddled over to the swan and nosed it to the other end and then back again before coming over to the stairs and sitting between Caroline and Savannah.

I raised my beer. "Cheers y'all. Welcome home."

Acknowledgments

As always, my thanks to my wife, Tara, for her love, patience, and encouragement in this project and everything else. She always reminds me that great things are possible. Thanks to my parents and sisters for everything. Thanks to my kids, Megan and Sean, for not reading my first book and waiting until they were an appropriate age to (hopefully) read this one. I owe special thanks to my friends Nancy Schofield and Jen White, who are absolutely relentless and would not let me give up on this book. In all honesty, I'm not sure I would have finished this story without their constant encouragement and badgering. Thank you both for not letting me off the hook. Thanks are also due to my friends Chris Self, Helen Patton, Tanya Sam, and others who would like to remain nameless, for reading early drafts and giving me invaluable notes, suggestions, criticism, and help. Thanks again to my friend Chris Gonsalves, the best editor there is, for constant encouragement and for telling me a long time ago that writing is a craft and convincing me that I might be decent at it. I'm not good at many things, but somehow I've managed to accumulate a group of friends that I wouldn't trade for the world. I truly believe that friends are the family we choose, and I'm eternally grateful for the ones who've chosen me. Thanks to my wonderful daughter Megan, who took the cover photo, and my incredibly talented pal Pete Baker, who designed the cover. My name may be the one on the front of this book, but it would not have been possible without the love, support, help, and encouragement of these people and dozens of others who aren't named here.

Greetz

George Pelecanos, John D. MacDonald, Richard Price, Dennis Lehane, John Sandford, Robert B. Parker, Don Winslow, Patrick Hoffman, Matt Bondurant, Iota Beta of Sigma Chi, Tanya Sam, Paul Judge, RSnake, Jeremiah Grossman, Adam Shostack, Kingpin, Weld Pond, Mudge, K8eM0, Adam O'Donnell, Window, Stepto, KymPossible, Dino Dai Zovi, Charlie Miller, Chris Valasek, Chris Eng, Dildog, Gary McGraw, Rich Mogull, Chris Hoff, Dug Song, Jon Oberheide, Jeff Wiss, Meredith Corley, Pete Baker, Zoe Lindsey, Fahmida Rashid, Duo Labs, Jamie Tomasello, Wendy Nather, Dave Lewis, Kim Brown, Chelsea Lewis, Ash Matthew, Hafsah Mijinyawa, Sarah Sawtell, Sarah Ovresat, Tracy Toepfer, Maddie Sewell, Thu Pham, Emily Niemann, Ben Armes, Rik Cordero, Martin Thoburn, Melanie Ensign, Ryan Naraine, Kelly Jackson Higgins, Christen Gentile, Katie Hogan, Lindsey O'Donnell-Welch, Chris Brook, Brian Donohue, Mike Mimoso, Paul Roberts, Jack Daniel, Jen Leggio, Kevin Kosh, Tim Whitman, and all of my Plymouth friends. You are my people. I love you all.

Made in United States
North Haven, CT
30 May 2022